DARK
PARADISE

For John F.

Acknowledgements

I want to thank everyone in the Tyrone Guthrie Centre, Annagh-makerrig, Co. Monaghan, for their kindness to me during the time I spent there.

I owe thanks also to the writers of the following books. Stanislav Graf, *Realms of the Human Unconscious* (E.P. Dutton, New York), Frederick Leboyer, *Birth without Violence* (Alfred A. Knopf, New York), Joseph Chilton Pearse, *The Magical Child,* Dr Thomas Verney with John Kelly, *The Secret Life of the Unborn Child* (Sphere Books).

DARK PARADISE

CATHERINE BROPHY

WOLFHOUND PRESS

First published 1991 by
WOLFHOUND PRESS
68 Mountjoy Square
Dublin 1

Wolfhound Press receives financial assistance from the Arts
Council/An Chomhairle Ealaíon, Dublin, Ireland.

British Library Cataloguing in Publication Data
Brophy, Catherine
    Dark paradise.
    I. Title
    823.914 [F]

    ISBN 0-86327-291-6

Cover design and illustration: Feargal Fitzpatrick
Typesetting: Wolfhound Press
Printed in Ireland by TechMan Ltd., Dublin.

Chapter 1

It had worked! The moment consciousness returned he could feel it. The blackness was still as profound, as enigmatic, as infinite. Suns long dead and suns vibrantly alive, glittered as remotely as before. Luminous nebulae swirled and wheeled, but there was a difference .... He looked around to check his bearings. He could not be certain in this disorientating nothingness. He had never had to remember the star patterns of a sky before. The Coweling had always protected him from its humiliating hugeness.

Yes, it was humiliating that he, Fendan, once the most revered, the holder of all knowledge, the preserver of the Laws, should be cast out here in space without any knowledge of his environment. It was humiliating to be unsure, to have no first principles, no certainties. He stared perplexed at star patterns so complex that he could not be certain whether they had changed since he had lost consciousness. And yet, somehow, in a frustratingly unscientific way, he was certain that they had, that the manoeuvre had worked. He sighed. He heard the sound of distant laughter and dismissed it.

He looked through the delicate grid directly in front of him. The filament of concentric circles and complex diagonals glinted faintly. His guess was right. It had something to do with direction. He chose a constellation at random and lined it up on the grid. He should try again. He allowed his eyes to go out of focus until the stars became a myriad eyes that stared back into his.

"Let us join our energies," he chanted in the old, old formula, his voice low for he feared abusing the rite. "Let us join our energies and take the leap of distance."

He felt a surge, a shudder and a momentary clutch of panic

5

but he did not lose consciousness. This time he could be certain that the craft had changed place. It explained a number of things. It explained why the Attic dwellers called themselves 'Star Vaulters'. He had always thought it a poetic but inaccurate name, typical of their impractical ideas. Perhaps Merculan was right and the Star Vaulters did travel other worlds. He had to admit he'd been wrong about the fuel.

"There is no fuel supply," he had told Merculan after examining the craft. "You'll find the space journeys of the 'Star Vaulters' were inside their heads. Trancers all of them, too much jiwa. In reality star vaulting would need a well-developed energy system. You're being taken in by hallucinations."

"You call yourself a scientist!" Merculan replied. "A true scientist accounts for all the evidence."

"But it makes no sense. Anyone claiming to travel such distances needs a fuel system. There is none here. This is no craft for vaulting space, Merculan. It's the fantasy chariot of a jiwa dream."

"We haven't begun to understand their systems," Merculan persisted. "How can you just refuse to consider it?"

Fendan dismissed it from his mind.

And he had been wrong. He knew that now. The technology was both simple and ingenius, a stroke of true brilliance. The joystick on the panel directly in front of him, just below the etched circle, rotated the craft 360 degrees in any direction. After that it was simple energy exchange, what Zintillians called mind-fusion. He had never even considered that it could be applied to inanimate matter. Mind-fusion with the stars! An extraordinary idea, but logical. What would the Assembly of Kristeran say? He couldn't see Farfar or Haupus or any of their cronies agreeing to investigate.

Farfar and Blana, Haupus and Dilh'. They all wanted to be the Supremes but the Assembly of Kristeran had elected Fendan and Joquah'. Farfar and Blana mind-fused superb educational methods but in the Chambers their chaos was average. They were appointed Education Kristeran and were happy enough. Haupus and Dilh' were not.

"We beat them," they had told their friends. "If they'd stayed any longer in the Chambers they'd have cracked. We could have gone on and on."

But everyone knew that Haupus and Dilh's mind-fusions did not compare with Fendan and Joquah's and everyone knew that Fendan and Joquah' had superb control. Haupus and Dilh' were appointed Justice Kristeran.

"You chose Supremes whose control is not supreme!" Dilh' told the Assembly.

But the Assembly didn't take kindly to having its judgement questioned.

On the Day of Inauguration when Haupus came to the dais to make urh to the new Supremes he looked Fendan in the eye.

"Spend time with me in the Chambers," he said, too quietly for the other Kristeran to hear. "Let's see who really is Supreme."

Fendan opened his hands and made urh.

"Accept the challenge if you dare!"

Fendan handed Haupus the Gemstone of Office. Haupus took the carved black beryl.

"Or know that you have shirked it."

He smiled his knife-like smile, bowed and turned away.

How are they faring now? Fendan wondered. He looked at the star-ciphered darkness and laughed.

He now knew how to move around. That was some achievement. Much better than hanging in space, alternating between paralysis and despair. He had been here for he no longer knew how long ... ever since he had been exiled, had exiled himself.

He played with his new-found knowledge, choosing groups of stars, or whorl-wheeled nebulae, or the faint glimmerings of a distant galaxy, fixing them in his direction finder, flitting from space to space.

"Mine to explore," he shouted and allowed his translucent hands to wave delicately at the galaxies. The Universe made no response. It surrounded him black and baleful. His shout died and chaos, fear and despair, returned and lodged in his chest. He could not return to Zintilla for he no longer knew which of the billion points of light might be its suns. Anyway he was finished there. Even if he could get back, all that awaited him was death. He needed another planet, one that could support his kind of life. Where could he go? The Star Vaulters had recorded many suitable planets but Fendan had neither their knowledge nor their experience of intergalactic navigation. He wished he'd paid more attention to the reports Merculan had shown him. The chances of finding a tiny planet in this ... this ... awfulness were next to impossible. It was ridiculous. At his age he should be in Great Halls teaching doctrine, supervising the applicants for Bajinj, receiving honour and respect, not flitting round the Cosmos as chaotic as a youngling.

The blackness pressed and the glitterings pierced his eyes. It was hopeless. He was condemned to be trapped in this bubble, floundering. He might as well have stayed to face the Levigation Chambers.

"Fendan, Supreme Krister of the Radiant Orb," a voice said, sudden and loud in his ear.

Fendan's head almost jerked out of his headrest in surprise.

"Noblest offspring of Breg, great teacher of Cah'ai, Aluu and Tsa, wise saviour of the youth of Xemplox, you have more to learn." It laughed.

"Stay quiet, can't you," Fendan moaned. "Be quiet, I command you to be quiet."

It only laughed again.

It was his own voice, he knew that, coming from that part of his brain which he'd been so careful to close off. The synaptic suturings had been loosening slowly since that first time when he had absorbed Emmerlade's chaos. That was the beginning, he realized that now. Holding his breath he went carefully through the suturing process. He needed now, more than ever, to be able to stay clear and logical. But the voice he'd come to fear seeped through.

"There's more to learn."

"Yes, yes, yes," Fendan answered impatiently. "But what can I do about it here? What can I possibly do?"

There was no answer.

His agitated fingers fiddled with the small wheel in front of him. A darkness, like ink, poured over, slid down the dome. It blotted out the stars and the blackness, giving the little ship a protected, intimate feel. Only the circular direction finder stayed clear but an extra turn of the control could shade that too.

Rolling the little wheel back and forth under his finger, Fendan realized that the shadow on the grid expanded and contracted like the iris of an eye. Intrigued by this discovery, he closed the shader until only the innermost circle showed. Inside this he centred a star. Suddenly the craft was lit with a white light that seemed to flow up and around the dome in waves. Fendan watched the light and thought how pretty it was.

He tried again with a different star. The light this time was emerald. He tried another, white light again, and another. Blue waves lapped the dome. As he shifted the iris of the grid from star to star he discovered suns to match the colours of the spectrum, red and yellow, green, blue and orange, indigo and violet and, the extra one, white. The colours flowed hypnotically up the dome, wave upon wave, overlapping, ebbing, flowing, each one fading and deepening into every nuance of itself.

He chose a red star and centred it, for on Zintilla red was the colour of potential. He pulled out his sleeping pallet. Easing himself out of his floater he lay down to watch the colour waves. They reminded him a little of the Coweling Day entertainments in the Great Halls of Xemplox. As he watched he relaxed and felt renewed. He forgot the paralysis, the chaos and the despair as tides of crimson, scarlet and flame swirled around the darkened dome. It was the first real colour that he had seen since leaving Zintilla. His eyes devoured it, swam in it, floated in it. He hadn't realized until now how much he'd missed the colour, the fretted lapis-lazuli of a balcony, the vivid emerald of a gown, the flash of gold when fountain water leaped. The flaunting flame-red soundlight of an airhorn concerto.

He had no idea how long he lay there watching, moving only to isolate another star in the direction finder, to have another colour inundate his world. Then a thought occurred to him. This colour difference in stars seemed to be a result of the filter of the directional grid. Was it also a navigational aid? Formerly, he could only move from one emptiness to another. Now he could isolate a single star. Perhaps it was a way to direct the craft? He centred the iris of the view finder. The luminous red pupil of the star stared him down. Fendan couldn't look at it directly, but by slitting his lids and shadowing his eyes with his lashes he could look and let his eyes unfocus.

"Exchange the energy," he whispered. "Take the leap of distance."

The movement was sudden and dizzying. Even with the shader closed the light was intolerable. It blinded him and his eyes streamed. He closed them tight and covered them with his hands. As he waited to recover, he realized that he had seen fire, boiling, seething, orange, red and yellow. He glanced again, great jets of purple streaked past, gouts of burning gases spouted from incandescent vortices. He must move immediately. But even as the thought occurred to him, he could feel himself drawn to the fiery depths. He wanted to plunge in, to be engulfed. Did it matter? Did it really matter if he died? There was a chaos in his body, a fear and desire, rendering him incapable of action, making it impossible to think. The voice spoke, urgently.

"More to learn, Fendan," it insisted. "More to learn."

Somehow, his fingers sought the joystick to swing the direction grid away. He opened the shader a pinpoint but the light dazzled him. He could get nothing in view, nothing with which to take the leap. He swung his craft from side to side hoping to get something, anything, in his energy line.

"Exchange energy, leap of distance," he screamed.

Nothing happened. He pushed the joystick round and round and screamed the words again. The light diminished. He could see nothing.

At first he thought the light had burnt his eyes. Then he had a fleeting impression of something huge and dark, hurtling towards him. He shut his eyes and shielded his head with his frail arms. When he looked again, it had stopped directly outside his window. Perhaps it was some kind of craft with beings aboard. He had been alone so long, he yearned to meet another living creature, no matter how alien. Perhaps they were watching him .... He dismissed the thought impatiently. It was one of those fantasies that slipped through to consciousness. Though he kept up rigorous and regular synaptic suturing, still they filtered through. There was no jiwa on board so there was little more he could do except be on his guard.

The object was just a huge lump of rock. Fendan stared at its pitted, greyish-brown surface. He wished he had a micromacromator so he could visulate a section to form a picture of the internal structures, formations, elements. There was always the possibility that it was some material unknown back on Zintilla.

The sun that had almost devoured him was there, larger than anything else in the sky, glowing pink and innocuous. He watched it for a while, relieved that he hadn't succumbed to the desire for self-immolation. And his craft had not melted either!

That meant the material must be resistant to incredible extremes of temperature. Those Star Vaulters! The more he discovered about this little bubble, the more respect he gained for them.

He put the pink sun in his direction finder and watched it turn bright red. He realized from his grid that the star was moving slowly to the left. The rock remained still, unmoved. Fendan laughed. The illusions of space! It was the rock that was moving. Some kind of meteorite that must have been directly in his line of energy. They were travelling together, he, caught in its gravity. It was a change to be moving in some comprehensible way.

He must have been asleep. He saw a pearly crescent rise behind the sun. Could it be a planet? It gave him a sense of hope. Despite his ability to travel in the void, despite the knowledge he was gathering, he had been losing hope of ever seeing anything but blackness and the mocking glitter of distant stars.

He watched the crescent rise for hours. He slept again. On waking it was still there, a little larger. For the next ten sleepings he watched it inflate from delicate ring to full-bellied sphere. For two more wakings there was no change, just a certain fading of the colour. Then he realized the meteorite to which he was gravitationally locked was now travelling away from the planet. He would have to get there by himself. Fendan had no desire for another dangerous adventure but it was the only planet he had seen.

He lined it up in his direction finder. Perhaps it would be habitable, somewhere he could live, the end of his journeying. The Star Vaulters' reports said most inhabitants of the planets they had visited had ignored them. Some were curious, some suspicious, some welcoming. But he could deal with that when the time came.

Another chaos of excitement rose in him. Careful, he warned himself, careful. He closed his eyes, held his breath and willed the sensation to leave him. He could no longer control these feelings the way he had on Zintilla, before helping Emmerlade, the way he'd taught the applicants for Bajinj, year after year when he and Joquah'... He wrenched his thoughts away from that. He needed a clear mind. This was only the first planet. It might not be inhabited, it might have beings in an early stage of evolution. He must keep his mind clear. He could think about

Zintilla later.

When he closed the iris of the shader, there was a faint grey glow in the craft. It was different from the light of the stars, neutral, steady luminous. He said the words of energy exchange.

At first he could see nothing. It was as though he had suddenly been plunged into a giant crucible, lost in its swirling gases. More fantasy, not helpful. Look, he reminded himself, look carefully, watch, observe. He could see nothing but grey cloud.

This is what the mists of the Outlands must be like. He'd heard the Rebels talk about it. It erased the world, they said, turning it into an illusion. The grey mists swirled and coiled, shifting, shimmering and eddying round his dome, the antithesis of the empty blackness he'd been in a moment before.

Lights came towards him. Pinpoints at first that slowly grew in size. Inhabitants of this marsh-mist come to investigate? But as they came closer and closer he realized that they were not the lights but glowing fragments. They streamed past and he could see that they hung together in clusters. Fragments of some mass suddenly arrested in mid-explosion? The clusters became more numerous, travelled faster and faster. Which of us is moving, they or I? All he could see were long white lines of light, crossing, separating, numbing his mind. The movement accelerated, Fendan felt dizzy. He had to close the shader to obliterate the view.

Then the noise began, a disquieting whine which rose in volume and in pitch. He put his hands up to protect his ears. The craft slewed into a large circular movement. He felt ill, very, very ill. The craft spun faster and faster until the centrifugal force had him splayed against the dome. The whine grew louder and higher and passed beyond his hearing range to become an excruciating vibration in the cranium. The sensation spread through every bone until his body was one monstrous wave of pain. He could not think. He could not act. He lost consciousness again.

When he came to, he was lying on the sleeping pallet in a heap next to his floater on the floor. Slowly, painfully, he climbed back on it and looked around. The movement had slowed. The sound had decreased and he was back again in the fog, luminous particles streaming past him.

This was some sort of spiral of coagulating gases he'd been

sucked into. A planet in the last stages of disintegration? Or the earliest phase of development? He opened the iris of his direction finder wide, focusing at random.

Back in the spangled cavern of the Universe he felt the relief of deliverance and a curious sense of gratitude.

Chapter 2

Each time he woke, Fendan stretched automatically for one of his jewelled earpieces to scratch another mark. The lines of grouped markings crawled steadily to the very top of the dome. Why do I continue them? he wondered. What do they mean? It had seemed a good idea when he had first thought of it. Keeping track of time, a sense of order, of logic, of being in charge.

Five hundred and sixteen sleeps. How long was that? A year? Two? By Zintillian reckoning it should be ... Fendan was surprised at his brain's delay in giving him the answer. Even younglings in their first school year could do that kind of calculation instantly. Let me see ... one year, one month, twenty-four days. But he did not know if his sleep-wake cycle corresponded to a Zintillian day. He only knew that it was a long time to be alone.

He considered the possibility that he might be completely deranged. How was he to know? There was no-one to measure himself against. Usually it didn't worry him but sometimes, like now, when he noticed an inconsequential cog-slip, a fractional delay, a minor fault in what should be automatic function, he experienced a sense of futility, that brought the chaos of fear in its wake.

And there was the voice.

"Number-juggling," it said. "A minor talent, irrelevant."

It was there all the time now. It had become familiar, ordinary, rattling round his head, recalling memories, giving orders, planning. Often unexpected surges of chaos came with it. Was this what younglings experienced before they learned control? After the oath of Bajinj he had totally forgotten the sensations of his early youth. Could this be the state that Merculan had recommended?

When he was possessed by the black chaos, he blamed the voice. He cursed it when the undertow of fear dredged his mind. But it was the voice that saved him.

"There's more to learn," it hissed when stars beckoned him to death in their incandescent hearts. How easy it would be to die.

"Do not give up," it counselled when, waken-time after waken-time, he lay paralyzed, curled and helpless as an implant in the Pool of Life. It kept him alive, kept him moving, kept him searching.

Eventually he had become used to the constant flow of unaccustomed thoughts, the surges of chaos. It was easier now. He ceased thinking of the voice as the interloper, separate from himself. Now it was his friend. He could argue with it to develop his notions about space travel. And when there was a crisis he could let it direct his actions. Merculan had insisted that he read all the Star Vaulter information. At that time he'd had scant interest, but he thought the voice remembered. Another fantasy perhaps, illogical but somehow comforting.

"Nothing that beings are born with is redundant," Merculan had been fond of saying.

Perhaps he was right. In any event, Fendan no longer bothered to dismiss fantasies that came unbidden.

He'd managed to discover more about the direction finder. The colours filtered from each star were related to that star's age and indicated the likelihood of a planetry system. White and yellow light came from stars so ancient that only their light persisted, still travelling from their long dead source. Orange and red were stars in the early stages of planetry formation, like that first one he'd visited. Green stars had satellites and planets spinning so fast that when he approached they whirled him dizzyingly into space. Indigo and violet stars had planets in slow-motion explosion. Blue stars were the only ones with planets that might be habitable.

He also discovered that star light, as well as tiding round his dome, showed on the direction-finder grid in a sine wave. Variations in the wave indicated planets in their relationship to their sun. By centring the grid to a variation, one could exchange energy and jump directly to the orbit of the planet.

He had been close enough to see signs of civilizations, clear evidence that beings dwelt there, but each time he said the words and tried to land, his craft juddered until he thought it must disintegrate. It was as though he were repelled in some way by the planet itself. Once the craft shuddered and shook so violently that he was thrown from his floater and left sprawling on the floor as the craft hurtled wildly with nothing to slow it down.

He had lain on the floor with broken arms, his face bruised and bleeding. He had never suffered pain before. One drop of jiwa on his tongue and he could shut the neural pathway, but there was no jiwa here. It was the voice that had saved him. It told him to lie quiet and recover. Each time he struggled to control his craft the voice spoke in his ear:

"Don't move," it said. "Lie still."

And when pain defeated him and he tossed and groaned, the voice sang the ancient lullabies of the Outlands.

He was glad then of his delicate bone structure which took so little to reset and heal. Nonetheless, it was eighteen-and-a-half sleep-waken-times before he felt well enough to look through the direction finder and steady the wild rush by taking a distance leap.

Fendan scratched the time mark on his dome. The five-hundred-and-sixteenth. How much longer could he go on? He was down to the emergency supply of nutrient pellets and did not know how much longer they would last. He refused to count them, for he knew that that would only add to his chaos. But the number was small, he knew that. He would have to find a planet soon and land there ....

He scanned carefully for changes in the star patterns while he'd been asleep. He had become quite expert at reading the skyscape, at finding reference points. Before sleeping he lined a constellation in the iris and blotted out the starlight with his shader.

Now he saw there had been a drift. He scanned the constellations and checked his direction finder carefully. Everything had changed. He could not explain it, but sometimes while he slept it was as though the craft slid down an oiled chute into another realm, a new universe with a whole new set of constellations. Fendan stayed perfectly still, noticing what was happening in his body. He could feel a change in the vibration. This meant he was hovering on the edge of a new galaxy. He could feel it quite distinctly in his body. He smiled at himself. What would the Kristeran say if he offered a mere physical sensation as a proof? Probably lock him up and send him to the Chambers. And, all that time ago when he was Supreme Krister, he would have done the same himself. The arrogance of ignorance!

It had taken him so long to recognize what the strange sensations in his body meant. At first he ignored them as an irritating intrusion on his mental processes, but the voice refused to let him off so easily.

"Pay attention," it told him. "Pay attention, feel."

Reluctantly he'd learned that each new galaxy, each star, each planet had its special rhythm, its own vibration which his body reflected. And even more reluctantly he'd discovered a certain pleasure in these rhythms. Sometimes he thought he heard, faintly, a kind of music. He'd experimented systematically and now he knew that when he let his body adjust to the new rhythm, travel within the galaxy was easier, smoother. He relaxed and paid attention.

"This is it," the voice told him excitedly. " This is it."

Fendan felt a pleasant, invigorating chaos. He scanned the new galaxy for blue stars and found three. Two were relatively close and one so distant that at first he wasn't sure if it really was there. But as he focused the iris, a tide of bright blue waves flowed up the dome. Many stars were blue, but no blue was as beautiful as this.

For a long while he watched the colour lapping gently. He could not rid himself of the certainty, the absolute and complete certainty, that this was where he'd find a home. No matter how logically he argued, no matter how he reminded himself of earlier disappointments, he just knew.

"This is it," the voice insisted.

Perhaps it was his own wisdom speaking, the part he had sutured off at Bajinj. Maybe that's what Merculan objected to, the reason why he'd rebelled. Fendan felt a great sense of sorrow that the wisdom had been there without his knowing, that he'd taught so many generations to ignore it ....

The blue light of the most distant sun surged to the apex of the dome, drawing his attention. Or was that just a trick of the eyes? The wave variations on the grid indicated nine planets. He jumped closer and checked again. The planets were of widely varying sizes. Some were encircled by orbiting satellites, others travelled alone.

Fendan had developed a routine. He started with the planet farthest from the sun, took the leap into its orbit, circled and observed. His scientific training stood to him. Even with the naked eye he could identify what substances were in the atmosphere from the colours and configurations that they made around the planet. He was surprised to find the same identity indicators everywhere he travelled. He'd expected strange and alien substances, chemicals beyond his experience, but there was nothing he had not learned of in his first-level school laboratory. Having checked the atmosphere, he looked for landmarks, points of interest and signs of habitation.

But this time as he scrutinized the sine-wave pattern, he felt pulled to one planet in particular. A chaos of excitement rose in him as he looked at the tiny squiggle, and the certainty of journey's end. Without further thought he leaped into its orbit.

There it was — hanging like a jewel, blue and white and beautiful. Planets came in every hue, but only those surrounded by a high proportion of nitrogen and oxygen and the necessary minute amounts of carbon-dioxide, argon, ozone and so on, showed signs of habitation. These were always blue and white, but this was different. It had something special, something he could not define. He forgot the black void, the ceaseless glitterings, the lonely wanderings from sun to sun and wondered if he'd come back to Zintilla. He watched carefully, but this was not Zintilla. There was no sign of the Coweling. This was another planet but it was home.

Now that he'd found it, Fendan was assailed with doubts. How would he communicate? Would there be any common language? What if the creatures had some inconceivably different type of body structure? What if they took him for a monster, a curiosity, locked him up for investigation. He remembered experiments done on Zintilla ....

He circled the planet, trying to find the courage to attempt a landing. More than once he aligned the direction finder with some distant constellation. But each time he did, a feature on the globe attracted his attention and he stayed in orbit. Then his doubts would return. The place seemed to threaten sanity while promising a refuge.

"Jump," his wise voice told him. "Jump."

He chose an area of the globe at random, pointed the direction finder and let his eyes go out of focus.

But he could not do it. His eye lids drooped and closed, although he was not sleepy. He shook his head, hard enough to rattle his headrest, blinked a few times and concentrated once again. Again his eyelids drooped. Perhaps he needed rest. He leaned back to close his eyes. They refused to close fully. So he stared unfocused, through the haze of eyelash. His mind went blank. For a fraction of an instant, he saw something. A kind of mist around the planet. He shook himself alert to concentrate but it had disappeared.

"Relax," his voice told him.

He lapsed once more into an unfocused stare. He saw it again, this time clearly. A sort of halo, an aureole of pale shifting colours fading to white at the edges. In all the planets he had visited he had never seen this phenomenon before. Without thinking, he focused on the halo, said the words, and leaped.

*

He was on a great green plain. Fendan turned round slowly. It stretched as far as he could see in all directions, broken only by an irregular pattern of low, circular, green walls. Beings wandered singly or in groups. They reminded him of the bipeds back on Zintilla. As he watched, Fendan decided they were primitives. Then he remembered Merculan.

"Our minds have atrophied," he'd said. "Just like our bodies."

Perhaps these beings were as advanced as Zintillians. Certainly no-one seemed concerned by the appearance of his space rider.

Fendan cautiously opened the door of the craft. He shivered as the first draught touched his skin. He sniffed cautiously. He could detect nothing unusual or noxious about the atmosphere, though it seemed to have a taste, a texture almost. He stayed at the door for a few moments, breathing, before he lowered himself carefully to the ground.

Immediately he wanted to get straight back inside his craft. He felt exposed out there, it was too chilly and too big. The stale air of his transparent dome offered security. He waited in the lee of the craft fighting the urge to go back.

The sky was black, star-scattered, just as it had been on the journey. A silver-fretted cupola, soaring from the circular horizon. But here, hanging like a promise in the sky, was a golden crescent. Fendan watched it rise imperceptibly, some kind of satellite? A nearby planet? Fendan could not remember what he had seen before he'd landed.

He adjusted his headrest to look at the ground. It was springy, textured as the carpets in his and Joquah's home. A sudden longing for her overwhelmed him. He lowered his floater to touch the surface with his hand. To his surprise it seemed to be some kind of plant. Its leaves were small, round and glossy, like polished jade-stone, and it had a pleasant odour. Under the leaves there was a complex, dust-brown stem system. Fendan knew little of plants.

Beings passed close by, talking quietly. They took no notice of Fendan or his craft. Occasionally a group came together and talked but most of the activity was centred round the circular walls. Individuals and groups came to them, leaned over and gazed downwards. Curious, Fendan moved to the nearest one.

He looked over the wall. There was a deep hole, something like the water wells bipeds constructed, but there was no water here. The carpet-plant grew up and over the surrounding wall and hung down the inside. There was nothing else, just the creeper trailing down and further downwards, swaying slightly as it disappeared into darkness.

A being, female, Fendan thought, came and stood beside him. She looked down and gave a cry. Fendan looked to see the cause but saw only darkness. The female climbed the low wall, laughed and threw herself down the shaft. There was no sound, no scream, no thump, no splash. It was as though she'd never been. Fendan couldn't understand.

He moved from well to well. They all appeared identical.

"What are these things?" he asked a being who came to stand beside him.

"The hylization tubes."

"You speak Zintillian?" Fendan was surprised.

"Zintillian, Queltar, Hangian ... it doesn't matter. Here, each one speaks, all understand."

This was something else to puzzle him.

"What is their purpose?" he continued.

"You don't remember?"

"I've never been here before."

The being looked at him long and hard and laughed.

"Well ... perhaps you don't remember," he said. "Many don't. You're on the translation station?"

"I thought ..."

"You don't remember anything!" the being laughed.

"I come from another galaxy, another planet."

"Obviously. If you wish to live on the planet here you must enter by these tubes."

"But ..."

"You could try direct landing, but in my experience the population will either discount you, demonise you or deify you. Take my advice, be hylized."

"How?"

"There are millions of tubes here. Each one leads to a different place, a different set of circumstances. Choose one you'll learn something from."

"How will I know?" asked Fendan. "They're all identical."

"You'll know."

The being drifted away.

Fendan reached a place where the glossy leaves showed clusters of tiny flowers. He had only once before seen flowers. Merculan and his rebels grew them as a symbol of their aims. He examined them curiously. Four delicate, almost transparent white petals with faintly traced mauve veins. They gathered in a deep pink heart. In the centre, a miniature bouquet of creamy-coloured stamen. Even the finest work of the best jewel-makers could not compare.

Fendan noticed more flowers farther on. These ones were turquoise with lapis-lazuli centres, farther on they became amethyst, and then the scarlet of flame-diamonds, then sapphire, cerise, orange, brown, even black. He recalled the jewelled gowns, the bright armlets and the gem-studded earpieces of Zintilla. Then he saw a hyzilation tube with extra space around it. It was carpeted in ruby-red flowers that hid the jade-green leaves. The veining glowed like flames in the petals, their black centres glittered. He remembered who he had been: Fendan, Supreme Krister of the Radiant Orb. He had worn the jet and ruby robe and, as he moved towards the wall, he could hear it tinkle, feel it sway around him once again.

The flowers clustered up the sides, over the parapet and tumbled down in shimmering cataracts. For an eternity he did not dare to look for fear of disappointment. Then his eyelids opened.

Instead of darkness there was light, instead of nothingness, a swirling brightness changing colour. It drew his eyes into its brilliance. He saw Joquah'. Her eyes were shining the rainbow hues of invitation. Overwhelmed with longing, with the pain of missing, with happiness and fear, he flung himself into the flower-hung shaft, the multi-coloured light.

Chapter 3

He had a profound sense of urgency. He knew he was swimming. He knew he was one of many. He knew he must survive. There were no thoughts. No images. Nothing to hear. Nothing to see. No questions. Nothing. Only the instinct to merge ... to meet ... to complete. And to survive.

He met it. Instinctively he pushed, demanding synthesis. The urgency ceased. He surrendered.

*

Fendan had no data. The Supreme Krister of the Radiant Orb was powerless without data ...

*

Explosion ... death .... He surrendered to it .... It was the only way ...

*

Fendan dreamt he had dissolved into blue, radiating fire, ringed with white. Volts of something — electricity or energy — pulsed through him, tore him asunder only to remake him.

Again it happened and again. Explosion, shock, reunion.

Without proper data he couldn't judge. No images. Nothing to hear. Just these dreams .... Were they dreams? With each explosion, each dissolution, the shock diminished. System adaptation to this strange environment? Gradually there was a calm. And suddenly he knew.

He knew that the old life which had been Fendan's was over and a new one was taking root. He felt secure, safe, certain that his needs were cared for, that he could rest, rocking gently in the darkness. But one task remained. He must remember and forget. Remember his past so that somewhere, deep in the cells of his new being, it would be embedded, a hidden history informing the present. And forget, to be free to start afresh.

Yes, he could do that. He wanted to do that. Now that he knew, he could relax. Relax and be rocked. Faintly he wondered what was rocking him but the thought melted and he let himself be rocked and soothed and lulled into remembrance.

Remember to forget ... remember .... Oh yes, to forget ... remember ... remember .... Yes, hylization tube, yes, Joquah's eyes and before that ... yes, the translation station ... and before that ... yes ... the little craft with its transparent dome and all that endless time in space and before that, yes, Zintilla, his beloved Zintilla ....

It had looked blue and white and delicate hanging there in space. And as he orbited he had seen serrated coastlines speckled with cities, mountain ranges veined with rivers and their tributaries. Deserts as orange as carnelian, as yellow as beryl, as white as powdered lime. And then he saw the large dark patch, irregular as a continent on a map. The outside of the Coweling, the great roof that covered the five continents and their crystal cities. The place where the inhabitants of Zintilla lived. It puzzled him.

He had always believed that the crystal continents covered most of the world, for who could live outside the roofed areas except bipeds? So they couldn't be cities he had seen, could they? The Outlands was covered with wild plant growth where feral animals roamed free. The herds of foodbeasts grazed there too, tended by the bipeds. But bipeds were little more than animals, living in shacks in the wilderness ....

And there was his home, his work room with its bank of recorders. All the learning of the planet at the touch of a key.

What did they tell about the Coweling? Was there anything to show how small it really was? He must remember, it was vital to know. He looked round the bank of recorders. The official histories would tell him, he must remember them.

EXTRACT FROM

THE OFFICIAL HISTORIES OF ZINTILLA

The forces of time and nature have endowed Zintilla with continents of crystal and it is here that beings have always been attracted to live. Our first engineers built a city of spires and domes and steeples so shining and so beautiful that it drew every intelligent being on the planet. The city, Breg, expanded to become the continent and eventually the other continents were developed and all civilized life on Zintilla was contained in the five continents of Breg, Aluu, Cah'ai, Tsa and Xemplox ....

*

... There was a long line of people, some cut and bleeding, dressed in rags. They shuffled past, chained to one another at the waist, shoulders weighted with a yoke to carry buckets filled with rock. The sound of their feet, shuffle, shuffle, shuffle, and the creak of the yoke and the shouted commands of the overseers, the crack of the overseer's whip ....

*

Where had that image come from? It wasn't the histories. Fendan struggled to forget the rags, the blood, the sullen shuffle, shuffle, shuffle .... The Coweling, what about the Coweling?

25

*

Wol the Coweler. Father of Engineering. 69(?) B.Co. 52
A.Co.
Educators: Liftha and Da'hil.
Major Achievement: Designed the Great Coweling.

The urgent issue of the day was the problem of weather. A population exposed to heat, wind, mist, snow, ice and rain expends much time and many resources protecting beings and buildings. This reduces time for study and research, experimentation, teaching and practice of new skills. Thus, weather hinders progress and hinders intellectual function.

Wol proposed building a great roof to cover the continents. He submitted drawings and an outline of methods. They were greeted with derision. Everyone believed a roof was desirable but no-one thought it feasible.

Wol was not disheartened. His suggestions were innovative and daring, and needed research, but he was convinced that his theories could be made into a reality. Quietly he continued his work.

He conceived the idea for 'constructagrow' and experimented with larger and larger units. When he was sure of its feasibility he submitted his design for coweling Breg. Interlocking frameworks were to be riveted into the granite borders of Breg and supported by stemple-steel pillars throughout the continent. Over this he proposed to grow a crystal canopy.

The Guild of Engineers was divided but the Supreme Krister, Batzan Adot, (see Ref. Recorder 7 a.c. Code e8g447) encouraged new concepts. He commissioned Wol to cowel Breg. The great experiment was a success. Wol used crystalline heat and light refraction to provide a controlled environment. The citizens of Breg were delighted and immediately Xemplox, Cah'ai, Aluu and Tsa demanded roofing too.

Despite the success of the Cowel, there was a vocal coterie

of dissidents and malcontents ....

*

"They were right!" Merculan's angry voice penetrated his recall.

"The pursuit of knowledge is unnatural?" queried Fendan.

"No. Isolating ourselves from the rest of the world is. And they were right. Look what's happened!"

Fendan concentrated, he would not have Merculan interfere now. Not while he recorded the histories for ... for ... for the future ....

*

Advocating physical labour, exercise and contact with 'the forces of nature', the malcontents objected to the Coweling. They travelled the crystal cities preaching their eccentric doctrine and gained converts among the young and the chaotic. The Assembly of Kristeran treated them with benevolence and the dissenters left to live in the Outlands. Without access to the Pool of Life they had no children and died out within a generation.

It took sixteen years to complete the Coweling. During that time some problems arose but Wol's genius and the co-operation of the Assembly of Kristeran overcame them ....

*

... A large unfinished section of the Coweling jutted out over Fendan's head. As though he were there, watching. There was a huge rumble, the roof began to crack, the rumble got louder, the Coweling crashed. He could see nothing for the clouds of dust. It clogged his nostrils, made his eyes smart and stream. He heard screams, moans, pleas for help. A voice shouted some-

27

thing unintelligible, there was another rumble .... White scribbles flashed on black.

*

... Somewhere close somebody spoke. It was low and difficult to distinguish.

"There's been another revolutionary" ... the voice became indistinct "... the Coweling ... danger .... "

Another voice, strident.

"... increase Wol's guard ... Jakus must not speak to him, imperative. Arrest the following: Jakus of Aluu, Burne the Hammersmith, Feelane of Aluu, Merdor the Cartographer, Qentian Speedman ... take them to ... arrests must be discreet, *repeat,* absolute discretion ... Broadcast that the Rebels have escaped into the Outlands ...."

*

No, no, not right! That was not the histories. That was ... that was something else. Something not to be remembered. It was not true. It was visitapes! He was remembering Merculan's visitapes! Fendan refused to remember them. No, he would only remember the true histories, those guarded and verified by Kristeran over centuries.

*

The Coweling was completed on the 37th day of the 8th month in the year 2054 by the old Star Dating system. The start of a new era. Batzan Adot introduced the new system on the day of completion. It is what we know as the A.Co B.Co. system, After Coweling and Before Coweling. And he honoured Wol with the title 'Father of Engineering'.

(Details of Wol's research, experiments, drawings and note-books may be viewed in the Hall of Teachers, Breg. Ref. Recorder 4 c.c. Code p9h534)

SUMMARY OF
THE BENEFITS OF COWELING

1. Provision of a stable environment
A huge increase in intellectual activity followed leading to:

2. Innovation and development of design and the decorative arts
Weather-worn streets were converted into elegantly smooth corridors of highly polished crystal. Design and decoration of buildings developed to create exciting reflections in the crystal corridors. Elegance gained importance.

3. Invention of the Floater
The prototype of our air-cushioned personal transport system, originally designed to prevent the corridors becoming scuffed.

4. The Evolutionary Programme
Use of the floater made lower limbs redundant, thus inspiring the Evolutionary Programme (see under Seej'ha of Xemplox).

END OF HISTORICAL EXTRACT

*

"Do you realize," Joquah' called, "that it is almost two years since our last pupil left home?"

Fendan, in the pleasuroom, unimpressed by the latest composition of a showy musician, switched off the sound.

"I was right in choosing you," he smiled, going into the work room. "You always know my mind. I was thinking that same thought."

Joquah' checked information at a recorder.

"Emmerlade is due to retire soon," she continued. "She'll be looking for educators for the Child of her Life. What do you think? Should we talk to her about it?"

"Emmerlade, of course!" exclaimed Fendan. "I have been thinking for days about whose child to choose. I'd completely forgotten about Emmerlade, too busy concentrating on suitable people here in Breg. She'd be ideal, High Krister of Aluu, impeccable reputation for intelligence ... superb logician ... who better? Joquah', you're a genius."

"You'd have thought of her yourself," she smiled back, "eventually."

"When do we formally inspect her reports and histories?"

"Let me see ..." Joquah' turned to the recorder and touched a key. "She will be 100 years old in two months' time. We should go as soon as possible."

"Fine then, I'll send her official notice immediately. We can see her on the first of next month."

A communicator capable of making contact with every being on the five continents stood against one wall of the work area beside the bank of recorders. Fendan went to it, spoke a message and pressed a key. It would transmit his words visually and orally to Emmerlade's home, an official notification, verifiable by voice and hand-print.

*

Emmerlade, the High Krister of Aluu, knew about the gossip. She knew that the squares, the crystal corridors, the workshops, the places where the people of Aluu met, were buzzing with speculation. She knew that in the research laboratories too, the experiment rooms, the schools, even the Auditoria, rumour and counter-rumour were rife. She was pleased and amused. The cause of the excitement was the birth and adoption of the Child of her Life. The continent was bubbling to know who'd be chosen to educate the child of the High Krister. They wondered too, who would replace Emmerlade after Crystallization, but that was a minor issue.

She had had requests to adopt the Child of her Life from many Kristeran, but as yet she had not made a decision. She knew from the records that Fendan and Joquah' must be due to take another child soon and she still hoped they would choose hers. What a heritage to give her daughter! But perhaps they had other plans. She knew in any event that she must wait for them to ask. That's why she was unwilling to decide just yet. Perhaps when they came to review her life's work?

Dressing in her ceremonial robes in preparation for the formal inspection, Emmerlade thought about the Birthing. For the first time since Bajinj Day, when she took the vow and learned the Suturing Process, she felt a rising of chaos. Not about the Birthing, but about afterwards. Hurriedly she sutured her mind and cut off the sensation.

"It is logical," she reminded herself aloud, "and it is the Law. This is no time to doubt the belief and practice of a lifetime."

She concentrated on her dress, ensuring that the topaz at the point of her headcover rested in the exact centre of her forehead. She clipped on matching earpieces and armlets, adjusted her headrest to hold her head high and checked that her robe of graded emeralds hung in aesthetically pleasing folds.

At the sound of the five chimes, Emmerlade was already waiting in the reception hall, erect on her tall ceremonial floater. She opened the door to Fendan and Joquah', swaying gently five times in the formal greeting of Krister to Krister.

"We have come in friendship and kinship," they said.

"And I receive you as friends and as kin."

Emmerlade led the Supreme Kristeran into the hall. The walls of uncut crystal were lit to appear transparent, green hints in the depths. They made the perfect setting for a group of peridot sculptures opposite the door. The Supreme Kristeran smiled their approval.

"They're the last works which Kur and I mind-fused before his Crystallization," Emmerlade said quietly. "There's been nothing new since. It's been ...."

Her voice lost its measured tone and trailed away. She felt another surge of chaos. Sudden images of Kur and their life together flashed through her mind. She took a breath and held it fast while she cut off the chaos and those disturbing images.

"It ... It's been, well, strange," she continued, "not to have a regular change of artworks."

Fendan and Joquah' exchanged glances. Emmerlade's only misjudgement had been to choose Kur as her co-creator. They had not been gestated in the same Pool of Life and he was her senior by two years. Despite their disparity in age, their co-creation had been more than usually successful, so their misjudgement was overlooked. Nevertheless it was illogical that one partner should leave for Crystallization before the other, untidy. Fendan and Joquah' looked curiously at the sculptures, wondering how Emmerlade could live for two whole years with the same pieces. Didn't they bore her?

"You've come to see my records?" asked Emmerlade, cutting through their speculation.

"Yes, yes, of course," answered Fendan, "but before that there is an important matter we wish to discuss with you." He gestured delicately at Joquah' to continue.

"It's a request," she said.

Emmerlade opened her hands in the polite sign of willingness to listen to a petition. A twinge of chaos made her heart beat unevenly. Joquah' continued.

"It's about the Child of your Life. But first, be assured that we will not misconstrue a refusal. You may have chosen already, though the continuing rumours in the corridors of Aluu lead us to hope.

"Fendan and I are now ready to educate another child. We have thought carefully about it and we would be honoured if you would allow us to adopt your child."

"It is I who am honoured by your request," answered Emmerlade. "Let it be as you desire, my child shall be yours. May she bring you credit, may she grow in knowledge, in logic, in reason, and may she always have a solemn respect for the law."

Emmerlade's heart was lurching again. She took another deep breath, held it to start the suture but she couldn't stop her mind racing ahead. Other Kristeran would want to adopt her daughter, senior Kristeran, High Kristeran.

"I am grateful for the honour of your request," she would say, gently, calmly. "But I have agreed to Fendan and Joquah's application."

She would enjoy the respect on their faces as each couple withdrew their petition. The Supreme Kristeran! This was reward indeed for a life of conscientious dedication to the laws. A tribute to her just and sober rule of Aluu. As her heartbeat steadied with the Suturing Process, she remembered her guests. This request changed the nature of the visit.

"Would you care for an entertainment? A light display perhaps?"

"Well now that we've agreed the adoption," Joquah' said briskly, "I think we should celebrate a little. Afterwards we can review the reports. What do you think, Fendan?"

"Oh yes, we must celebrate first!"

All three smiled, pleased with the outcome and the Supreme Kristeran followed Emmerlade to her pleasuroom.

The circle of the wall was a smooth, translucent alabaster, flushed pink. Gem-mosaics and sculptures, designed to complement one another, had been arranged around one half of the circle, low couches around the other. The carpet, the same pale shade as the walls, was thick and soft, with a subtle pattern which led the eye back to the artworks.

"How delightful!" exclaimed Joquah', and she got off her Floater to lie on a couch.

"This was our last room design, Kur's and mine," Emmerlade said almost to herself. She went to the panel of buttons and pressed a selection.

Joquah' frowned. This was the second time that Emmerlade had mentioned Kur and their last creations. It wasn't ... well ... appropriate. For a moment she wondered if they were right to adopt her daughter. The lights went down, she dismissed the thought and waited in the darkened room.

A sound of chimes, delicate, stung their ears exquisitely. A turquoise glow hovered round the ceiling. For a long moment they held and then cascaded down the walls, flowed to the centre of the room and spiralled to the ceiling again. Colour and music flowed together, overlapping, rippling, curling and intertwining until the minds of the Kristeran saw colour create sound and heard music create light.

Slowly, subtly, the turquoise transformed into every shade of itself from a pale whisper of aquamarine to a resonant bass, blue-black. Harmonies became subtler, more complex. Colour gradations shone with the glitter of jewels, the iridescence of rock-pearl, the encrustations of raw azurite. Harmony and colour, surface and counterpoint, arabesqued the walls, the ceiling, the floor, until, with a great crescendo, they intensified to an exquisite soundshape, spangled with gold.

It hovered in the centre of the room, opening, changing, turning in on itself, contracting to a dancing spark which pierced the heads, the eyes, the ears of the Kristeran. Suddenly it exploded in a shower of tiny soundshapes. These burst into further showers and on and on until the watchers felt that they too had been transformed into sound and colour.

When it ended Joquah' and Fendan remained silent.

"We called it 'Crystallization of Being'," Emmerlade said quietly.

"Wonderful. Quite wonderful," Fendan said slowly.

"It was our last ...." whispered Emmerlade.

Fendan didn't hear her.

"It will be shown in the Auditoria of Aluu to celebrate your motherhood," he said.

"That would be an honour," said Emmerlade.

But Joquah' had heard.

"Now," said Joquah', rising from the couch, "we should take a look at the records."

The work room was dark. Emmerlade turned on the screens mounted round the wall. They made a faint humming noise and cast a glow on the instrument panels below. Fendan and Joquah' moved from recorder to recorder, checking here and there, flicking through programmes, getting a sense of how Emmerlade organized her information before settling down to more thorough examinations. Joquah' pressed the key that accessed the records of Emmerlade's Food Programme.

She read details of Aluu's production levels for allish and falkin. The nutrient extracts from these plants showed little variation in output during Emmerlade's term as High Krister. Very satisfactory. The herds of foodbeasts had fluctuated considerably, but that was to be expected. The herds were affected by external conditions and by bipeds. But this had never affected Aluu's food supplies. Emmerlade had ensured that a surplus of animal nutrient was always in storage. It compensated for the fluctuations in the herds. Nothing pleased Joquah' more than well-presented detail and Emmerlade's reports were a delight.

Fendan preferred the histories. It was important to check them before a change of High Krister. It was his duty to Zintilla to ensure that no Krister tampered with the facts or their interpretation. He keyed the recorder.

EXTRACT FROM

THE HISTORIES OF ZINTILLA

Heldar the Great: Krister of Aluu. 120 A.Co. 202 A.Co. *Educators*: Fedark and Hena.
Major Achievement: Founder of the Food Programme.

At the time of Heldar's appointment to the Food Labs of Aluu, there were two major difficulties. We were dependent on the unreliable produce of the Outlands and twenty per cent of each adult's working day was wasted in food-related activity. Scientists researched methods to improve the production of allish, falkin, inger-weed, neff and the edible animals. But progress was slow.

Heldar discovered that research was being duplicated and there was no inter-continental communication. He rationalized research and arranged for each continental Food Lab to concentrate on one specific area of research. Aluu worked on animal food production.

A number of animals were used for food but each presented problems. The arglik had too much fat. The carcass of the mengs, while high in nutrient value, had a tiny proportion of edible flesh. Fetelswele meat, tasty as it was, had a low nutrient level and so on. Heldar's ingenius experiments in cross-breeding produced an animal which had everything: high nutrient value, a high proportion of edibility and a particularly fecund reproductive cycle. He called it the foodbeast.

But the foodbeast thrived only in the Outlands. It needed attention when calving and had to be fed during times when plant growth was poor. Heldar tried to overcome these problems but the foodbeast was not amenable to further modifications. It developed abnormalities, disease and became sterile. But Outlanders lived in squalor beyond the Coweling. Heldar contacted them and arranged a treaty. They would tend the herds in return for a proportion of the animals. The agreement was signed in 131 A.Co. and remains unbroken to this day.

The rationalization led to exciting developments, new edible plant strains, growing and harvesting methods, better understanding of nutrition. Heldar created the first plant sheds dug deep in the granite of Breg. He had each chamber lined with crystal, lit and heated to the ideal growing temperature.

He used Pool of Life rejects and deviants to study nutritional needs and evolved the precise combination and balance necessary for beings to live healthily. The Coweling ensured an even temperature, therefore Heldar could standardize liquid needs. He developed a capsule containing all essential nutrients and liquid. Two to three daily, adequately supplied one being.

*

Black and white scribbles flickered. A blurred image jerked into vivid focus. Crowds stood unnervingly silent in the square of Aluu. A female, mute and sullen, held a dead child in her arms. A youngling supported a gasping old male. A group of ragged beings covered with weeping sores huddled together. Healthy ones pointed silently to an emaciated child, a youngling coughing up blood, a female gazed with huge burning eyes. Someone shouted, someone shook a fist, someone raised a dead child and howled. The crowd erupted in a roar of anger ....

*

No, no no, I refuse to remember the visis. I refuse, I refuse. Fendan wrestled with the images of illness and death and disorder. He sutured his mind and the crowds flickered away. Darkness came, enfolding all. Fendan rocked there and was soothed. Remember ... remember ... he must remember ....

*

SUMMARY OF

THE BENEFITS OF THE FOOD PROGRAMME

1. Development of the intellect
Time wasted on food-related activities could be devoted to learning and research.

2. Lowering of chaos levels
Beings no longer depended on the sensation of abdominal satiation or full-belly syndrome. This reduced indulgence in unnecessary body sensation, thus improving chaos control.

3. Reduction of energy needs
With Complete Food Capsule there was no excess waste matter to be expelled from the body. Thus the time and energy devoted to sewage disposal was available for more important projects.

4. Advances in the Evolutionary Programme
The organs of waste elimination became redundant. The Evolutionary Programme could therefore improve body form, giving us the shape we enjoy today.

END OF HISTORICAL EXTRACT

*

"Congratulations Emmerlade," Fendan said at the end of the day. Her records were in perfect order, reports completed, the histories updated in the accepted form. "I have seldom seen reports so beautifully ordered. You can go to the Crystallization Chambers in peace knowing that your life has been an example to all." He bowed to her as a mark of respect.

"Your words are undeserved, I fulfilled my duties according to the Law," answered Emmerlade. "But there is a request I'd like to make."

"Ask what you will."

Fendan and Joquah' both opened their hands, willing to listen.

"You know that Kur is already gone from me."

"Yes, we know that he is forgotten," interrupted Joquah' with a slight emphasis on 'forgotten'.

Emmerlade looked at her a moment.

"Yes," she answered calmly, "he is a forgotten one. I have no-one to accompany me on the journey, and no-one goes there alone. You will adopt the Child of my Life, would you also accompany me to the Crystallization Chambers?"

"The honour is ours," said Fendan, and Joquah' smiled agreement.

They left Emmerlade and made their way to the Glider Station. The corridors, lined with beings out to greet the Supreme Kristeran, buzzed with speculation. The citizens of Aluu swayed their greetings, bowed their respect and opened their hands in urh. They were willing to listen to anything Fendan or Joquah' might say. They hoped for news. But, though the Supreme Kristeran smiled and bowed, they made no announcement and kept moving. It was not appropriate to make a statement in the corridors.

"Look, the Supremes are wearing the ceremonial dress."

"It's an official inspection, what else would they wear!"

"Both of them! There's more to it than just an inspection, you can be sure of that."

"The Supremes are adopting Emmerlade's child!"

"The Supremes don't want that Education Krister near the child!"

"The Supremes have refused to adopt the child."

" Emmerlade begged them."

"The Supremes refused."

"No, they didn't, the Supremes did the begging."

The Supremes ... the Supremes ... the Supremes ... rumours

rushed through the crowd.

When Joquah' and Fendan arrived at the Glider Station a young Krister of Aluu showed them to an empty compartment. He hoped they'd notice and remember him. No-one joined them in the compartment, but that wasn't surprising. Although transport was public, there was a custom that only a Krister would join another Krister in a compartment and nobody, not even High Kristeran, would join the Supreme Kristeran without a specific invitation.

Fendan and Joquah' eased themselves out of their floaters and lay on the couches. They were content, pleased that the adoption had been arranged satisfactorily.

"It's about time those fountain patterns were redesigned," said Fendan as they crossed Lapinderal, the freshwater sea that divided Aluu and Breg and supplied water to both. "They haven't been changed in ages. I must mention it at the next Assembly."

Joquah' looked out at the fountains spouting high jets of water in complex patterns, catching the light, flinging off rainbows and throwing shimmers on the ceiling of the Cowling.

"Leave the Waterlight Path to Engineering," she said. "One of us had better go to the ICS before we go home. We should inform people about the adoption. You know how uncertainty disturbs the slow-brains. It makes them restless."

"No doubt the wildest stories are already flourishing in the corridors of Aluu," said Fendan.

"Precisely."

"I suppose you're right," replied Fendan. "I'll go. Though I'd much prefer to celebrate."

He looked at Joquah', admiring her big broad head supported by the jewelled headrest, her eyes were large, luminous, he could feel the urge to mind-fuse come upon him. His own eyes were beginning to enlarge.

"Fendan," she reprimanded, "this is not a suitable time nor a suitable place."

And she closed her eyes against him.

He was tired when he got home. They had kept him at the Intercontinental Communicating Station longer that he had anticipated. He had wanted to give a short statement covering the facts, but the communicards had further questions. What were his future plans for his daughter? What would be his reaction if she turned out to have mere normal intelligence, what some called a slow-brain? Did he have ambitions for her to become a High Krister, perhaps even a Supreme Krister? Fendan thought the questions were illogical and ridiculous. There was no way to know how the child would turn out. Anything he could say was mere speculation without basis in fact but the communicard assured him that these were the questions most ordinary citizens would want to ask.

Fendan found these reminders that people saw his and Joquah's life as different from their own rather stupid. The citizens of Zintilla were all equal. They ate identical food, lived in similar dwellings, had equal opportunity for education. The only differences were in intelligence. Those of superior intellectual and academic achievement did the more responsible jobs. That was logical. Positions held by the Kristeran demanded knowledge and intelligence. The more complex and responsible their role in society, the more intelligent the being must be. Simple, obvious, logical. But slow-brains thought Kristeran led different lives. Would that ever change?

Joquah' lay on the couch in the pleasuroom. She put on a soothing soundlight-tape and waited.

"Come Fendan," she called, "take food and rest."

She held out a small jade cup with the nutrient capsules in it. Fendan swallowed them quickly and eased himself out of his Floater to lie beside her. The light patterns were restful and the music peaceful.

"We should create something to celebrate our new daughter," Joquah' said, and he saw the first faint rainbow gleam in her eyes. She took the phial of jiwa from the shelf above the couch and placed a drop on each of their tongues. Her eyes grew larger, and the urge to mind-fuse rose in him once more. This time her eyes did not close.

"Yes, yes," he whispered, "let us create something beautiful to welcome our daughter. What will it be Joquah'?"

Now his eyes were enlarging, his rainbow hues shone straight into hers, hers beamed back to him. Their colours combined, glowed deeper and brighter, kaleidoscoping the room, enfolding them both in a spiral of colour.

"Oh Fendan, my Fendan," she said urgently. "Let us combine

our energies to create what we want most."

"Yes, Joquah', for her, for our daughter, what we want most."

She drew his eyes deep into hers and he drew hers back into his. Deeper they went and much deeper. Then their chanting began.

"We exchange energies,
May our energies exchange.
The gift of perfection
For the daughter to come."

Over and over they chanted it in ecstatic union until the whirling colours locked suddenly in phase, intensified and exploded in a blinding brilliance.

And when the climax had passed they smiled and held eyes. Mauves faded to blues, blues to pale in the silence. Eyes disengaged, returned slowly to normal. They now knew what they had created. From the shelf above the couch they each took a board and a fine drawing tube. In unison they sketched the blueprint and specified its composition. A knuckle-wide ring of the rare blue jade, set with a crescent-cut diamond. The ring of a Supreme Krister.

"May she prove worthy of it," Joquah' said quietly.

"Zhenta, zhenta, zhenta," added Fendan devoutly.

Chapter 4

Darkness was total, endless as space, starless as the womb of the world. He hung there rocking gently, amorphous, blind, drifting towards some distant shore of awareness, cauled in Fendan's memories and mind. And there was a presence. Something he neither heard, nor felt, nor even sensed, though it permeated his very centre. A rhythm, a security, a sense of sacredness, of self.

*

Fendan, remembering, sensed something in the darkness around him. A new galaxy, perhaps? He adjusted to its rhythm automatically, rocking, remembering.

"Remember, remember, remember. We remember!" The crowd chanted it over and over and over.

"Remember, remember, remember. We remember!"

They trudged through the streets, chanting, grimfaced. Thousands of them, with their children. Five or six females came out on a balcony. They held out their younglings. The children seemed sickly, and lay lifeless, limbs splayed, across the females' arms. The mothers screamed to the crowd. Fendan couldn't make out what they were saying. The crowd growled some reply. Some beings lifted infants aloft, others clutched them to their breasts, more carried them on their shoulders. The little ones looked frightened. They watched with wary eyes. He could see their faces puffed and streaked with crying. One knuckled her eyes, another opened his mouth and howled. The crowds trudged on.

"Remember, remember, remember. We remember!"

A huge square. He knew from the buildings that it was the centre of Xemplox City. Crowds poured in, jostling, pushing, running now.

"Remember, remember, remember. We remember!" The chant got louder. He could see mouths wide and black with rage.

"Remember, remember, remember. We remember!"

They punctuated the chant with cries and howls. Their faces were all askew and every face was turned towards the huge doors of the Hall of Science.

A dozen or so younglings of Bajinj age pushed their way to the front. Some climbed to a window ledge and shouted to the crowd. Some pounded the doors.

"Kill, kill, kill Bewal," they chanted.

More younglings joined them, beating the doors with sticks and clubs.

"Kill, kill, kill Bewal. Kill, kill, kill Bewal," they chanted.

"Remember, remember, remember. We remember." The crowd rumbled back.

But more and more beings joined voice with the younglings. "Kill, kill, kill Bewal. Kill, kill, kill Bewal."

Soon the whole crowd took up the new chant.

"Kill, kill, kill Bewal," they roared again and again.

The younglings attacked the doors. Cutters, drills and burners appeared from nowhere.

"Kill, kill, kill Bewal," roared the crowd, punctuating each word with their fists to urge the younglings on. Then the doors collapsed. The mob ran screaming through the hall and into the laboratories.

Fendan watched with sorrow. They looted everything, tore up records and burned them, broke delicate equipment, smashed furniture, destroyed artworks, yelled and screamed and fought until the Hall of Science stood dark and silent, littered with things torn and broken, and hurled aside in anger.

"Bewal and her conspirators have escaped," a voice said. "They have taken all records and materials relating to the Pool of Life. But we will pursue. They cannot hide from the wrath of beings .... "

"Not accurate," protested Fendan. "That visitape's not accurate ... not from the histories ...."

Another of Merculan's accursed visitapes ...

"Remember, kill. Remember, kill. Remember, kill, kill, kill Bewal ..." The chants of the crowds came back.

"NO, NO, NO!" protested Fendan and hauled his consciousness back to the starless space, the rhythm. His mind calmed down again ....

*

EXTRACT FROM
THE HISTORIES OF ZINTILLA

Bewal of Xemplox: Mother of Beings. 250 B.Co. - 146 B.Co. *Parents*: Festal and Hawb Takh'bisa.
Major Achievement: Developer of the Pool of Life thus the Mother of Beings. First Krister to be named Supreme.

When thinking about Bewal, it is important to remember the circumstances of the times. Although the crystal cities had developed a highly sophisticated society and culture, most of the advances which inform modern thought had not yet been developed.

Bewal was born two-and-a-half centuries before the Coweling and three-and-a-half before the initiation of the Evolutionary Programme. Beings looked rather like today's bipeds. They moved awkardly on articulated lower limbs, their heads and features, especially eyes, were smaller and their bodies were large, squat and muscular.

Infants were created by couples, male and female who lived together for this purpose. Reproductive cells could be fused only through union of the reproductive organs, a physical intimacy which we today would find bizarre and repulsive. Gestation occurred in the atavistic female organ of the womb.

Although society had evolved intellectually, it was still acceptable to indulge in chaos. These irrational sensations were acceptable even in adults. Nowadays we know them to be the underdeveloped being's reflex response to external and internal stimuli.

'Natural' methods of reproduction were a major concern of the time. Females complained that reproduction took their time and energy from work and studies, and as a result they did not reach the highest positions of influence. Males complained that the females had total power over reproduction levels and the earliest education of infants. Everyone agreed that the imbalance should be corrected.

Bewal was born through the old 'natural' methods. Her parents were Festal and Hawb Takh'bisa. (Parents and their children used surnames to indicate groups of beings related by blood. The nearest modern comparison would be the kinship of the same Pool of Life. See: *Education Recorder*, History ref: 3**46098.) Both were scientists, though not of the highest grade, and both worked in the laboratories of Xemplox. They reared Bewal strictly according to scientific principles and, from the moment of her birth, treated her with reason and logic, discouraging any expression of chaos.

So Bewal was reared in an atmosphere closer to ours than that of her contemporaries. She developed a logical overview rare amongst younglings of her day. Coupled with a powerful intelligence, it ensured that she would become one of the moulding minds of the crystal cities.

After graduation Bewal sought a field of specialization to challenge her. She had been an outstanding student and each of the prestigious research programmes was anxious to recruit her. Her parents encouraged her to travel to Cah'ai to work on the Space Travel Programme. (See: *Star Vaulters*: Education Recorder, History ref: ***58694.)

Space travel was attracting intercontinental interest and the brightest young graduates because of the wide range of disciplines it involved. Bewal had always considered it a waste of resources, especially when more basic and pressing problems had to be solved. But it was here that the pioneering research took place. So, she decided to work on it and learn as much as possible.

When the Space Programme had no more to teach her, she left. Her superiors were dismayed. They offered her a more senior post and better facilities, they foretold a brilliant future, but she was determined to go. "Space research is foolish," she wrote in her resignation, "while females are tyrannized by biology."

In Tsa and Xemplox research on the fertilization of the reproductive cells of infertile couples had been established. The process was delicate, difficult and demanding. Bewal spent some time with these researchers and made these notes:

DRAWBACKS OF

LABORATORY FERTILIZATION

1. Couples infertile therefore possibilities of developing live infant decreased.

2. High level co-operation from couple essential.

3. Infertility causes increase in chaotic feelings. The possibility of fertility offered by Programme increases chaos to even higher levels. This interferes with success rates.

4. Chaos levels of scientists raised by uncertainty of success are exacerbated by the chaos levels of couple. Therefore, scientific objectivity impossible.

5. Couple claim any resultant child therefore further observation and experiment severely limited.

Bewal set up her own research department in Xemplox and the scientific community was happy to give her facilities. She let it be known that she wanted to concentrate on infertility and began to recruit her staff from among the most brilliant students in all the cities. A principal requirement was the ability to control chaotic feelings. All were sworn to the strictest confidentiality.

THE GOALS OF BEWAL'S RESEARCH.

1. A deeper understanding of the reproductive system with a view to producing infants by artificial means.

2. Recovery of genetic material from the deceased.

3. Development of the artificial womb.

4. In-depth study of laboratory infants.

5. Development of an easily administered sterilization agent.

Bewal used criminals and social deviants for experiments. When they were no longer useful to her alive, she had them levigated and used their remains to develop efficient recovery of genetic material from the dead. All children resulting from her work were raised in the laboratories for observation. Many of these grew up to be scientists.

Within 10 years, recovery of fertilization substances by the crystallization method became routine, researchers trying to isolate specific genetic material made a breakthrough and Bewal turned her attention to the womb simulator. She developed gestation tanks large enough to hold five foetuses and planned for larger.

She had long been interested in studies on multiple births. Evidence of strong mutual support between twin younglings was impressive. There was mounting evidence also of a high incidence of thought fusion among them.

"In the ideal, rational society," she argued in her thesis, "co-operation, mutual support and consensus would predominate. We can achieve this if we extend to all our children the advantages which have been available only by accident of conception. Now we can create the Pool of Life, a communal womb where all our children can be bred."

Bewal also studied neurohormones. She discovered that maternal chaos was translated into neurohormones in the womb. This meant that mothers could communicate their own chaos to the foetus. Sometimes neurohormones damaged neural and glandular development and predisposed the child to chaos. Now Bewal was certain that all children should be gestated in a large neutral womb.

She wanted to produce a generation of intelligent, rational beings, biased towards mutual co-operation, who would enhance and develop science and the arts. On the day the first Pool of Life gave birth to 800 new infants, Bewal went on Visinews to broadcast the results of her years of work ....

*

... A picture jerked to life.

A woman at the top of the steps addressed a crowd. Below her, beings shoved back against the pressure of the crowd.

"I don't care what Bewal says," she screamed, "they're freaks, freaks of nature. No — freaks of science. Science cannot replace nature! Look what happens! Pool of Life, she calls it! Can it sing a lullaby? Well, can it?"

"No," the crowd roared back.

"Can it cradle, feed and love?"

"No, no, no, no."

She shook her head in anger and frustration. "What kind of automatons would Bewal have us rear?" She paused and looked round the crowd defiantly.

"No more, I say. No more!"

The crowd cheered and clapped. "No more. No more. No more," they chanted, clapping to a rhythm.

There was a flurry at the front of the crowd. Three beings wearing rough tunics leapt up the steps. They grabbed the woman and bundled her into the building behind. The crowd howled in anger and surged up the steps. But the first ones up drew burners from beneath their tunics and turned to the crowd.

"Stay back or take the consequences," they shouted.

People yelled defiantly and threw missiles. The self-appointed guards switched on their burners. Flames shot into the crowd. The injured screamed and the crowd panicked. It churned and swayed, everyone pushing to escape the flames, the crowd, the fear .... Many fell.

The guards turned the flames on the surrounding buildings. Smoke plumed from windows. People ran down the side streets. Someone stopped and leaned against a doorway coughing and clutching his chest, another tried to drag him on. "Come on, come on, you can't stay here."

"Bewal's doing ...." he spluttered. "She's sent her children to impose her will."

The square was cleared now. There were only guards and bodies, flames and pain ....

*

Fendan wrenched his mind from the smoking buildings, the coughing people. He brought himself back to the dark. The safe and pulsing dark. He squeezed the scenes of violence from his mind and thought only of the starless dark, pulsed with its rhythm, rocked and rocked ... remembering ... remembering ....

*

Within a very few years, the majority of beings accepted Bewal's plans for voluntary parenthood. Now a couple could adopt an infant from the Pool of Life at a time convenient to them.

*

...."Fifteen more bodies", the voice said, "have been found on the steps of the laboratories of Xemplox. Latest reports indicate they were trampled to death." Broken bodies lay piled in a heap. Above them a hastily written notice fluttered. It was skewered to the door with a stinchiron.

"DEATH TO BEWAL'S SPIES"

*

These scenes would continue to interrupt his recall. Fendan realized that. He would just have to return calmly to the pulsing blackness and remember ....

*

By the year 211 B.Co. the sterilization of all citizens had been completed and the Pool of Life was in full operation. Those who did not agree with the Programme were free to leave the crystal cities and live elsewhere. There were some initial problems but, after a period of adjustment, the children of the Pool of Life were adopted.

*

Black and white scribbles ... visitapes .... Fendan wanted to go back to the blackness but the image caught his attention. A male, haggard and lined.

"We wanted to give our children a chance," he said, turning his head away.

He was tall and thin and he shaded his face with his hand. His wife stood beside him. She plucked at her tunic and kept glancing round. They were nervous, afraid they'd be caught talking.

"We're hoping it hasn't affected them," the wife said, eyes darting from side to side. "Maybe they'll lead normal lives. Maybe they'll be all right." The children were very young. They were pale and distracted and pulled at their parents, crying and demanding attention.

"She put it in the water!" the man said. "How could she do it! How could she neuter us all without saying!" He broke down and cried like an infant. Fendan sought the darkness again but it eluded him.

Another couple. They sat listless on a rock.

"You're going back?" someone unseen asked.

"Yes," the woman said in a toneless voice. "We're going back."

"We'll co-operate," the man said. It's the only way."

"We have not drunk the water of the crystal cities for five years now," interrupted the woman. "We've been out all that time and still no sign of a child."

"We're not the only ones," the man said. "It's not just us. It's everyone. Not one couple we know has had a child."

"Since we drank the water not even a miscarriage. It's evil, so it is," said the woman. "Downright evil." Her eyes flashed for a moment. Then they faded again and she started plucking viciously at her clothing. Tears streamed down her face. The man tried to calm her by stroking her shoulder.

"We'll adopt from the artificial womb," he soothed. "We'll have a child soon." The woman shrugged his hand away.

"And we've lost all interest in sex," she shouted.

"Hush, hush," said the man glancing round. "Anyone could hear you, chaotic mothers don't get babies." The woman put her hand over her mouth.

"Maybe it is as Bewal says," the man continued. "Maybe it's a side effect of chaos, of anger, of disappointment."

"Well everyone's the same. We have all lost interest, even the ones who didn't want children."

"We're hoping that getting the child might help," said the man.

"Are you not betraying your friends who opposed Bewal?" the unseen voice asked.

"Bewal! Hah!" the woman spat on the ground.

"Hush, shhhh," said the man.

"It's a victory for Bewal," snarled the woman. "You don't need to be a genius to realize that. Total victory for her and her spies."

"So," her husband interjected quickly, "we've decided to make the best of it."

"What about the revolutionaries?" asked the voice.

"What's the point?" answered the man. "The revolutionaries are sterile too."

*

Merculan's visitapes. How wrong were they really? Fendan wondered. It hardly mattered now. There was nothing he could do about it. The memories came, bidden or not. He would just remember as best he could.

*

DEVELOPMENTS RESULTING FROM
THE WORK OF BEWAL
THE MOTHER OF BEINGS

1. Standardization of Child Education
As all children were now the property of the laboratories, Bewal and her team designed the Education Laws to ensure their proper education.

2. Population Control and the Law of Life
In order to stablize the population and provide the raw materials for reproducing children, some control over lifespan was essential. Bewal and her team designated one hundred years as the ideal lifespan.

3. The Assembly of Kristeran
Bewal and her team of scientists gradually came to be recognized as a loose assembly of leaders, the Kristeran. Bewal was appointed the first Supreme Krister.

4. Reduction of chaos levels
Children born of the Pool of Life had reduced levels of chaos and, as more disciplined adults, grew to become scientists, artists and workers dedicated to the improvement of society.

5. Deformity control
As reproduction was in the most advanced scientific hands, defective children could be identified early and removed from the Pool of Life.

6. The development of Mind-Fusion
Children of the Pool were infertile and asexual. Sexual differences were defined in the differing intellectual qualities of male and female. And these were now recognized to be complementary. The foundations for mind-fusion had been discovered.

END OF HISTORICAL EXTRACT

*

The corridors leading to the Birthing Theatre were crowded. Beings, tall and solemn, moved in glittering decorum. This Birthing was special. Today the Supreme Kristeran would adopt the Child of the Life of Aluu's own High Krister. It was an honour for the continent and the Aluuvians were proud. They raised their floaters to ceremonial height so that their jewelled robes hung in elegantly sculptured lines. Everyone wanted to be there to get the first glimpse of the chosen child.

The theatre filled up. Beings chose their places and adjusted their headrests to look around. It was like entering the very brain of a jewel. The walls were mosaicked in zircons, and rose in a great circle to a glittering dome. Aluuvians were proud of their jewellers' secret method of faceting stones. Its effect was to refract light into the colour spectrum so that a rainbow sprang between any two stones put together. In the Birthing Theatre this was magnified and huge bands of colour danced from wall to wall in complex patterns. The floor sloped gently to the Birthing Dais in the centre and, because it was made of polished crystal, reflected the swathes of colour and the glittering dome. Naturally it was the showpiece of the Auditoria of Aluu.

The delicate strains of a new concerto for chime and airhorn filtered into the theatre. The buzz of conversation quietened and people looked expectantly towards the central dais. Joquah' and Fendan waited among the adoptive parents. The locked Lifeway stood on an alabaster table. Only Orgolon, Krister of Birthing, knew how it was opened. The last notes of the concerto faded and, from somewhere high in the dome, the Birthing Chime sounded. It made the jewelled robes ring in sympathy.

The doors opened and Orgolon entered. He was dressed in vestments of sapphire and pearl and held the birthing instruments aloft. The Givers of Life followed in procession. It was the final public ceremony for these Siblings of the Pool. Emmerlade was last. Many Aluuvians tried to catch her eye to make urh but she looked only at the crystal floor.

Orgolon placed the birthing instruments on the table while the Givers of Life formed a circle on the lowest step of the dais. He waited for the silence to deepen. When the silence was holy he raised his arms in the air.

"Behold, New Life comes," he intoned.

Music swelled while he removed the jewelled dome of the Lifeway and lifted the lid. The first child was visible, floating in the gestation fluid. He gave the Lifting Spoon to the first Giver of Life. The Giver of Life lifted the infant out of the fluid and circled the dais with it.

"Greet the New Life," Orgolon chanted.

"New One, you are welcomed," the audience sang back.

The Giver of Life replaced the spoon and held the child high for all to see.

"See that this child is perfect," he chanted in a cracked voice.

The large head flopped, the dainty, translucent arms twitched, the tiny body finished in a perfect U-shape. Not even the residual bumps where the lower limbs used to be — a perfect child. The Giver of Life lowered it to the table.

"I, Merculan the Elder," sang the Giver of Life, "name this perfect he-child." He waved the cocooning robe over the child three times. "Son of my Life, Merculan."

Orgolon beckoned a couple from the circle of adopting parents. He laid the cocooning robe on their arms and led them to the table.

"Teach him well," said Merculan the Elder, handing over the child. "Raise him up in logic, in knowledge and in respect for the Law. May he bring renown to your house." He bowed to the new parents and moved to the edge of the dais.

"I have seen the Son of my Life," he shouted to the crowd. "Now I can leave the Radiant Orb. Now I become a Source of Life."

"Zhenta, zhenta, zhenta," responded the audience.

He moved with infant and parents back among the Givers of Life.

The Birthing continued all day. Each child was welcomed, and named. During breaks everyone was talking about the infant Merculan. "Very highly evolved," remarked Joquah'.

"Match-making already?" said Fendan. Joquah' ignored him.

"All the rest have residual limb-bumps," she said.

"So far," added Fendan. "There are more to be born."

But they all had the bumps except for the last. Her body, like little Merculan's, was perfectly rounded. She was Emmerlade, Daughter of the Life of the High Krister of Aluu, adopted by the Supreme Kristeran of Zintilla. Emmerlade held her aloft. The crowd gasped. The new infant seemed to recognize her good fortune, for she smiled.

After the ceremonies the corridors were crowded.

"Did you see?" they questioned one another. "Did you see?"

"A match for Emmerlade if ever I saw one!"

"But who are his parents?"

"Are they even Kristeran?"

"What matter, it is a sign."

*

It was time to call to Emmerlade, the elder, for the last time.

"Your time of regeneration has come," Fendan said formally.

Emmerlade just bowed in silence and followed him. As she reached the door she stopped and looked back into her home.

"Emmerlade!" said Joquah' quietly. "It's time."

But the moment went on.

"Emmerlade," Fendan reminded her, "it is time for your regeneration ...."

"I am not sure that I want to go," said Emmerlade, still gazing at her home.

"Watch yourself, Emmerlade," Joquah' said sharply. "What you're saying is treason."

Emmerlade looked directly into Joquah's eyes.

"Your manners!" said Joquah', looking away.

But, Emmerlade continued to stare at her.

"Ah, Joquah'," smiled Emmerlade, "you do not know what this is like. I thought that when I took my infant in my arms that my life would reach completion but ..." She paused a moment and sighed.

"Now that I've done it I want to stay. I want to watch over her, to see how she turns out. I want to teach her things she'll need to know."

"Are you suggesting," asked Fendan icily, "that new Emmerlade will not learn all she needs to know from the Supreme Kristeran?"

"No, no," protested Emmerlade. "Of course I don't mean that. Your adoption has honoured me more than I can possibly tell you."

"What is it then?" snapped Joquah'.

"It ... It's just the final chaos of an old woman and ... I've indulged it. That's all."

The Supreme Kristeran were shocked.

"But, Emmerlade," said Joquah'. "You can conquer chaos. You know how to suture it, hold it in check. You've done it all your life. Why do you indulge it now?"

Emmerlade said nothing.

"You could be sent for Levigation, you know."

Emmerlade smiled. "What does it matter?" she asked. "Levigation, Crystallization, I must still go."

"But it does matter," argued Joquah'. "It is very serious. It matters to your memory."

"In a few months I'll be officially forgotten."

"But you live on in your child, you know that."

"Do I?"

"It matters to your child. It matters that it sets an example for the slow-brains, for the younglings."

Fendan moved towards Emmerlade.

"You have been a Krister all your life," he said, "and a High Krister, too. You know the Law of Life."

Emmerlade sighed, her hands fluttered. "Don't worry, I will go," she said. "I just ask one favour before I do."

"What is it?" asked Fendan.

"Just hear me, this last time."

"It's time to go," said Fendan, moving away.

"No," said Joquah', "I want to know what this is all about."

"Levigation," said Emmerlade, "Levigation causes death. So does Crystallization. It is irrelevant how I die."

"I know we talk of the honour of Crystallization, the honour of first receiving a child, and then the honour of donating our cells to create new life. But now, with my allowance of years lived and life still vibrating in my veins, Crystallization is only death. The method is irrelevant, I will still be dead. What matter praise or ignominy? I will not see my daughter as she grows. This is why I am not ready to go."

"I don't understand," said Joquah'.

"You will. You too, Fendan. You will understand it when your time comes."

"Enough of this nonsense," said Fendan. "It's time to go."

"Is Law always right?" Emmerlade persisted.

"Silence, Emmerlade." Fendan was disconcerted by her eyes. "You have said unlawful things, but the Child of your Life is now ours so I will overlook it."

"You must promise," added Joquah', "to conduct yourself as is proper in public."

"I am resigned," said Emmerlade. "I will conduct myself as I have always done, with dignity. I thought the final thoughts of a Giver of Life would be useful data." She adjusted her headrest to hold her head high. She did not speak again.

The citizens of Aluu crowded the corridors. In some places there was barely enough room for the Kristeran to pass. Despite the crowd there was no murmuring, no talk, just an awed silence and the rustle of clothing as each one bowed to the Giver of Life and fluttered both hands in farewell.

Every one of the Kristeran of the Assembly of Aluu was

present. They gathered in the reception area of the Crystallization Chambers. When Emmerlade arrived they bowed. She bowed back but did not give the usual final speech. The Kristeran were surprised but Fendan and Joquah' were relieved. Emmerlade fluttered her hands and the Kristeran fluttered back. The door to the Crystallization Chambers opened.

"Emmerlade, once High Krister of Aluu," a voice called. "You now become the Seed and New Life shall spring from you."

Emmerlade went into the chambers, followed by Fendan, Joquah' and the other Kristeran. When everyone was within, the Krister of the Chambers held up a blue cup. Fendan took the cup and handed it to Emmerlade. She smiled and stared at him over the rim as she drank. When she fell the attendants came to remove her body.

"A dignified parting," remarked the Krister of the Chambers.

"Yes, indeed," said Fendan.

On the return journey Fendan was silent. He hardly noticed the crowd at the Glider Station or the Krister who gave him valuable earpieces for his infant daughter. He didn't notice that the fountains on the Sea of Lapinderal had been changed.

"What did you think of Emmerlade's last thoughts?" he asked, turning to Joquah'.

"Worrying," Joquah' answered.

"Yes, I thought so too," he said. "Do you think we should do anything?"

"There's hardly any need," replied Joquah'. "She's safely crystallizing by now."

"I must say I'm glad of that," said Fendan.

"I think she's been deteriorating since our first visit. Remember her constant references to Kur?"

"Do other Givers of Life think like that?" asked Fendan.

"I hardly think so."

"It could disrupt the order of our ways. What if a being near life's completion campaigned to live longer?"

"Is that really likely?" asked Joquah'.

"We have no indications, have we?"

"We had no indication what Emmerlade thought until today! If someone of her stature and position can think like that, what might the slow-brains think? If it got out of hand – questions only lead to more questions. That's fine for science, but hardly the Law! Next they would be questioning the Levigation Rules! I think it is far more serious than just Emmerlade."

"Perhaps you're right," said Joquah' thoughtfully. "Maybe we should consider creating some kind of thought surveillance."

The infant Emmerlade lay in her sleeper, sucking the feeding nipple. When Joquah' and Fendan looked in at her through the viewing screen she laughed and waved her delicate little hands before her face. Joquah' checked the temperature control and the feeder, then she and Fendan withdrew to the pleasuroom. They took the jiwa but their eyes failed them and the colours refused to come.

For three long weeks they tried to co-create and failed. Then suddenly it happened. As the climax came they knew what they must create and when the colours faded the plan was completed in their minds.

The Assembly of the Kristeran was sceptical. Many members thought it unnecessary. The last great rebellion had been so long ago it seemed more myth than history. But Fendan and Joquah' convinced them that a chaos detector, capable of picking up all chaos above a certain level, would be invaluable for training younglings.

The laboratories of Breg developed it. Soon every wall of every building in the five continents had a system of sensor implants finely tuned to pick up gibble-wave activity in the brain. Once gibble activity reached 8* glyts per second the wall sensors glowed green. It did not respond to immature brains but as they reached the age of Bajinj, younglings began to register. It would ensure the future harmony of Zintilla. Fendan and Joquah' were conferred with the title of 'Defenders of the Law'.

Meanwhile, with every day that passed, the infant Emmerlade grew more delightful and more interesting in the eyes of the Supreme Krister. Somehow she was more attractive than his other four children. Certainly she was more intelligent.

Chapter 5

There was some shift, a momentary disturbance. A tiny reflex synchronized his rhythm with the cradling dark.

*

Fendan noted the change. He could feel a shift in his awareness of the rhythm. Not a galaxy, he was not in space. But in something like it, all-surrounding. He seemed to have been here a long time, but time could do strange things. Anyway he just wanted to rest, to rock and to remember ....

*

"I want a floater," she kept repeating. "I want a floater."

Fendan looked at his little daughter as she rolled over, waved her arms and persisted with her demand. She was far too young for a floater, but then she was far too young to be talking as she did, understanding as she did, asking questions. Fendan smiled as he watched. He'd entrusted the early education of his other children to a suitable Krister, but not this one. She was so precocious!

"I want a floater," she interrupted his thoughts.

Fendan watched her chaos rise as her voice got louder, more insistent.

"All right, all right, Emmerlade, I'm getting it now. Just calm down."

The child immediately relaxed, and watched her father. Fendan was pleased that she could control her chaos so easily — another sign of maturity. He got out the padded headrest and the trainer-floater he'd used for his other children and programmed an elevator.

Emmerlade remained silent and alert as the elevator lifted her. Fendan fixed the headrest to support her drooping head and adjusted the floater's suction cup to her small body. When he had made sure she was secure and comfortable, he took the dual control to guide her round the room. She squealed and laughed with the movement. She clapped her frail hands together and would have toppled over if it had not been for the automatic adjuster.

Fendan let her play around the room, moving her faster and slower, then faster again. She soon discovered the knack of holding her head erect in the headrest and adjusting her balance to the movement. But he knew he shouldn't leave her on the floater too long or her skin would be chaffed.

She screamed when he took her off and continued to scream while the elevator lifted her to her couch. She screamed while he removed the headrest. She screamed while he guided the elevator to its place, and when he turned on her couch rocker. He hushed and admonished her, he slapped her hands sharply but she still howled for the floater.

"It's logical," Fendan argued aloud with himself. "If she can go on the floater she can go in the chamber."

The Anacoeic Chamber was very useful for developing chaos control in young children. Inside the chamber all noise was absorbed, thus they were deprived of the stimulus of hearing their own cries. It interrupted the cybernetic cycle of their chaos. Besides, it was totally dark and that, too, helped control. He recalled the elevator and set it to pick Emmerlade up and put her in the chamber while he left to do some work at the recorders.

Later when he opened the door of the chamber, Emmerlade started to howl again. This was unusual. It's because she's precocious, he decided. Then another explanation came to him. Perhaps her chaos levels are unusually high? He hoped not. With the potential she was showing it would be ... a waste. He decided to leave her in the chamber a while longer. He closed the door and went back to work.

The image of Emmerlade screaming prevented him from concentrating on his review of the research reports. What if her chaos rating was abnormally high, what then? She could fail her Lower School entrance exam on her chaos-control. They'd accept her, of course, but she'd be noted. She'd get through on her other abilities, her intelligence. Fendan had no doubt that she'd be well above standard, one of the most advanced students. But what if the chaos continued? He and Joquah' would be blamed. The Assembly of Kristeran would demand their resignation.

"Well, we'll just have to make sure it doesn't happen," he told himself. "Between Joquah' and I, she'll be fine."

He opened the door of the Anacoeic Chamber and secured Emmerlade into the floater again. She was still sobbing.

As she sobbed, she rocked. Forward and back, forward and back, as though she would never stop. Fendan switched the dual control to 'unaided', curious to see what would happen. The floater jerked forward when Emmerlade rocked forward, and back when she rocked back. Suddenly she stopped. Her eyes were alert, her little hands rested on her safety rail. The floater remained motionless.

"Move," she shouted impatiently to it. "Move, move, move." When the floater didn't respond she shouted again, louder, the blood rushing into her face. Fendan thought she was about to have another bout of uncontrolled chaos. Instead she leaned forward. The floater moved. At first she was startled, then she made the connection. With a cry of delight she threw herself backwards and the floater reversed.

She began to explore the room, heading straight for the wall. Fendan used the dual control to save her from hurting herself but she screamed at him.

"Myself. I want to do it myself."

She enjoyed the movement so much that she didn't seem to mind even when she bumped her head or crushed her hands between the safety rail and the wall. He watched her attempts to control the machine, fascinated at her quick understanding and her willingness to experiment. He was still watching her when Joquah' came home from the Halls of Teaching.

She was tired after a day spent with a team of young Kristeran of Engineering, so enamoured with their latest idea that they were unable to think it through to its logical conclusion. She had intended going straight to the pleasuroom to rest but the sight of her infant daughter controlling a floater put everything else out of her mind.

"I wonder how the other one is getting on?" she mused, watching Emmerlade halt just before hitting a recorder.

"What other one?" asked Fendan, smiling at the child's tactics.

"The one who was born first, Merculan."

"That's right. I remember, he had no residual limb-bumps."

"Perhaps he's as mature as our Emmerlade?"

"Joquah'! You're match-making again!"

"No, it's plain logic. If Merculan is as advanced as this, wouldn't it be sensible for us to encourage a friendship?"

"'Planning indeed makes project succeed?'" Fendan quoted. "Isn't that what we teach our children?"

"I think it's worth investigating," Joquah' persisted.

"If this Merculan's chaos levels are as high as Emmerlade's, they're going to be a handful."

"'Too much delay ....'" warned Joquah'.

"You're right, we should find out about this Merculan."

The reports of the Kristeran were very promising. If what they said was true, Merculan was highly intelligent, as good even as Emmerlade. The Supreme Kristeran couldn't wait; they decided on a visit to Aluu. While there they could visit the parents and see the child.

Jenta and Jergul wore their ceremonial robes to greet the Supreme Kristeran. They were Grade 1 Engineers, employed to service Kristeran recorders. "Welcome to our humble home, your Supremacies." Jergul made an exaggerated obeisance.

"Supremacies," echoed Jenta.

They knew there had been a report and they expected some kind of investigation. But the Supreme Kristeran!

"This is an informal visit," said Fendan. "Address us by our names."

"He's impossible, this child," Jenta began, suddenly.

Jergul nudged him to stop.

"You must see a light show," she cut in.

She was anxious to do the right thing. A number of the Kristeran she worked for had asked about Merculan. Reports must have reached Breg. Those Kristeran told one another everything.

She led Fendan and Joquah' to the pleasuroom and put on a pretty interweaving of light. It was competent, uninspired and derived from the famous 'Tapestry of Light' composed by the Supreme Kristeran for last year's Coweling Celebration.

"Lovely, lovely," murmured Joquah' and Fendan.

No doubt it was intended as a tribute.

"How is the infant Merculan?" asked Joquah' as soon as she politely could.

"Oh, your Supremacies," said Jergul, "I hardly think you'd be interested in him."

"We are interested in all children," Fendan smiled.

In theory, thought Jergul, but did they call to every house? "He's a very difficult child," said Jenta. "Full of chaos, unresponsive ..."

"I expect he'll be for Levigation soon," said Jergul.

They had decided to volunteer him if he hadn't improved before going to school. It was better that way. They didn't want to risk being failed educators and lose everything. This way they could get another child. If Merculan's chaos grew and they couldn't curb it they would not be eligible again.

"We hear he is advanced for his age," said Joquah'.

"I don't know about that, your Supremacies," Jergul said.

"Well, that's what we hear," continued Joquah'. "That's why we wanted to visit you."

So, the Kristeran had passed on the news.

"He's good enough, I suppose," Jergul said. "But it's the chaos that concerns us, we think he's an untrainable."

"He's young yet," said Fendan.

"And he can talk like an adult," said Jenta. He drew breath to continue, but a warning sign from Jergul stopped him.

"I'd like to meet this remarkable youngling," said Fendan.

Jenta didn't like the sound of that but he went to get the child. Jergul was uneasily silent. She did not know what to say to the Kristeran. The silence went on.

The child's scream of protest was a welcome intrusion.

"What did I tell you?" Jergul exclaimed. "He is so difficult, that child."

Merculan appeared at the door on his own floater. He seemed

to have perfect control of it.

"Who are they?" he asked, pointing at the Kristeran.

"Sorry about the noise," said Jenta, with pride in his voice. "He was experimenting with the recorder and didn't want to come."

"Who are they?" the child asked more loudly, waving his arm for attention.

"Merculan!" admonished Jergul. "These are the Supreme Kristeran! Show some respect."

She introduced them while the child looked at them curiously. Then he came over to feel the fine veldan of Joquah's robe and trace the embroidered pattern.

"Stop that at once, Merculan," ordered Jergul, "Greet their Supremacies properly."

But the child just stared a while and floated out of the room making a rhythmic gurgle.

"See what I mean?" Jergul sounded satisfied. "The child is impossible, absolutely impossible."

"Isn't he very young for a floater?" asked Fendan.

"Yes, yes he is," Jenta agreed, "very young. None of his Pool peers can do it."

"I hardly expect so."

"And they can't talk as well, or read."

"He can read?" asked Joquah'.

Jergul allowed herself a small smile of satisfaction.

"Yes. We taught him how to."

Joquah' and Fendan glanced at one another. "We have a suggestion," said Fendan.

Jenta and Jergul opened their hands in the gesture of urh.

"Your son shows every indication of considerable intellect," Fendan continued.

The parents bowed in agreement.

"We are interested in him because our child Emmerlade is similar."

"The same chaos?" asked Jenta.

Fendan ignored the interruption.

"Children like that have special needs."

"Certainly, they need to be kept in check, watched all the time," said Jergul. "That's what we are doing. That's what we intend to continue doing, sir."

"Yes, I'm sure you will. But these children also need competition from equals. And they need constant stimulation if their talents are to develop."

"We want him to develop."

"There is a position available in Breg. We need a couple for our maintenance team. Perhaps you might consider moving?"

"Oh, your Supremacies!" exclaimed Jenta.

"What kind of maintenance?" asked Jergul.

"Recorders. The move would benefit both children."

"That would be a great honour," said Jenta.

"Are you trying to take Merculan from us?" interrupted Jergul.

"No!"

"Are we not quick-brained enough for him?"

"No, no. It's not that."

"What is it then?"

"Jergul, please," Jenta pleaded.

"Emmerlade and Merculan," Fendan said patiently, "will be bored by their peers and that will cause endless problems. If you lived nearby they could be companions, go to school together, study. They would stimulate and challenge one another. I think it is worth considering."

"I don't know—" said Jergul.

"I understand your doubts, but we'd be grateful if you'd give it some thought. Would you do that?"

Jenta agreed immediately.

"Jergul?"

Jergul frowned and cast down her eyes. "I appreciate the honour," she said, "but we need some time to decide."

"Take as much time as you like," said Joquah', "but let us know as soon as you've reached a decision."

"What's wrong with you?" asked Jenta as soon as the Supremes had gone. "That is an amazing offer, we'll never get anything like it again."

"There must be a catch," said Jergul.

"Imagine! Working for the Supremes!"

"I don't trust them. You never know what those bright-brains are up to."

"But this is *the* Supremes, not just any old Krister."

"Maybe they want to prove we're not fit parents. Then they'll take Merculan for themselves by pleading special circumstances," said Jergul anxiously.

"That's breaking the Law of Life. You can't have two children at the same time!"

"Hah! They have the Assembly around their little fingers! If they suggest it, the Kristeran will agree.

"Why would they do that? What would they gain?" said Jenta.

"They'd get all the credit. And where would we be? No, Jenta, we have to be careful here."

"The Supremes have always upheld the Law."

"How can we know for sure? We don't know what goes on behind closed doors."

"All right, but what if the younglings can't control their chaos?"

"Exactly. We could be blamed. They can say Emmerlade spent so much time in our home, that she was unduly influenced. We'll be to blame."

"You're making too much of it," said Jenta. "Don't you want to work in Breg?"

"Well ...."

"Think of it, mixing with the best technicians, on friendly terms with the Supremes. Think of the benefits for Merculan's future. Anyone with half a brain would take the offer."

"I just think we should be careful," said Jergul quietly.

*

LOWER SCHOOL AIMS

1. To expand the pupils' knowledge of cultural and scientific subjects.

2. To facilitate pupils to carry out their own experiments and projects.

3. To identify and encourage pupils of superior intelligence.

4. To identify and remove pupils of lower than average intelligence.

5. To develop, in association with the parents, pupils' chaos control.

*

"Did you see his report?" Jergul asked.

"What does it say?" Jenta responded.

"Brilliant but chaotic."

"He's young yet," said Jenta.

"Those Education Kristeran are too mesmerized by intelligence. They're too lenient about his outbursts."

"They know what they're doing," said Jenta. "I'm sure they do."

"They're not the ones who'll answer for it! You'll have to see Fendan."

"Again? But we're doing everything he told us."

"He'll just have to think of something else — and try to find out about Emmerlade."

Emmerlade's report was identical.

"I'm tired of Jenta calling constantly," said Fendan.

"He's right to be worried," said Joquah'.

"I know. We'll just have to plan more techniques."

It was Joquah' who designed the breath-holding and muscle-tensing exercises. She insisted that Emmerlade and Merculan practise regularly, so that they would improve enough to be accepted for Middle School.

*

MIDDLE SCHOOL AIMS

1. To expand knowledge in all subjects.

2. To encourage pupils to choose their specialist areas.

3. To develop rigorous chaos control with advanced non-breathing and the use of jiwa.

4. To prepare pupils for Bajinj.

*

What Joquah' did not know was that for every control technique she taught, Merculan designed its opposite, and he practised his loosening exercises just as diligently, in secret.

"Control should be both ways," he explained to Emmerlade. "You should try it."

"Why should I?"

"It's logical, isn't it?"

"I suppose so," she said. "But what about the warning system? Don't the walls glow green?"

"We're still too young, our brains are too immature. They won't register. It won't affect us for a few more years."

"What then?"

"Maybe by then they'll agree with me," he grinned.

The idea intrigued Emmerlade. She repeated Merculan's argument to Fendan as though the idea had just struck her. Her father was pleased, it had intrigued him briefly as a youngling.

"Let's take that argument a bit further," he said, turning from the visitapes he was editing. "What would happen if everyone were to loosen control?"

"They'd be learning to keep control at the same time — that's the point — keeping a balance."

"All right, suppose that everyone learned how to keep the balance. There would be times when some are out of chaos control and some are not, right?"

"Right," nodded Emmerlade.

"What happens to control surrounded by chaos?"

"During chaos the brain emits gibble-waves", Emmerlade quoted from her neurology primer, "at the rate of 24.006 glyts per second. Wave accumulation loosens the subject's suturing and creates sympathetic loosenings in surrounding brains."

"Precisely. Chaos causes chaos. That's why parents are only allowed one child at a time. The combined chaos levels of two or more children could loosen even an adult's control! Even with one child, adults often have to use the Suturing Process as a safety precaution."

"Yes, but — " Emmerlade interrupted.

"Let me finish. Think this through. What happens to logical thought in chaos?"

"It becomes impossible."

"And if, say, ten per cent of the population were out of control at the same time?"

"The glyt count would rise dramatically."

"And?"

"It would loosen the suturings of another twenty per cent of people."

"Exactly. That's now thirty per cent out of control. That would loosen more suturings. The entire population would be in chaos in no time. Think of the effect. There'd be no logic left!"

"Yes," said Emmerlade thoughtfully, "I see what you mean ...." But the reservation stuck stubbornly in the back of her mind, an obscure sense of something missing.

It was the same every time she came up with arguments that questioned the Law. Fendan listened carefully and prefaced all his answers with: "Let us think this through ...."

Joquah' listened carefully and prescribed more control exercises.

Jenta and Jergul did not listen, instead they would put Merculan in the Anacoeic Chamber for the rest of the day. So he stopped sharing ideas. He went his own way, keeping out of trouble as best he could. "It's all right for you," he told Emmerlade.

But Emmerlade still wondered.

Once a week Joquah' monitored the results from the Chaos Detector. She had been doing it ever since it had been installed. And it showed some surprising results. Everyone registered chaos from time to time, even the most senior of Kristeran. That must be what they had witnessed in the elder Emmerlade before her Crystallization. It was not information she wanted to have broadcast. Fendan did not believe her at first and had to examine the results himself.

"Most of this happens during sleep times," he pointed out.

"And in neighbourhoods where slow-brains live," she added. "You'll have to decide on an average level of acceptable chaos and calibrate the instruments to take that into account."

"And we'll have to re-locate the slow-brains."

The slow-brains were delighted to be moved to live among the intelligentsia. They saw it as a rise in social status. And the Zoning Kristeran were happy to co-operate. The concentrations of chaos averaged out though there was still a small number of insane beings who up until now had avoided detection. These were put on a rehabilitation programme and, if they showed no improvement, were levigated. Joquah' could then recalibrate the Chaos Detector.

She instucted the Education Kristeran to develop improved control techniques and encouraged the Birthing Guild to search for the genetic key to creating a new generation of beings with high control. Neuro-psychology and genetics became the most popular sciences.

"Can I come in?" Jergul asked from the door of the work room.

Joquah' was not pleased to be interrupted, but she needed all the information she could get about Merculan.

"Please do," she said.

"I suppose Emmerlade is still full of those crazy ideas," said Jergul.

"I'd expect that from younglings."

But Joquah' was concerned. Emmerlade had more chaotic notions than were good for her.

"I'm glad to say Merculan has stopped."

"Really?"

"Yes. You see, I was right. A few shifts in the chamber soon put an end to it."

"Mmmm," said Joquah', and wondered how she could monitor his chaos ratings more closely.

"You could try it with Emmerlade."

Really, Joquah' thought, Jergul was pushing her familiarity a bit far. Joquah' looked at her for a long moment.

"I'm not sure that all her crazy ideas are her own," she said.

Maybe she could use the Chaos Detector. They were too

young to register accurately, but in view of their precocious development it just might be possible.

Their readings were very unusual. First, they were the same as an adult's, none of the meaningless scratchings normally received from an immature youngling. The averages were within acceptable limits, but the score was made up of huge swings. At times their chaos levels went to 10.3 glyts per second, way over the legal limit, but at other times their control was tighter than a High Krister.

"It's a feature of their exceptional abilities," Fendan suggested. "Everything they've done so far has been unusual. It's just their pattern for control development."

"But their brains register like an adult's," Joquah' argued.

"They're still learning."

"I hope so."

"We've had no complaints."

"Except for Jergul boasting that she's the better educator!" Joquah' pointed out.

"At least we don't have Jenta here every other day."

"Still, I'm worried, Fendan."

"There's time yet before Bajinj."

"I'm not overly concerned about Emmerlade, but Jenta and Jergul's chaos readings are not ideal."

"They're slow-brains, Joquah', what else can you expect?"

"Merculan may need more help."

"Merculan knows that," Fendan reassured her. "He talked to me recently."

"What did he say?"

"He knows their limitations and has no intention of letting it hinder him."

"Good," said Joquah', somewhat reassured.

What Merculan had actually said was: "My parents want to limit me, they don't understand what I'm doing, but I won't let it interfere." It amused him to know that Fendan had got it wrong.

*

They had been all day in the Food Laboratories. The Breg Guild of Educators was curious to know what project their two best pupils would choose as a result of the visit. Already they had come up with startlingly sophisticated experiments for younglings of their age.

Merculan called to Emmerlade as she came through the doors with a group of class peers.

"What is it?" she answered. He gestured to her to follow him.

"Typical!" sneered one of the other students as she left the group to join him. "I suppose it's about something you think the rest of us wouldn't understand."

Merculan stopped to consider the remark, frowning. "I believe you wouldn't," he said seriously.

"Oh, you geniuses, you're all the same."

"Chaos, chaos," admonished Emmerlade, imitating one of the teachers by waving a warning thumb.

"Come on, let's go," said Merculan, making the secret sign that told her to ask nothing until they had privacy.

"There you go, always rushing. You'll both end up in the Chambers if you go on like that," Jergul scolded as they burst in. They greeted her politely. She was always like that and they pretended to be chastened.

Merculan carefully closed the door of his room. "Did you know," he began.

Emmerlade gestured to him to be quiet. She opened his robe closet and went inside, beckoning him to follow.

"I've been looking at Joquah's current work," she said, when he'd closed the door. "Both of us register. She's watching us closely."

"Of course she is, but what are we doing in here?"

"Closet walls were not fitted with sensors. We're safe in here."

"Are you sure?"

"I found the specifications. It's safe now to talk."

"Did you know that bipeds could talk?"

For a moment Emmerlade was stunned. "Don't be ridiculous," she said. "How could they?"

"I don't know, but one spoke to me."

"Oh, I know they can hold a simple conversation but —"

"No, this one could converse intelligently!"

"Tell, tell," she urged.

"Remember when we were in the plant sheds?"

"Yes, go on." Emmerlade's chaos was rising.

"Remember when the Krister was talking about crop rotation, nutrient levels, all that basic stuff?"

"Yes."

"I slipped away to watch the biped feeding plants. When I greeted him he answered perfectly. No mumbling, nothing. So I asked him about genetic harvesting."

"Did he understand?"

"Not only that. He explained it correctly!"

"You mean like in the books?" asked Emmerlade.

"Not exactly. He uses a roundabout way, laced with stories, but he was right all the same."

"With a horrible accent and grunts!"

"No, in perfect Zintillian."

Emmerlade thought for a while. There must be some explanation. "Perhaps he is particularly intelligent .... "

"That's not the point, Emmerlade, don't you see? It's proof."

"What proof?"

"That they're teaching us lies."

"But he's only one. What about the rest?"

"He said that they can all talk!"

"But ...."

"They like to give us the impression that they are dull. It makes it easier for them to work here."

"But that's ridiculous. How could it be easier?"

"All he'd say was that I might understand sometime."

"Maybe we could civilize them and become famous for our work!"

"Maybe ...." said Merculan.

"I must ask Joquah' and Fendan about this."

"Would they believe you? They'd think you were mad. Let's find out what we can first."

All the other students wanted to work with the Food Laboratory scientists. However, Emmerlade and Merculan proposed a project to observe growth cycles of plants and assess the vulnerable phases.

"That means work in the sheds!" their Krister reminded them.

They explained that they intended to observe how bipeds worked with a view to charting their methods and suggesting improvements. The Krister smiled.

"Bipeds work best when their methods are unquestioned," she said.

"What will we do if they ever refuse to work for us?" asked Merculan.

The idea of bipeds withdrawing their services was laughable but it was theoretically possible. If any other student had suggested the project the Krister would not have agreed, but Emmerlade and Merculan were special. She approved their project.

*

The biped moved from plant to plant, testing the soil, checking the leaves, spraying and mumbling under his breath. From the top of his head a thick black growth sprouted, streaked with white. That must be hair, Emmerlade assured herself. And he was as tall as any being on a high floater, maybe taller, with bulging arms and trunk and those extraordinary lower limbs. Emmerlade couldn't stop staring even though she thought him grotesque. Still there was a curious grace in the way he moved.

"Let's talk to him," she said to Merculan.

"Patience, Emmerlade, wait a bit."

"I want to find out what he's saying to himself."

"We know nothing about bipeds. Let's just take it easy. We have plenty of time."

Merculan went up and down the plant beds moving gradually closer to where the creature was working. Emmerlade followed him. They pretended to examine leaves but they were listening intently. The biped was singing! A strange little tune and ... the words made no sense.

"The first thing to learn is to care," a voice said unexpectedly.

Emmerlade and Merculan looked round. They were alone except for the biped and he was still working away.

"You must care for plants or they'll die."

The voice was deep and resonant, the accent strange.

"Who's speaking?" Emmerlade demanded.

"I am." The biped turned round. He looked straight at them

and they didn't know if he was mocking or not.

"We have come to learn about plants," Merculan said politely, showing the same respect he would to a Krister. "We'd be grateful if you'd teach us."

The biped put the spray down deliberately. He did not wear a headrest and his head could move freely. He wore a rough veldan robe tied at his middle and exposing the lower part of his walking limbs which were wrapped in more veldan and ended in rough leather slippers. The younglings stared, fascinated.

"Well, well, well," said the biped. "There's a tergiversation for you!"

His body began to shake and he made a sound. It looked like laughter, but it sounded like no laughter they had ever heard before. They felt dishonoured, disconcerted, as though they had said something particularly stupid. The sound seemed to affect them and they too began to laugh, gently at first and then in high-pitched screams which made them gasp for breath and clutch one another. They were not even very sure what they were laughing at.

"Emmerlade and Merculan, well, well, well. The bright hopes of Zintilla want to learn from a biped."

"But we do, we really do," said Emmerlade, and realized that she meant it.

"How do you know our names?" asked Merculan.

"This might be difficult for you to believe but ...." he paused and rolled his eyes from one to the other, "bipeds listen! We understand more about you Glitterflies than you do about us."

"Isn't that what I told you?" said Merculan.

"Glitterflies?" Emmerlade asked. "What do you mean by Glitterflies?"

"That's hard to explain." The biped thought a moment and leaned against the plant beds.

"Outside your all-purpose dome," he began, "there is another world. It is a place of life and death, energy, excitement. There are fields and villages, and trees, and plants, and all kinds of animals. There are cloud-mottled skies for the birds. There are blue-rippled lakes for the silvery fish. There's a bed for the traveller, food for the worker, sun after storm and dark, dark, deep, jungly woods."

Emmerlade and Merculan listened, hypnotized.

"And deep in those jungly woods," he continued, "lives an insect. It flits through trees where the sunlight dodging through the leaves makes it shine and glitter like a jewel. We call it the Glitterfly."

The biped laughed again.

"You call us Glitterflies because of our jewels?" Emmerlade asked.

"That's one reason."

"There is another?"

"You're sure you want to know?" the biped asked, smiling.

"Yes."

"Remember the deep and jungly woods?" he began in his hypnotic voice. "In those dark and jungly woods there are trees. Trees of many kinds. Trees with blossom and trees with fruit, spiky trees and smooth, with names you've never even heard of. One tree weeps tears of sap and this is the food of the Glitterfly. The insect lights on the bark and glitters in the sunlight and sips the amber tears. But when a Glitterfly leaves the woods, forsakes the weeping trees ...." The biped paused and sighed.

"What happens?" Emmerlade asked.

"It dies."

"I don't understand all you say," Merculan said, "but I think you mock us."

"A little, yes," answered the biped.

"Have you a name?" asked Emmerlade.

"I am called Festal Takh'bisa."

"Takh'bisa is the name of the Mother of Beings!" exclaimed Merculan.

"We keep family names just as you keep the name of your Life Giver."

"But that's Bewal's name."

"I know," smiled the biped. "I'm a descendant."

"Bewal children were all from the Pool."

The biped laughed.

"She married a husband and gave birth to a child."

"That's not true! The histories say ...."

"I know what your histories tell you but it's true none the less. Her husband disagreed with her so she condemned him. But he had friends. One night that was dark, very dark, he escaped. He fled from Xemplox with their child in his arms and lived with those who rejected the lure of crystal."

Emmerlade and Merculan looked at one another. They did not
know what to believe. Festal just smiled and took up the plant
spray.

"Now, what is it you want to learn?" he asked.

"I'd like to see an insect," said Merculan.

"All in good time, when the plants need them. You'll see
enough of them then."

"Why do they need them?" asked Emmerlade.

The biped faced them.

"Think carefully," he said, "before you listen to the lessons
of Festal Takh'bisa. Think very carefully. The Kristeran may
not like what you learn."

"He's a strange being full of chaos," Emmerlade said when
they were alone again. "It affected me. I was in chaos all the
time there."

"Yes, isn't it interesting?"

For a moment Emmerlade thought she saw something in
Merculan's eyes that reminded her of the biped.

"Was it true about Bewal?" she asked.

"I don't know but I'm going back."

"So am I," said Emmerlade.

Over the next two months Emmerlade and Merculan worked
with Festal. They learned to know when the plants needed water
or food. They learned which shoots were weeds, the warning
signs of blue-tick, dry leaf and boreworm, the times for pollina-
tion. And they listened to Festal's tales of the Outlands.

"Far above the Cowel," he told them, "is another roof. It is
the roof of the world and we call it the sky. Your cowel-roof
gleams and glisters according to plan. Your plan. And you
change it whenever you choose. This sky-roof has its own plan.
It changes itself. This morning it was high, wide and pale, but
who knows how it will be when I leave. It might be splattered
with green or bursting with orange or dark and dirty as the
coat-tail of a wandering story-teller.

"All morning the double suns climb up and up through mists
and trees and birdsong to the top of the blue, blue dome and slip
back down behind the mountains in the afternoon. The sky goes
black. And now the Red, the Ringed and the Broken Man rule
the sky.

"Our dome gives heat and light, the air we breathe, the rain to quicken plants. Mind you, it also gives us torrents, shiver-rains, spin-winds and snows," Festal added.

"It must be difficult to live outside," said Merculan.

"You get used to it, enjoy it even."

"What's the cause of all these sky changes?" asked Emmerlade.

Festal laughed.

"Enough clather for today," he said and held up a box. "I've brought insects. The plants can't wait to hear from them."

"Insects!" Merculan exclaimed. "Let me see."

Festal put the box aside. "First," he said folding his arms over his chest, "there are some things you need to know."

Emmerlade and Merculan concentrated.

"Some insects sting, and for you two a sting could be fatal. So don't try to touch them. Look all you like but don't touch them, ever. And remember, they can fly and they obey only themselves."

"If they fly they might land on us," Emmerlade suggested nervously.

"If one does, just stay quiet. It will fly away again."

Festal opened the box and the insects flew out. They circled the ceiling in a black buzzing cloud.

"I can't see them up there," complained Merculan.

"Be patient," said Festal.

Then one by one the insects settled on the plants. They had never seen anything like them.

"Flying jewels!" exclaimed Emmerlade, leaning close to examine one. "They're so tiny!"

"Look at this!" cried Merculan. "A live topaz."

"Watch how they flit from plant to plant," said Festal, smiling at the younglings' excitement. "They whisper messages into its leaves."

"Tell us properly, Festal," said Emmerlade.

"The plants here grow far from their kin, they get lonely for news of the Outlands. When that happens they droop and they die. That's why I bring the insects. For company. Listen ...."

"I can't hear a thing."

"Shush ... listen .... Can you hear the leaves sing?" They held their breath to listen.

"There's nothing to hear."

"Perhaps your ears are too dull."

"Oh, Festal, be serious, please," begged Merculan. "They don't really talk to one another, do they?"

"They do. And they pollinate too, see how ...."

Merculan screamed and held up his hand.

"It stung me. I just moved my finger towards it and it stung me."

"What did it look like?" Festal asked.

He took Merculan's little hand in his own big one, examined the bite on the finger and put it in his mouth.

"Stop that, how dare you," shouted Emmerlade. "Leave his finger alone."

She was shocked. It was an act of gross intimacy.

"He'll die if I don't," Festal answered. "What kind of insect was it, Merculan, tell me, it's important."

"It was a topaz."

"What size."

"Big, a big one, I think"

"Good. You've a chance."

He pulled out an old mattress from a press and carried Merculan to it.

"Lie here and don't move," he said, "Emmerlade, don't let him move. I'm going to get something for him."

Merculan's finger swelled and swelled. Emmerlade was afraid it might burst. It grew red and he seemed to be running a fever. Festal was away a long time. Emmerlade wondered if she should go for Fendan or wait. She tried to think logically what was best, but a chaos of fear took over. She couldn't think, couldn't decide. And all the time Merculan got sicker and sicker. She was afraid he might die.

At last Festal came with a lumpy wet compress. He wrapped some round Merculan's finger and bathed his head with the remainder. Merculan slept.

"Go now," Festal said. "He'll be all right now, he only needs sleep. I'll watch him. You'll have enough on your hands."

Emmerlade told Fendan and Joquah' the whole story. Even the bit about Festal speaking. They took an elevator and went with Emmerlade to the plant sheds. Merculan lay on the mattress with Festal still bathing his head.

"Thank you for your care," Fendan said.

Festal grinned and grunted and bobbed up and down.

"I'd hold him responsible if he weren't so obviously incapable," said Joquah'.

"Hush, Joquah', he understands," warned Emmerlade.

Festal grunted and grinned.

"I doubt it," said Joquah', looking at the biped.

"Speak, Festal. Please, speak properly," Emmerlade begged.

Festal grunted and looked at the ground.

Jergul and Jenta were not pleased when they heard the news but they agreed to keep the whole incident quiet.

When Merculan was better again, Fendan called the two younglings to his work room and described precisely what was involved in Levigation.

"That's what awaits," he warned.

Chapter 6

His only awareness was of comfort, a rhythmic comfort and a presence. He stretched, weightless, and kicked. He touched something and recoiled quickly. Touched it again and then again. It was safe. He continued kicking. Then there was another something, a different something. He squirmed away, startled, and it was gone.

*

There was a limit, a frontier, Fendan knew that much. He was inside something. A chamber, a tank? He thought he saw a soft orange glow in the dark and then it was gone. There it was again. Light! From where? From what? But it disappeared and he was in darkness again. He waited until he didn't know if he'd dreamt it or not and the rhythm took him over. Remember ... remember ... he had no control. The memories flowed through him like – water through a fountain – histories, visitapes, Merculan ....

*

Merculan woke with the plan in his mind. It had excited him so that he couldn't sleep for turning it over. He'd have to see what he discovered in the Levigation Chambers. It would take nerve and a cool head. He laughed. Thanks to Joquah's control exercises that was not a problem!

*

Emmerlade practised her exercises diligently but still chaos took over more often than was proper. That business with Merculan in the plant sheds had changed her mind. Merculan was wrong to go against the Kristeran, she realized that now.

"Help me," she appealed.

Joquah' looked at her and frowned. This was getting serious. She made a decision.

"You're too young for this, but in the circumstances ...." She took a bottle of jiwa from a shelf.

"Open your mouth," she said and squeezed a few drops onto Emmerlade's tongue. "Now, go through your exercises."

Emmerlade held her breath and tensed up her muscles the way she'd been taught. In a moment she felt as though her head floated free, disembodied. She could think clearly again.

"Use it only when you have to," Joquah' advised. "In time the synapses will learn the procedures."

"Thank you."

"And ... you might mention it to Merculan."

It was unorthodox to give jiwa before Bajinj but Joquah' felt it was justified.

Emmerlade was quite concerned about Merculan. He was different now.

"Just forget about the bipeds," she advised.

"I'm no longer on that plant-shed project," he countered. "You know that."

"Yes, but —"

"But what?"

Emmerlade didn't know what to say. Merculan talked but he seldom shared his ideas.

"Try jiwa," she urged. "It really helps with the control."

"Control's not a problem," he said.

But Emmerlade had seen his chaos results.

"Please," she said, and handed him a phial. She was gratified when he smiled and closed his hand on it.

"I should meet Joquah' and learn to use it properly," he said.

"I'll arrange it immediately."

Afterwards Merculan said or did nothing unorthodox but something was not quite right. Emmerlade thought his control seemed too perfect. She knew how he had wrestled with chaos. And the things he said .... It seemed everything had more than one meaning. Sometimes, though, she longed to share his wild ideas again, plan experiments, discover more about bipeds. What an extraordinary co-creation couple they would make.

"How do you find the jiwa?" she asked after classes one day.

"I've discovered some interesting things," he said.

She wished he'd tell, but he said no more.

"Tell me," she asked.

"You wouldn't want to know."

"But I would, you know I would."

Merculan studied her for a long time.

"All right," he said, "I'll describe the method. If you want you can try it yourself."

"What's the result?" she asked.

"I thought you were a scientist," he grinned. "If I told you, the result would be prejudiced."

Emmerlade waited until Fendan and Joquah' were away on one of their visits. She went to her closet and closed the door. Just in case. She got off her floater and lay on a cushion as Merculan had told her. She checked the breathing instructions and followed them one by one. Then she took the jiwa.

At first nothing happened and she wondered if she should get up on her floater again. Then her brain seemed to expand and her mind wriggled out through a fissure. She floated through time, through matter and space, and watched barriers break. Everything flowed. The lines that divide things, that separate building from fountain, crystal from being, all dissolved. Everything was one. She could see it and know it. Elegant as a mathematical formula, balanced, beautiful and breathtakingly simple.

Then slowly it faded and the wisdom of Zintilla, the histories, the knowledge, traditions, all flooded back. A war waged in her brain that left Emmerlade shaken, confused, inarticulate. She was glad Fendan and Joquah' were away.

"It's dangerous," she told Merculan.

"You saw it, didn't you?" he said.

"Saw what?"

"You know."

"I saw more chaos that I ever want to know again."

Merculan looked deep into her eyes and for a tantalizing instant she glimpsed unity again.

"You've made your choice," he said gently.

*

"Guilty," said Haupus, President of the Guild of Justice. "Guilty on all charges." He loomed over the accused in his high floater.

"You are condemned to Levigation."

He waved a hand at an assistant.

"Have her removed at once."

His assistant removed the unworthy from her low criminal's floater and scooped her up on an elevator. Then he brought her to the Chambers.

The Bajinj younglings watched and held their breath. Haupus looked from face to face, satisfied to see the ripple of chaos.

"Follow me," he said, and led the younglings to the Chambers. Haupus had heard rumours about Emmerlade. Brilliant but faulty control, they said. He wondered with a smile if she might not dishonour her parents. If Fendan and Joquah' were removed, the Kristeran would recognize that it was he who was the true Supreme.

The younglings watched Haupus's assistants strip the unworthy of her clothes. They hung them on a long rack already three-quarters full. Floaters stood against the wall in neat rows.

"Any questions?" Haupus asked, and without waiting for a reply moved on.

"What happens to their things?" asked Merculan.

Haupus turned back. "They're cleared at the end of every month."

"Where do they go?"

"Floaters are repaired and reissued. Robes go to the Guild of Jewellers who destroy whatever they cannot use."

"Thank you, Haupus," Merculan said.

Something about his tone irritated Haupus.

They entered the Levigation Chamber.

"Take a good look," Haupus said. "Take note of everything."

One wall was blank, dull stone but the rest were lined with shelves. Deep shelves that were filled with unworthies. They lay there naked, rolling from side to side, crying and moaning. Arms waved, hands clenched, opened and clenched, opened and clenched and their faces all contorted. The chaos level was intolerably high. Higher than anything the younglings had ever experienced. They fought for control. Emmerlade held her breath and closed her eyes.

"So," said Haupus, looking around the group. Emmerlade opened her eyes and saw that he was staring straight at her. "So, you are this year's crop for Bajinj. Watch carefully. Maybe we'll meet here soon."

He smiled like a knife, never taking his eyes from Emmerlade. He could see her chaos flicker. The knife became longer, sharper. Chaos flickered higher. Emmerlade struggled.

"You have a high number of prisoners here," Merculan said.

The interruption startled Haupus. He looked round for the speaker. They never asked questions at this stage. "I did not expect so many."

Merculan! Haupus had heard about this one. Always asking smart questions.

"Are there really this number of unworthies in Zintilla?"

"We levigate for the whole world," Haupus answered, looking hard at Merculan. He saw only a calm, cool, intelligent interest. He shifted his gaze and stared slowly at each youngling in turn. "And, yes, there are more unworthies than usual. An exceptional number of younglings like yourselves, even some from the same Pool of Life, are here. Some are very intelligent indeed but ...." He gestured towards the shelves.

"Look at them," he said. "See the chaos. Their unpredictable behaviour disturbed everyone around them, reduced efficiency, retarded progress."

He smiled and pressed a button on the blank wall. The wall slid back to show transparent doors. Through them the younglings could see horizontal rows of griddles.

"The Levigation Chamber." He opened the transparent doors. "Unworthies are placed here. Then — let me show you." He signalled to an assistant.

The elevator started at the top shelf and shovelled the unworthies, five or six at a time, into the Chamber. When it was full, Haupus closed the door.

"Now who'd like to start it?" he asked.

Nobody volunteered, so he chose Merculan. It would be interesting to see how the youngling dealt with this. Merculan pressed the button and returned to his place without a flicker. He'd make a good Krister of Justice, thought Haupus.

The unworthies in the oven glowed suddenly red and then flashed white before disintegrating into dust. Haupus pressed another button.

"That rakes the ashes through," he said, still smiling. "They make good fertilizer for the plant sheds."

On their way home the younglings were subdued.

"That was not pleasant," said Emmerlade. "Not pleasant at all."

"It wasn't supposed to be," Merculan answered. "Haupus enjoyed humiliating us. Especially you."

"He's jealous of my parents," said Emmerlade, not realizing just how deep Haupus's hatred of Fendon and Joquah' went.

"He's hoping you'll dishonour them," said Merculan.

*

Fendan was concerned by what Emmerlade had said.

"Haupus saw my control weakening, I know he did. If it hadn't been for Merculan ...."

"You've been using jiwa?"

"Yes."

"Exactly as Joquah' told you?"

"Exactly."

"Keep doing that," he reassured her. "It will help." But he was not sure that it would.

"What if it doesn't?"

"I'll think of something."

But when he talked to Joquah' she was not very helpful.

"Send her for Levigation," Joquah' said. "We can't let her go on like this. Haupus knows she's shaky. What if she fails the

Bajinj test? There could be nothing that would please him more."

"I'm sure she won't."

"But you've seen her chaos results, they're much too high!"

However, Fendan couldn't bear the thought of all that intelligence being lost. Ever since she was small he had done all he could to encourage her, to develop her abilities, certain that given time she would be all right.

"Not yet," he said.

"We'll be failing in our duty."

"Merculan is doing well, maybe he could help," said Fendan.

"His results are very odd, I think he has enough to cope with."

"I'll think of something."

"It had better be quick," she snapped. "I'm not prepared to be pilloried as a parent and lose the Supreme Kristership because some youngling can't control herself."

Fendan did have an idea, but it was unthinkable.

But Emmerlade's control did not improve and Fendan's idea kept tweaking his mind until he had to pay attention to it. The more he thought of it the more he felt that it might work. After all, who would know? Just himself and Emmerlade. And he'd make sure that even her memory of it would be gone. He began to work out the details. When the plan was complete he called for her.

"What are you prepared to do to be ready for Bajinj?" Fendan asked.

"Anything," said Emmerlade.

"Anything?"

"Anything that would give me control," she replied.

He closed the door of his work room and turned off all the instruments. The room was suddenly very still.

"The help I offer is uncertain but there's a chance it might work," he said. "Are you prepared to take a risk, a big one?"

"I said I'd do anything, didn't I?"

"Even exchange energies with me?"

"Exchange energies?"

"Yes, exchange energies to remove the chaos from your mind and take it into mine instead."

"But that's —"

"Illegal. I know. And if it were ever discovered .... But it also may be the answer."

"Would you be able to keep my chaos in control, on top of your own?"

Fendan had no doubt that he could, his concern was that the exchange might not work, for it was never done between father and daughter. He looked at Emmerlade and, as he did, he saw that her eyes were already enlarging. The rainbow hues had begun to glow. He locked her eyes to his.

"Go to Joquah' now," he said when it was over, "and take a control test."

It had worked. Emmerlade's control was perfect. Fendan noticed a slight loosening in himself but nothing to be concerned about. He did a Suturing Process and was in control again.

*

Merculan waited until his parents went to the pleasuroom, and then made his way to a small disused shed off one of the laboratories. Anyone seeing him enter the Food Laboratories would assume that he was going to study. But he was going to meet Festal Takh'bisa. The shed was a long way from the place where Festal tended the plants, but the biped had ways of getting into Zintilla.

"I have a plan," Merculan burst out as Festal came into the shed. "Will you help me?"

"So, like the stickleleaf you turn in the warmth."

"What's a stickleleaf?" Merculan could never hear enough about the extraordinary things that lived in the Outlands.

Festal chuckled at his ignorance and his desire to learn. He was quite a Glitterfly this one.

"Amongst the trees that grow in the Outlands," he began, "there is one that always grows apart. It grows apart because it must have sunlight. Warmth and sunlight keep it alive and it cannot tolerate the shade of other trees. We call it the stickleleaf. Its leaves are long and narrow and their undersides are covered with needle-sharp spines. When the suns are shining and the earth is stretching with the warmth, the stickleleaves turn slowly to the suns, the prickling spines grow soft and downy as a baby's swaddling robe, and they drink in heat and light to feed the hungry tree."

"Oh I want to see that," exclaimed Merculan.

"In good time, in good time. Now tell me your plan."

*

Joquah' was surprised and relieved to note the sudden improvement in Emmerlade. She wouldn't have to hand her over for Levigation. She was pleased, too, to find that Merculan's control had become consistent. Neither of them should have any problems now with the final Bajinj tests. In the future they should make ideal co-creation partners.

The first set of Bajinj test reports came in from Cah'ai with a higher failure rate than usual. It was the same in Tsa and Xemplox, even in Breg. Many of the failures were younglings of high intelligence.

*

Emmerlade studied herself in the mirror. It was her first time on a high floater and she was pleased with the effect. Her Bajinj robe had an intertwining pattern of flame diamonds and her armlets, headrest, earpieces and headcover were made of smoky earthshines. Her parents agreed that she looked spectacular.

*

Merculan, too, studied himself carefully in the mirror. He wanted to be sure that the veldan garment was not obvious under his Bajinj robe. He looked at himself from every angle until he was satisfied that nothing showed and that his robe fulfilled the requirements of ceremonial dress. It would be very warm wearing both of them, but it wouldn't be for long.

*

The great central square of Breg was surrounded by some of the most historical buildings in the world. The Halls of Teaching, the Hall of the Sacred Crystal and the workshops of Breg's most eminent artists. In the centre of the square the Singing Fountain sprayed water in multicoloured jets and sang its tinkling music. The square was crowded with parents and younglings and the crowds who had come to look. Beings greeted one another with meticulous formality and the talk was subdued. Bajinj younglings, about to be received as adults, fixed their headrests to hold their heads high and floated towards the Hall of the Sacred Crystal, conversing quietly with their peers.

As she made her way with Fendan and Joquah' to the ceremony, Emmerlade was very aware of the responsibilities of adulthood. To uphold the Law, to continue traditions, to make changes only when there was a logical need ....

Jenta and Jergul could hardly take their eyes off Merculan. He looked so good in his ceremonial robe and they were so proud of him.

"Aren't you glad that we made the move to Breg?" Jenta asked. "If it weren't for the Supremes, Merculan would be fertilizer for the plants in the plant sheds by now."

"The Supremes, the Supremes, why give them all the credit?"

"Fendan was very good to him."

"He's our son, we educated him." Jergul believed that Merculan was by far the best of all the younglings. He'd gained control long before Emmerlade. What a wonderful couple they'd make. They might be the next Supreme Kristeran. She had checked to see when Fendan and Joquah' were due for Crystallization. It would be six years before it was time for Jenta and herself. Six years as the only living parents of a new Supreme! That would change the attitudes of certain people .... Particularly that young Krister just out of College. He thought he knew everything. Well she'd like to see his face when she became the mother of a Supreme.

"Excuse me," Merculan interrupted her daydream. "I just want to go over and talk to Emmerlade."

"Certainly," said Jergul, smiling.

Merculan moved through the crowds, bowing to peers and greeting neighbours, making sure he was seen. He talked to Emmerlade and the Supreme Kristeran for a few moments and then excused himself. He slipped down a narrow side corridor and made his way to the Hall of Justice and waited.

Only the candidates for Bajinj and their parents were allowed into the Hall of the Sacred Crystal. The adults were ranged round the amethyst walls, talking quietly and waiting for the ceremony to start. As the younglings took their places about the central dais they tried to catch a glimpse of the Sacred Crystal of Breg hanging high in the ceiling. But it was difficult to do without moving their headrests. It was the first time any of them had been in the hall. Fendan and Joquah', magnificent in garnet, ruby and jet, stood on the dais one at each end of a panel of instruments. The hall doors were closed and the music began.

The younglings moved round the dais in a formal dance sequence based on the movement of foetuses in the Pool of Life. The patterns of the dance became more complex, and then the solos began. Emmerlade was first, for tradition had it that the last out of the Pool of Life was the first to take the Oath. She danced to the music of a Kuhlaharp until it reached a long crescendo. When the orchestra joined in with a great chord it was the signal for Emmerlade to take the Oath.

Joquah' removed Emmerlade's headcover and attached electrodes to her skull. Immediately the screens displayed her brainscan. Her pattern ran in the smooth elegant curves of an ideal brain. Not a trace of wobble, no lack of focus. The adults present murmured among themselves. They had never seen such perfection.

When her headcover was replaced, Fendan raised his arms. Everyone adjusted their headrests to let their heads fall backwards. Now they could gaze at the Sacred Crystal in the roof. It was enormous, at least four denka wide and must have weighed about three perd. Fendan slowly lowered it into the expectant hush. The place where it had been was a gaping hole in the ceiling.

"Behold the abyss!" Fendan cried.

Some closed their eyes, some looked and glanced away, but Emmerlade gazed steadily. Beyond the roof of the hall was nothing, blackness, the hideous Outside. Emmerlade remembered stinging insects, a biped sucking Merculan's swollen finger and the days of fever. She would do anything to preserve Zintilla from that.

"Now tear your gaze away, behold the Sacred Crystal," said Fendan.

Each spectator adjusted his or her headrest. Emmerlade gazed at the crystal shining bright, colours glinting, suspended just above the panel of instruments.

"It is time to take your Oath of Bajinj," said Fendan.

She opened her palms at shoulder height.

"I, Emmerlade," she said, "Daughter of Fendan and Joquah' of Breg, swear by the Sacred Crystal to obey, protect and uphold the rule of logic, the discipline of knowledge and intelligence. Be witness to my Oath."

*

Merculan removed his Bajinj robe and hung it up among the garments of the unworthies. With the weight of his jewels gone, he felt freer to move. He examined the rows of floaters, chose one which was in excellent condition and exchanged it for the high floater he was on. He entered the main room and stood in the darkness listening to the moans and cries. This was the most difficult part.

On his last visit he had noticed that not all the unworthies were rolling around distraught with chaos. There had been at least four who had watched everything steadily, learning right up to the end. He hoped there were more like them.

*

Joquah' placed a tiny drop of jiwa on Emmerlade's tongue with a fine glass rod. Emmerlade stared into the Crystal's colours and swallowed the jiwa. Her first proper Suturing Process. She held her breath and willed her synapses into submission, never once taking her eyes from the colours. Her brain was clear, unhampered like pure crystal and she knew that she could achieve the highest office in the world.

*

Festal Takh'bisa sat waiting with three of his friends in his battery-driven carrier. It was a clear night and pleasantly warm for the time of year. It should be safe enough for the Glitterfies. He saw the first beam of light pierce the roof and chuckled to himself.

"There they go," he said, pointing to the light. "That'll be the first of them on the Oath. Not all the mad go wandering wild."

"I hope he doesn't keep us here too long," said one of the friends. "I want to get back to my hearth and my downy bed."

"Don't worry, friend, you'll be back by your hearth before the moon-men are halfway up the stairs of the sky."

*

Joquah' placed a fine chain round Emmerlade's neck. On it hung a phial of jiwa and her personal crystal, the aids to suturing.

"May these protect you against any threat of chaos," she said.

"Zhenta, zhenta, zhenta," agreed the onlookers.

"Zhenta, zhenta, zhenta," said Emmerlade reverently and went to join the adults.

The dance recommenced again and another youngling took the Oath and did the suturing. It was some time before Jenta and Jergul realized that Merculan wasn't there.

"Where is he?" they asked one another.

They wanted to cry out and stop the ceremony, but that was impossible. Instead they repeated the Suturing Process to themselves to keep the chaos at bay.

Fendan noticed Merculan's absence and ended the ceremony as though nothing were amiss. Even the people in the Hall of the Sacred Crystal realized that one youngling was missing, and when the ceremonies were over there was a buzz of speculation. Jenta and Jergul got away as soon as possible, but by then everyone knew that it was Merculan.

Rumours spread through Breg and to the other continents. Many people remembered seeing him in the corridors before the ceremony. Some said that he had been overtaken by a fit of chaos and was hiding in disgrace; some that he had had an accident and was fatally injured; others that he had made a scientific breakthrough and had gone by the laboratories to check something. Perhaps he was so engrossed that he had forgotten to turn up for Bajinj. The rumours were as numerous as they were far-fetched.

Emmerlade wondered if he had escaped to the Outlands with that biped, Festal Takh'bisa. But she realized that no Zintillian could last anytime out there, so she said nothing about her suspicions.

Chapter 7

Intrusion! Another rhythm, jerky, uncomfortable, imposed itself, disturbing him. He squirmed away in protest but could not escape. He kicked and kicked and kicked and it continued. He turned and flailed, trying to regain the peace, the comfort. Then it stopped. Another rhythm began, calm ....

*

The new rhythm interrupted Fendan's memories. He listened carefully. The old internal one was still there, simple, unchanging, *ba-dum, ba-dum, ba-dum, ba-dum.* Sometimes faster, sometimes slower, but always there, protection, a sign that all was well.

This one was different. It was external, he was sure of that, intrusive, complex and unpleasant. Where did it come from? Who was out there?

And it was no longer total darkness. For long periods there was a faint light, as faint as the glow inside the eyelids when the light is quenched. Sometimes he saw the orange radiance he'd seen before. An experiment, perhaps? Were they checking on his state of readiness? Testing his reactions?

The external rhythm stopped suddenly. Then it started again, calmer this time, soothing, weaving gently through the internal one. Fendan relaxed and surrendered to the motion. It was pleasant just to float here ... rock ... remember ....

*

Merculan opened the door cautiously. The chamber was dark and the moans and cries seemed louder, wilder, more abandoned than the last time. He stayed quite still a moment to check on his control. When he was sure that it was strong enough he turned on the light.

The cries stopped abruptly and the room seemed full of eyes. Rows of large, folorn, wary eyes, staring at him from the shelves.

"Who are you?" a voice asked.

"I'm Merculan." The eyes stared. He couldn't make out who had spoken.

"Another of Haupus's tight-minded minions come to mock?"

"No, I'm Merculan, I —"

"Merculan! What do you want with us?"

"I've come to save you."

"The Supreme's protégé!"

"Yes, but I can save you."

"Save, save, save," another voice interrupted.

"That's if you want."

"Oh yes, you all want to save us! Forget it. We're beyond redemption."

"No, I —"

"We will not use the control systems. Better to die."

"That's not —" Merculan tried again.

"Remember this, we are only the beginning. There will be more like us, many more. What will you and your kind do then? Kill us all? But sometime, somewhere, some of us will escape."

"You could escape now," Merculan interrupted."All of you. But you must be quick. We must be out of here before Bajinj is over."

"This is a plot," the second voice laughed bitterly. "A subtle punishment thought up by Haupus. He enjoys this kind of torture. Leave us alone."

"Yes, leave us alone," begged another.

The rows of eyes began to close, and the moaning began again. Just a scattering stayed open and alert.

"Please listen," Merculan shouted. "There isn't time to explain it all. Just know this: I should be in the Hall of the Sacred Crystal taking the Oath of Bajinj. Instead I am here. I can free you and take you to the Outlands. There'll be help waiting."

Some more eyes closed.

"What have you to lose?"

The moaning grew louder. Merculan did not know what to do. Perhaps his plan would fail.

"I will send the elevator along the shelves," he shouted in desperation. "If you want to come, roll on to the scoop. I'll get floaters and clothing."

"It's a trick," a voice said. Others took up the phrase, rocking themselves to it.

"A trick, it's just a trick."

"Maybe not. Maybe Merculan's right," the first voice broke in. "What have we to lose?"

Five came down from the shelves, all of them younglings.

Merculan helped them onto floaters and led them to the rack of clothing in the outer room.

"I must find my own floater, it has to be here somewhere," one of them, a female, said.

"There's no time for that," urged Merculan. "Get dressed quickly. Any one will do. Hurry now."

"You might be glad of mine later," she replied. "I've adapted it for the Outlands. There's a tool kit strapped to it. I can adapt yours as well."

"You've been in the Outlands?" asked Merculan, surprised.

"A few times, yes."

"What's your name?"

"Chareem."

"Let's find your floater, then," he said.

The corridors were deserted, everyone had gone to celebrate Bajinj. Even so, Merculan avoided the corridors and led the younglings through back lanes, just in case, but there was one corridor which could not be avoided.

They moved silently along the Arcade of Engineers. Suddenly there was a noise on the other side. A door opened and Haupus came out with two other Kristeran. Merculan did not know them but he guessed they were in the Justice Guild. They came towards the Arcade. The younglings froze behind the pillars, grateful that they were the wide, old-fashioned kind. But the Kristeran were engrossed in a conversation about types of stemple-steel. They passed without noticing.

When they arrived in the plant sheds, Festal Takh'bisa was

waiting. He looked at each one.

"See who's here!" he said and laughed."I might have known ... Chareem of Cah'ai, Tingaal of Aluu, Stipo the Smuggler and the White Hopes of Xemplox, Kwas and Pipanda."

The younglings looked at one another confused.

"How do you know their names?" asked Merculan.

"Outside first. Come on. Follow me." He opened the door to the Outlands and waved. Two biped friends waited in a vehicle.

"I win my wager," he called.

The bipeds came to meet them.

"What wager is this, Festal?" asked Merculan.

"They all came?" one biped asked.

"I told you they would. Now, you owe me a day's work each!"

"Tell us about the wager?" asked Stipo. He was two years younger than the rest of them and had a reckless air.

"I had a bet with these bipeds here that I could guess which of the younglings would join Merculan."

"How could you know?"

The bipeds laughed.

"Oh, it wasn't too difficult. It's just that my friends are more pessimistic than I am."

"I still don't understand," persisted Stipo. "None of us ever met before the chambers ...."

"You each think you're unique, and that's what your Kristeran want you to think."

"But how do you know us?" asked Merculan.

"We have been watching dissenters for generations, observing, recording."

"There've been dissenters for generations?"

"Yes, and the number is increasing."

"Are you sure?"

"Of course I'm sure. Most have made some contact with Outlanders. We help when we can."

"There are more of us out here?" asked Stipo.

"No, you're the first to escape." Stipo twirled around with delight.

"Pioneers!" he cried. "We're pioneers!"

"And you've Merculan to thank for it. He's the first Glitterfly to learn from a biped!"

The Outlanders laughed.

Inside the Cowel it had been daytime, but out here it was night. The younglings stared at the starry blue Cowel above. Low in the sky, above the lacy silhouettes of trees, hung three fat moons.

"The Red Man, the Ringed Man, the Broken Man," Merculan sighed.

"Yes," said Festal, pointing. "The Three Men of the Heavens are waiting to welcome you to the Outlands."

"You bipeds!" said the female called Tingaal with a smile. "You say the most ridiculous things for the sake of a story."

"I don't know," said Pipanda who had been silent up to now, "I like the idea." She spread her arms towards the moons. "Thank you for your welcome," she called.

"Oh Pipanda," snorted Tingaal. "I know your parents are poets, but this is ridiculous."

"I like the idea too," said Kwas.

"No wonder you ended up in the Levigation Chambers!"

"So did you, Tingaal," reminded Merculan.

Festal put his hand on Merculan's shoulder.

"Time to go," he said. "Come on."

He led the younglings to the All Purpose Transport, the APT, as Outlanders call it. Merculan had heard about these sturdy vehicles. They ran on solar batteries and were highly adaptable. He had expected it to be ungainly and was surprised by its neat lines. Not exactly beautiful, but pleasing. The Outlanders lifted the younglings into the back. The seats had been moved to accommodate the floaters.

"Grab hold of the siderails," called Festal.

The APT made a dull humming noise and began to move.

"The road is bad here," said Festal," but we don't have far to go." The APT bumped around, throwing the younglings onto one another. None of them was strong enough to hold onto the siderails. Not even Tingaal, who had been practising arm muscle exercises for three years. Festal stopped the APT and looked into the back.

"Tossed around," he said, "like rainbirds in a spin-wind!" He spread a blanket on the floor for them to lie on and secured their floaters.

Merculan was disappointed. This was his first real journey in the Outlands and he wanted to see everything. He couldn't see much from the floor but he could see the sky. It was nothing like the empty blackness, the chaotic void the Kristeran described. It was nothing like the dark cavern he'd imagined. It was both more beautiful and more awesome. A living thing that mocked his puniness, that could do what it willed with him. He felt defenceless as an infant just taken from the Pool.

The moons, red, ringed and broken, rose imperceptibly and, as he watched, their markings became faces. The faces of three scarred, wise, old men. Now he understood how they got their names. Festal turned right onto a smoother road. Merculan could no longer see the moons but now he could see the stars. Festal said there was an infinite number and they were millions of kenka away. He shivered at the vastness.

"Why did we choose the Coweling when we were roofed by this?" he asked of no-one in particular.

"Why did we chose this when we could be lying on the shelves?" said Tingaal. "At least it was comfortable there."

"I'm sure Festal could bring you back," said Merculan.

She was silent then.

"We'll never get around with our floaters on this bumpy terrain," said Kwas.

"Don't worry," called Chareem from her corner, "I can adapt them for the Outlands."

At last they came to a halt outside a house. The younglings got on their floaters again.

"This is where I live," said Festal. "Look."

Festal's home overlooked a valley. Contoured terraces undulated to a gleaming narrow lake on the valley floor. Each terrace was water-filled, bordered in black shadow. And each reflected the sky, the stars, the three pale moons. The younglings stared. A breeze ruffled the reflections into ripples, silver and blue, then dropped again. Sky, moons, stars shimmered into place once more in every pool. Somewhere close they heard 'cruk-cruk, cruk-cruk'.

"Cruk-cruk the pond-dweller!" exclaimed Kwas.

"Shhh ..." whispered Festal.

They watched the valley silently. All around them were the sounds of running water, hidden streams, and the air was filled with scent. Then tiny points of gold flickered in the black verges of the water fields.

"Lights?" whispered Merculan.

"Candle-moths."

"At last!"

One landed on a bush beside him. He saw it glow and fade and glow and fade. Another joined the first and they glowed together with five times the light. He looked to the valley and it was ablaze.

"How do you get this effect," asked Chareem.

She had automatically begun to think about the technical problems involved in producing such a scene. Festal hooted with laughter and the candle moths faded with the noise.

"She wants to know how we get the effect!" he shouted to the others. The other bipeds laughed too, bringing people to the door of the house behind them. The laughter spread as this information was passed on. The younglings laughed too, though they had no idea why.

"It's just a fish-farm," said Festal. "The slopes were terraced and irrigated many generations ago by our forebears. Nature does the rest."

"Who is 'nature'?" asked Pipanda.

"I think you call her 'Chaos'."

"Come on, Festal," someone called from the lighted doorway. "Don't keep them out there in the cold. Bring them in, bring them in."

There were steps up to the house, but Festal had fixed a sloping ramp beside them and the younglings were able to get up to the wide, lighted verandah. A woman stood there smiling.

"My wife, Maya," said Festal, drawing her forward by the hand.

Maya was as tall as her husband, and as dark-haired, dark-skinned and muscular. She wore a fine-weave veldan tunic, the colour of pale amethyst. It had none of the beauty or craft of the robes of the Kristeran but, disconcertingly, it seemed to give her something of the same dignity. She opened her arms in a familiar gesture.

"See," she grinned. "I've learned the Glitterfly greeting! Now you are going to have to learn ours." And she laid a hand lightly on each side of Merculan's face. "Welcome," she said.

Merculan smiled uncomfortably.

"You do the same to me," she said, and hunkered down so

that he could reach her face.

He put a hand on each side of her face. It was soft and warm.
"Thank you," he said.

Tingaal made a strangled noise and Pipanda frowned at her.
"Don't be so rude," she whispered as they entered the house.
"But they touched!" Tingaal answered.

Inside the house the younglings stared. The floor and walls
were of some textured material, neither hard nor soft. A stone
section in the end wall housed a fire. And there was furniture.
They recognized it from historical visitapes. A table, some
chairs, specialized storage units. And plants everywhere, each
one different, each with its own growth pattern. Some grew in
sprays, others in clusters or trails of foliage. Globes of soft
golden light shone from among them and cast long leaf-shadows
on the walls.

"Do they grow on the plants?" asked Kwas.

"The lights?" smiled Maya.

"Yes."

"No, they don't grow, they're made."

The younglings found the room disconcerting. By the standards they'd been brought up with it was crude and inartistic, but
despite this it was pleasant and ... somehow comforting.

"I have some questions," Chareem began.

"Before you start quizzing me," Festal said, "it's made en-
tirely of wood and stone, the power is solar, the plants are mostly
decorative but some are used in the preparation of food. You'll
be able to examine it all better in daylight. Now, come and meet
my children."

Festal's children, a female of about Bajinj age and three
younger males, came to greet the younglings. They all had the
same look, these bipeds, muscular and brown with thick dark
growths of head hair. Each was dressed in neatly tailored veldan
trews and tunic. But oddest of all were their facial features. Each
face was remarkably different from the next.

"Stop staring," Afon, the eldest, chided her brothers.

"You've very big heads," said Sedon as he greeted the younglings in the Outland way.

"Yes, we have," said Pipanda with a smile.

She pitied the bipeds with such big bodies and such relatively
small heads.

"Your faces are all the same!" said the next one.

"I think not," said Tingaal.

"Hush, Irthon," said his sister.

"But how do you know one from the other?" Irthon persisted. "You are all identical."

Tingaal smiled at him.

"It's the result of genetic research," she explained. "We sought co-operation through uniformity. In fact there are many differences but they are subtle. You may get to recognize them in time."

"They squeak," giggled the youngest in that low, resonant voice that even biped children have.

"Don't be rude, Rithon," said Maya. "I'm sure they find you strange, too."

"I'm sure we all have things to learn," Merculan said kindly.

"You must be hungry," Maya turned to the company, "Are you ready to eat?"

The younglings did not know how to reply. Eating was an essential function performed in private, never discussed with others.

"They don't eat like us," interjected Festal. "They just pop their pellets."

"Of course, I'd forgotten," Maya laughed at herself.

The younglings smiled uneasily.

"We consider it polite to offer food to travellers. Forgive me. Come and sit by the table anyway," she laughed again. "I forgot, you don't sit. I can't imagine how uncomfortable that must be."

"It's perfectly comfortable," said Tingaal.

"Well, come over and talk to us while we eat. Perhaps later Festal will tell us a story."

By all the standards the younglings knew this was a bizarre conversation, but somehow it didn't seem to matter. Maya had Festal's gift of making things seem all right.

She left the room and returned with food. It looked exactly like the unpleasant pictures they'd seen on visitape, but the visitapes did not reproduce aromas. They were at once elusive and strangely pleasant.

"What makes the smell?" asked Chareem, sniffing and peering into Maya's plate.

"It's just a simple stew, meat, vegetables and herbs."

"But the smell is so ... so ... I don't know ... complex. It makes me wish I could eat it!"

The younglings watched covertly as Festal and his friends and family ate. It didn't seem a chore to them. They appeared to enjoy it, chatting about their day, exchanging tit-bits, news of neighbours and friends, wanting to know the details of the younglings' escape. It was like some social occasion. Later, when the remains of the meal had been cleared, they sat round the fire and Afon brought out a mattress for the younglings to lie on. The boys, Sedon, Irthon and Rithon put the floaters aside, giggling and whispering and fingering them curiously.

"Tell us the history of the Outlands, Festal," asked Merculan. "You promised you'd tell me some day. This is a good time, the beginning of our new life."

"Yes, the beginning," said Festal, drawing his chair to the fire. "I'll start at the very beginning."

*

In the beginning, in the time before time, in the time before life and suns and worlds, in the time before everything, before anything, there was It. It was the Egg of the Universe. It remained, timeless, complete, suspended in Nothingness.

"Then deep within the Egg came a tiny stirring, a shift, a change. And then another. And a tiny crack appeared, for the Egg of All was wakening. Another crack appeared. Then another. And another. The cracks widened and widened .... They grew bigger and bigger until the shell split wide. And from out of the Egg stepped the One who is One Being.

"It was neither he nor she, but All. Neither human nor animal but All. Neither sea, nor land, nor sun, nor moon. Neither galaxy nor void, but All. Now the Egg was no longer and the Being who had come from it was It. It contained everything we know and everything we do not know. It was and is complete. It was and is Its self. And the name of that All, that One, is 'Aum'.

"We call It 'Aum' for, on stepping from the shell of the Egg, It shouted, 'Aaaaaoooooouuuuummmmm', the first ever sound. Aum heard the sound and was enchanted. It shouted once again and then began to dance. It danced the ordered ecstasy of calm, and Calm came into being. It danced the wild, unfettered ecstasy of chaos and Chaos was. It danced pain and it danced pleasure. It danced growth and decay, the ecstasy of life, death and rebirth.

"And as Aum danced, It sang. Its song was the trickling of streams and the bubbling of wells, the pounding of oceans, the crashing of tides, deep notes of the valley, high notes of white peaks, the twinkling of stars, the psalm of the spheres.

"'I am the All,' Aum sang to Itself, 'I am the All and all alone. Wouldn't it be fun to have Others? Others who would sing the song, dance the dance?'

"So Aum recalled Its words, recalled Its songs, recalled Its dances, recalled Its shell and became the Egg once more. Cracks dovetailed and disappeared, the Egg was once more It.

"Then It drew all energy deep into Itself until even the Egg was no more and there was only the spark of Being and Unbeing flickering between Void and All. And when all energy was gathered the spark of Being and Unbeing exploded. Exploded into stars, suns, moons and planets and scattered far throughout the Void. The beginning of the Universe.

"On every planet, mountains appeared and oceans, rivers and plains, deserts of burning sands and deserts of burning ice, rich marshlands, fertile plains. All held in place by the exulting mind of Aum.

"'I like this,' Aum said, well pleased with Its creations. Then It looked and found Its heart still intact.

"'My Universe is not complete,' Aum said.

"Aum took Its heart and blew on it. It shattered in a million, billion pieces. The fragments flew out through all the Universe and each chose a different planet as Its own. From the tiny fragments of Aum's heart sprang everything that moves and breathes. An infinite variety. Insects, reptiles, fish, birds, animals, those known and those unknown. And all the living people, female and male. Creatures of the world we know and of the worlds we'll never know. All of them the living heart of Aum.

"'Now you and I can sing together,' Aum said to Its creation, 'dance and play.'

"And Aum gave us the games of laughter and forgetting. The games of fear and the games of danger, of good and evil, creation, destruction, sorrow and despair.

"'When we have played them to their end,' Aum said, 'we will reunite again.'

"The Universe laughed its agreement.

"'Oh this will be the best of fun!' sang Aum.

"And the Universe sang too. Aum danced and the Universe danced with It. Aum played and the games of Life began."

*

Festal stopped speaking. The room was silent except for the small sounds of the shrinking fire. The listeners were bound in the echo of his words. He rose to throw a log on the bright embers. The children, ruddy faced, stared into the glow.

"This was not a history," exclaimed Pipanda. "It's just another creation myth."

"You think so?" said Festal.

"It was delightful, of course, amusing, poetic, but hardly founded on scientific fact."

"It depends which scientist you're talking to," said Festal gently. He shifted the logs to catch the blaze.

"There are many different ways to tell the truth," he continued, "all equally true. Each a fragment of All."

"But the history of Zintilla?" asked Merculan. "You didn't tell us anything about that."

"The story of the Beginning is the history of Zintilla."

"But ...."

"I will tell you more, I promise, but there's time enough for that another day. It's very late. There's work to be done on the fish-farm tomorrow and in the fields, and I have to go to the plant sheds."

"You'll be tired after your adventures," Maya said to the younglings. "I'll show you where you can rest. It will take a while to adjust to normal time out here. Do it gradually."

The friends who had come with Festal in the APT said good-night and left. Afon and her brothers retired and Festal and Maya lifted the younglings into high featherbeds. Although for them it was still early, they slept. Maya had been right, they were overcome with fatigue after the strange happenings of the day.

*

Another rhythm, strong at first then faint then strong again and faint. He stretched and kicked a little, then ignored it.

*

Fendan noticed the new rhythms. The louder one seemed internal, almost part of the *ba-dum, ba-dum, ba-dum,* the fainter one, external. And yet both had a similar quality and rhythm. Experiments probably. He drifted back to memories.

*

The Assembly of Kristeran could not agree what to do about Jenta and Jergul. If Merculan had failed the chaos tests it would have been simple: his parents could be publicly disgraced and prohibited from making any future adoptions. But this was different. Merculan had been successful by every criterion. He had simply disappeared.

They searched everywhere, from the underground passages that housed the servicing units to the spaces in the Attics. They searched the plant sheds and the storage rooms cut into rock but found no trace. The only thing they found were biped footprints in a disused shed off the Food Laboratories, far from any area where bipeds were permitted. Behind the shed they found a steep stairs impossible to negotiate by floater. Perhaps Merculan had been attacked. Or perhaps he had been kidnapped by some biped he'd discovered there.

The Assembly of Kristeran drafted a news bulletin.

"Merculan defended himself heroically against a biped attack," it said, "but he was overcome by brute strength."

The information was given to the ICS and broadcast to the five continents. Everyone agreed there was no point in investigating the bipeds. They were too dull to understand and too stubborn to co-operate. Merculan would be remembered for three months and then forgotten, like any crystallized being. And the Assembly would see to it that only the most senior Kristeran would have any contact with the bipeds in the future.

Some Justice Kristeran thought that Jenta and Jergul should be punished anyway but Joquah' reminded them that they could not logically accuse Merculan of any breach of the law so there could be no case against his parents. Besides, it would cause unnecessary speculation.

The problem was solved by Jenta and Jergul. They gave up their prestigious work in Breg and asked Fendan's permission to return to Aluu.

*

Haupus's chief assistant had been left to supervise the Levigation. He looked at his list. There should be one hundred and thirty-six unworthies for the Chamber. He guided the elevator from shelf to shelf and counted bodies as it shovelled them on the rack. But there were only one hundred and thirty-one. Maybe he'd miscounted. Well, he couldn't count again, all he had now were ashes. He knew that Haupus tolerated no mistakes, so he decided to say nothing. He struck the correct number of life-records from the recorders and dismissed it from his mind.

*

Malthu, High Krister of the Guild of Jewellers, happened to pass through the work room when the garments of the unworthies arrived to be stripped of jewels. One robe caught his attention. A celebration robe. How could it have got mixed up with the other garments? Unworthies were not permitted to wear such garments at their trial. He thought he recognized it so he took it with him to check his recorders for the design. He was right! It had been designed for Merculan's Bajinj.

"Extraordinary," Fendan said when Malthu showed him the garment. "The mystery deepens."

"No-one knows of this, Supreme Krister, except you and I."

"I think that's best, don't you?"

"The incident's forgotten," Malthu said.

But Fendan could not forget. He kept the robe hidden away, and when Joquah' was teaching and Emmerlade was at her studies he took it out and puzzled over Merculan's disappearance. He had ideas of his own but he did not share them, not even with Joquah'.

"He's left the Crystal Continents," Emmerlade assured him, "to live with the bipeds in the Outlands."

"That's ridiculous," Fendan smiled.

"It's not," she said, and confided all the details of Merculan's theories. Control and balance, jiwa, bipeds.

"Youngling nonsense," Fendan laughed.

"It's not nonsense, Fendan. You are the Supreme Krister. Do something."

"What can I do?" he asked. "If Merculan has fled to the Outlands, he's gone. He won't survive."

But he was disturbed. It confirmed his own theory. So disturbed that he had to do a Suturing Process to regain his equilibrium.

*

Some days later Joquah' called Fendan to her work room.

"Look," she said, pointing to data on the screens. "There's an increase this year in youngling Levigations. A marked increase."

"Slow-brains, I suppose?" Fendan glanced casually at the screens.

"No."

"You mean they were intelligent?"

"Very. As good as Emmerlade."

"But why? What's wrong?"

"The chaos level is rising."

Fendan looked more carefully at the screens and touched a key. New data came up. He read and touched the key again. "It's been rising for the past twenty-five years," he said.

"Yes, gradually," said Joquah', "but this year is the worst."

"We'll have to do something."

"I've already spoken to the geneticists."

But Fendan wasn't listening. All those younglings, just like Emmerlade .... Such a waste. "There must still be a way to save them," he said.

"Prevention is better," Joquah' answered.

She switched off her screens and made for the door.

"Come on, Fendan, we'll be late for the Assembly."

But during the Assembly Fendan could think of nothing but the younglings who'd been lost and Merculan who'd disappeared.

"I'll visit all the continents," he announced to the Kristeran at the end of the meeting. "I'd like to meet the most intelligent of your younglings."

And maybe on his visits he might find Merculan. It would give him an opportunity to search. If he were still alive Merculan must be under the Cowel. He must be hiding somewhere. He could not survive the Outlands, the gross food, the extremes of climate. Fendan wanted to talk to him, find out what had made him leave, save him.

*

Emmerlade waited eagerly for the geneticists' results.

"Well?" she asked as soon as Joquah' returned.

"I don't think they've got very far," her mother said, and went straight to her work room. Emmerlade followed her.

"They must have found something," she insisted.

Joquah' took a tab from her sleeve and pressed it to the screen. A report scrolled up. She scanned through it and keyed the other screens. Emmerlade watched as experiment after experiment appeared.

"You see?" said Joquah', waving her hands. "Nothing."

Emmerlade read each of the experiments. She could see the line the Birthing Kristeran had taken.

"Call if you need help," Joquah' said.

But Emmerlade had no problems. She spent the rest of the day reading steadily, going back and forth through the geneticists' work, comparing, calculating, checking.

"Look at these," she said eventually.

Joquah' read the four experiments on screen. Emmerlade pointed to some sets of figures.

"No-one seems to have noticed the correlation," she said.

Joquah' read the screens again carefully.

"You're right!" she said. "You must have a talent for this!"

"Will you tell them in the lab?"

"Of course I will. I think the programme should be upgraded, we need results."

"But you'll tell them I saw the correlations?"

Joquah' smiled at her daughter.

"You'll get the credit," she said.

"This is work I'd like to do." Emmerlade turned off the screens. "I want to lead the research team and ..."

"Wait now," Joquah' interrupted. "You've only started in Krister College, at least wait till you're finished!" But she was very proud of Emmerlade.

That night when she lay on her couch, Emmerlade thought about the elusive gene. She wanted to be the one to isolate it, to capture it, to breed the first generation free from chaos. They'd call her Emmerlade the Chaos Breaker, the Messenger of Peace.

*

The meeting of the Guild of Justice Kristeran was coming to a close.

"About this matter of Merculan," Haupus said. "We should take some precautions."

"It's over and done with, Haupus, leave it alone," Selucid

interrupted.

He was one of the most senior Kristeran. There was a general murmur of approval.

"I know it's over," Haupus continued, "but there are implications." He was not about to let it pass.

"What implications? He is officially forgotten."

"One of our finest younglings was attacked by a biped! It puts us all in danger."

The Kristeran moved uneasily and murmured among themselves. But Haupus's partner, Dilh', spoke up.

"They are physically stronger," she said. "What if they decide to invade?"

"They've never done anything like that," argued Selucid.

"It would be the end of our Crystal civilization," Haupus said solemnly.

"An isolated incident, that's all. Merculan may have aroused the creature's chaos. Who knows?"

"Who indeed?"

"So there you are."

"Bipeds may be stupid, Selucid. They are no doubt chaotic, but they do have eyes. They see our jewelled clothes, our 'magic' machines, the beauty of our buildings. Someday they'll want that for themselves."

"Haupus has a point," one of the younger Kristeran said.

"When that day comes they could easily overwhelm us."

"Perhaps .... " said Selucid.

"We must be on our guard."

There was a murmur of agreement. Haupus waited.

"You have a plan, Krister?" asked Selucid.

Haupus smiled. He was enjoying this. He took a tube from his sleeve and placed it on the table. It was made of stemple-steel, tough and lightweight. He looked around the room. These Kristeran, so smug, so short-sighted ....

"I'd like to remind you," he held the tube for everyone to see. "You may remember, Dilh' and I co-created it. At the time it was considered—" His knife-smile snicked around the room.

"—unnecessary."

The Kristeran shifted uneasily. No-one spoke.

"Your hand levigator," said Selucid eventually.

"Yes," Haupus agreed. "We've refined it since."

Dilh' went to the door and called an assistant. He entered guiding an elevator which carried a stone figure. He positioned it at the far end of the room and left. It was a rough replica of a biped.

Haupus held the tube to his eye, looked along its length and pressed gently. A streak of light startled the Kristeran. The figure glowed bright orange, then white and disintegrated.

There was silence.

"It could be useful," Selucid said slowly.

Haupus passed the instrument around and the Kristeran examined it.

"I'll get unworthies to manufacture them," Haupus suggested.

"Unworthies!" The Kristeran looked at him in surprise.

"Extend the length of time between judgement and execution. It should be simple enough to show them what to do. And when each unworthy has fulfilled a quota – well, Levigation as usual and we keep the information to ourselves."

"We have not used weapons for centuries," Selucid said uneasily.

"We have a treaty with the bipeds."

"Hopefully," said Dilh', "we won't have to use them."

"All in favour, raise your thumb," said Haupus.

Every Justice Krister raised a thumb.

*

The younglings lay in the high beds, confused and disorientated, until they remembered where they were. The sky was darker outside the large window, and the stars brighter than they had remembered. The last moon trembled on the horizon and disappeared. Their clothing and floaters were out of reach. Stipo was restless, anxious to be up exploring.

"This is as bad as the shelves," he groused.

The others murmured agreement.

"I'm sure Festal could arrange for you to go back!" said Chareem.

"And that's another question," said Tingaal. "What does he want with us? I don't trust him and that Maya, nor any of the bipeds for that matter."

"Merculan?" interrupted Chareem, "How did you avoid the Chambers?"

"Fendan and Joquah' protected him, of course," said Tingaal.

"No!" protested Merculan.

All the younglings had turned to look at him.

"Then how?" asked Stipo.

"It was mostly thanks to Festal."

He told them of their first meeting and how, later, Festal had taught him the use of jiwa.

"The Kristeran misunderstand chaos," he continued. "So it's dangerous to indulge in it. I learned all the techniques for control and secretly practised reversing them. But I could never be sure I'd have enough control when I needed it. Joquah' was suspicious, she had me under observation. It was Festal who suggested jiwa."

"Bipeds know about jiwa?" Tingaal was sceptical.

"Yes, Outlanders use it for healing. Joquah' gave me some, she thought it would 'save' me and she was afraid I'd disgrace her and Fendan."

"Show us how it's done!" enthused Stipo.

"There's no need now, we're no longer under the Cowel."

The younglings had a million questions which Merculan answered patiently.

"Enough," he said at last, "tell me about the rest of you. How did you end up in the Chambers?"

No-one said anything. Merculan looked around the younglings lying on the big high beds. None of them would look at him.

"We can't go anywhere until the Outlanders come," he said.

Still nobody spoke.

"If we're going to live together we should know."

The others shifted uneasily.

"I'll start," said Kwas eventually.

Everyone turned to look at him.

"I am the son of High Kristeran," he said. "Pipanda and I were the brightest of our Pool peers. Everyone expected that we'd become co-creators and astound everyone with our inventions. They said we'd get some prestigious position, that we might even become Supreme Kristeran. There haven't been Supremes from Xemplox for four centuries and Xemploxians are sensitive about it. They believe they are regarded as slow-brains by the other continents. We were their hope." He paused, remembering.

"But we didn't want to apply controls," added Pipanda quietly. "It seemed illogical, suturing off part of the brain. We thought it should be explored instead."

"Exploring might lead to some discovery, some greater understanding of intellectual function."

"But we know about the brain," said Tingaal.

"Let them finish," Merculan intervened. "Go on."

Pipanda smiled and continued. "We met bipeds, too. We thought we'd observe them, see if their behaviour gave any clues as to how the sutured part of the brain functioned when left untouched. That's how we began to realize that bipeds are not as dull as we'd been told. Anyway, my mother denounced me. She said I lacked control and she blamed Kwas."

"So my parents denounced me too," Kwas added.

"My mother wanted to do the same, but Fendan stopped her," said Merculan. "He promised to train me."

"I'd give my floater to know what he's saying about you now!" said Stipo.

They all laughed.

"I don't think even a Supreme's intervention could have saved me," Stipo continued. "I discovered a passage to the Outlands and got to know a few biped younglings. I was always bringing Outlandish things in to show to my friends. That's how I got the name Smuggler. But I was not one of the brightest, so they didn't think it mattered. Then for a wager I brought in a live foodbeast! It knocked over a junior Krister and excreted in the Hall of Education! They decided I'd gone too far."

"I'm not surprised!" said Tingaal. The others laughed.

"You knew Outlanders, too!" said Chareem. "I met them when I was experimenting with the floaters on rough ground. All of us met them, I suppose?"

"No," Tingaal said brusquely. "I had no contact with the bipeds. Until yesterday I had never been within thirty dinka of one."

"Why were you in the Chambers, then?"

"I questioned the wisdom of breeding beings so dependent on machinery. What if the services broke down? We couldn't cope!

I suggested that the genetic programme should be reversed."

"What!"

"They all smiled and remarked on my lively mind. Youngling enthusiasm, they called it. But I outlined a suggested reversal and circulated it among the other students. Some agreed with me, a whole debate got started. That's when they decided I was a dangerous influence."

There was silence.

"Look at us, the threat to Zintilla, and we can't even get off these beds!" Stipo's comment made them all laugh.

The night-blue sky bleached grey beyond the window. They watched as gradually it suffused with citrine, gold and orange.

"Why did you save us, Merculan?" asked Stipo. "You could easily have been caught."

"I wanted to change, to see what would happen if we use everything, without limitations. But I can't do it alone."

"But how did you know anyone would help?"

"Haupus implied that youngling Levigations were increasing and Festal hinted that there were others. The Chambers were the obvious place to look."

"Were you the only one in Breg?" asked Kwas.

"There was another but ... yesterday she took the Oath."

The door opened and Maya came in with Sedon, her eldest son.

"We'll help you out of the beds," she said. "There are nutrient capsules outside if you need them."

"Is Festal here?" asked Merculan.

"He's gone to the plant sheds. You'll have to look after yourselves today. I have to tend the fish-farm and the children have their own work to do."

"Don't they go to school?" Pipanda was shocked.

"Beings learn best what they most need to know," smiled Maya. "Our children work with adults, they learn from them. When they want more knowledge than the adult can give, we find a teacher who can help."

"How can you be sure they'll learn everything they need before they're adults?"

"They don't," laughed Maya. "There's too much to learn."

"But ...?"

"All of us, adults too, seek teachers when we need them....

Before I go, remember, be careful outside. Stay on the flat surface and don't attempt the terraces without help. You'd probably break your necks. Don't interfere with animals, birds, or insects, it might frighten them, and a frightened creature will attack. Be careful, too, about touching leaves and plants: some sting, and with you Glitterflies could be fatal. Ask Merculan, he knows about stings!"

*

He awoke, faintly aware of a pattern. A time to rest, a time to wake. The eternal rhythm comforted him, told him he was safe. Another rhythm soothed him, intermittent, belonging to the comforting one. He ignored all else and floated, cradled. And when an alien rhythm intruded he kicked against it.

*

Fendan realized that he must have been asleep. He could not be sure when exactly it started, but he knew there was a clear 'rest' and 'activity' pattern. The faint hint of light was during the activity time. And he realized something else: this container was not static, it moved round all the time, more so during light times. The comforting rhythm stayed constant and the internal rhythm was becoming more distinct, as though it might have a message for him, information.

*

Merculan and Stipo were the first back. They were both tired and excited. Before they'd left that morning, Chareem had adjusted the floaters, but travel on the bumpy surfaces of the Outlands was still difficult and tiring. They would need a lot of practice before they could negotiate Outland terrain with ease.

But everywhere they'd been Outlanders had welcomed them, telling them the names and uses of animals, the plants for eating or for healing, the fruits of the trees. So much new information. As Maya and Festal prepared the evening meal together, the other younglings returned one by one.

"What do you think of the Outlands so far?" asked Maya as she dished up plates of food.

The aromas awoke an unfamiliar sensation, a desire to eat as Outlanders did, but they knew it was impossible so they watched and talked of the day's adventures. When the meal was over they all gathered round the fire.

"The history of Zintilla," begged Pipanda. "Please Festal, you promised."

Festal settled himself in a deep chair. Sedon and Irthon placed logs on the fire. Maya sat with her hands in her lap and Afon arranged cushions and blankets for the younglings. Then Festal began.

"I'll begin where I left off, " he said in his story-telling voice.

The Universe was complete. Each galaxy in its appointed place, each being on its perfect planet, each tiny particle alive, aware. The Universe rejoiced and sang Its universal song. Everything vibrated to the music, every live thing danced in timeless celebration.

"In Zintilla, the Children of the Heart of Aum beheld the double suns and gave gratitude for heat and light. They watched the red, the ringed and broken moons sail stately over the starry sky and praised the night for its magnificence. They tended the fertile soil and blessed it for the good things that it gave. And every living thing that walked or flew or swam or flowed or stood firm had its song. And each refrain was necessary, essential to the whole. And there was no time, just eternity ... until Imo found the crystal.

"Imo was the Seeker for the Children of the Heart. He wandered the earth discovering new plants and trees, new animals and insects, new mountains and new valleys, sleeping in the shelter of a bush, eating of the bounty of the land. And after each adventure he returned to the Children of the Heart to tell them of his finds. And in the telling he had to give them names. So he became the Namer too.

"One morning he awoke at first sunrise. The little sun was just above the horizon and in its pale, white light he thought he saw a shimmer in the distance. He sat up, rubbed the sleep from his eyes and looked again. The shimmer was there still. Leaning against the tree where he had slept, he waited. The second sun rose gold and strong and Imo saw the shimmer become mountains. But like no other mountains he had ever seen.

"He travelled all that day and all the next and well into the third, his eyes fixed all the time on the shining mountains. The colours changed as the suns rose and set. At night the moons shone white upon the peaks, turning them into fantasies.

"As Imo came closer he saw the mountains radiated many hues, rainbow colours in arcs and beams and shafts that shifted and trembled in the sunlight.

"'Where can they come from?' he asked the sky.

"So taken was Imo by the sheen and shifting colours that he forgot. He forgot the Children of the Heart, forgot who he was.

"He called the mountains Crystal and wandered them for days and days. He went on half-crazed with hunger and thirst, for nothing grew in the Crystal mountains and he was far from home.

But Imo didn't care for food or drink. His eyes stared from their sockets, his arms hung loose and useless and his feet bled. He cared only for the Crystal. He wanted to touch it, feel it, possess it. To him all else was dross.

"The Children of the Heart sent out scouts to look for him. They found him starved and fevered, tattered, raving, and they brought him home. He babbled about crystal, its colours and its shine. The Children bathed and fed him, they made sweet compresses to soothe his fever, but nothing calmed him.

"'We are not the Heart,' he cried. 'The Heart is in the Crystal, let us pay due homage.'

"And because he was their Seeker and their Namer, the Children listened to Imo, and they believed him.

"And that's when Time began.

"Beings who had been eternal began to age and die. Their

aging and their dying semed to prove Imo right. The Heart was not within them anymore but in the Crystal. Imo returned to the mountains.

"One by one beings who had been the Children of the Heart forsook the lakes and trees, the fertile plains, the lapping seas and went to live with Imo in the Crystal mountains. They cut crystal to build round huts and, as more beings came, they gathered into villages. The villages grew into towns and then to spiring cities. And the grandeur of the mountains was destroyed.

"Many still stayed by the lakes and the fields but the dwellers in the Crystal called them stupid, dullards, slow-brains. Yet the ones who stayed knew something had been lost, forgotten, and they hoped that by staying they'd remember. It flitted ghost-like in deep chambers of their minds, smiled in a loved one's face, flowered briefly in a hedgerow. So they stayed to stalk it, catch it unawares and bring it home."

Festal's voice faltered.

"It's beginning to sound like the start of history," said Merculan. "Go on, Festal, please go on."

"No, not now, the next part is too sad, I'll keep it for another time." He stood and stretched.

"Besides I have to go to the plant sheds," he added smiling. "It's daytime there, remember. They'll expect to see me."

"It's not like any history I've read," said Chareem.

Festal smiled at her and went out into the night.

Chapter 8

There was something else. Something extra — more rhythms and something else as well. He turned and stretched and touched something. He floated away and touched it once again. He turned and listened — *Ba-dum, ba-dum, ba-dum, ba-dum.* Safety. *Ba-dum, ba-dum, ba-dum, ba-dum* .... A base, foundation .... *Ba-dum, ba-dum, ba-dum* ....

He curled up, thumb in mouth, listening.

*

Fendan tried to ignore the noise and hold onto the memories, but they slipped away. What a lot of noise! Odd, he hadn't noticed it before, as though it was there from the beginning, the volume imperceptibly increasing. *Ba-dum, ba-dum, ba-dum* .... He listened, trying to identify the sounds. *Ba-dum, ba-dum, ba-dum, ba-dum* .... It was more than just a rhythm. It sounded like a pump. There were gurgles too, rumbles, squeaks, clicks like some great boilerhouse. Like the pump rooms where they had searched for Merculan.

Was that speech? He listened but could make no sense of it. It came from somewhere inside this craft. Sounds, muffled and indistinct, came from somewhere beyond. He got tired trying to work it out, lost interest.

*

"The Star Vaulters lived there," Maya told the younglings as they travelled towards Cah'ai. "You'll like it."

The Outlands were exciting and exotic but the younglings felt a need for familiar surroundings, a period of rest. Festal had suggested the Attics. They lay in the back of the APT while he and Maya took turns driving. It was a long journey.

"How did Outlanders and Star Vaulters get along?" Stipo asked.

"An uneasy friendship," Maya said.

"They told us travellers' tales," Festal added, "of stars and galaxies and other worlds."

"Did Outlanders believe them?"

"Sort of."

"What kind of stories?"

"Oh, tales of Thasree-Sukro-Thong — where the suns' light never shines and every living thing glows phantom phosphorescent. Of Laktrof's starburst skies and cerise shores. Of mysterious deaths and disappearances, of lifeforms seen or glimpsed."

"The Kristeran say they were jiwa fantasies."

"We were awed. They wanted us to fly with them."

"Did you?"

"No, we refused politely."

"Why?"

"We wanted no part in such strangeness. We were suspicious. They wanted to teach us their knowledge. Better mark it down, we told them, store it in your recorders."

It was halfway through the second day of travel when Maya stopped the APT. A grey-green cliff rose jagged from flat land.

"The continent of Cah'ai," she said and led them through an opening in the cliff face.

Inside there was a staircase with wide and shallow steps. The younglings jumped their floaters up to a landing. Daylight shone through glazed gaps in the rock. Here the stairs divided. Two flights of steep and narrow steps twisted out of sight.

"We can't make those," said Merculan.

Festal touched a lever on the wall. They didn't notice the door until it slid open. It was an elevator similar to those in some of Breg's older buildings. It took them up to a long bright corridor glazed down one side. They could see herds of foodbeasts, ogra and cloplinger, grazing below in their wide, corralled pastures. They looked tiny from here. In the distance, mountains stained the pale horizon mauve.

At the end of the corridor a door led to a maze of interconnected rooms. Some were empty, some were stacked with broken things, some were furnished like the ancient rooms they'd seen in visitapes, and all of them had large glazed sections in the walls or roof that let the sunlight in. They could see the rough exterior of the Cowel and the wide and shifting sky.

Festal led them on through the maze of rooms into a huge circular hall covered over by a dome. In the centre there was a transparent ball, large enough to hold three Outlanders. It stood on a high pedestal, resting in a cradle of stemple-metal. A stairs led up to its door but the younglings couldn't climb it. They moved around it, touched, examined, stared upwards.

"What is it?" Merculan asked.

"A space rider."

"This travelled space!"

"That's what I've been told. And still it's on its launch station."

Around the walls there was a continuous bank of instrument panels. Sloped study seats stood at angles as though just abandoned.

"See, we've kept everything clean and in good condition," said Festal.

"What is this place?" asked Merculan.

"The heart of the Star Vaulters' laboratories," said Festal.

The younglings moved around the room, examining. Chareem pressed a button and another. Indicator lights glowed.

"It's showing active!" she exclaimed.

"I told you we had taken care."

"Tell us, tell us everything."

Festal looked uncomfortable.

"We never tried to understand. We feared contamination with their knowledge, their craze for naming and for things."

"Knowledge is the key to understanding," said Tingaal, quoting the Kristeran.

"Is it?" Festal's question made Tingaal hesitate.

"Well ... yes," she replied.

"Perhaps we're too influenced by the past," he said, and

moved his hand as though to brush away the thought. "The rooms are warm and dry and energy comes from the great sun and the small, same as ours. You should be very comfortable here."

But the younglings were more interested in the instruments.

"What is all this?" Merculan asked.

"What they were working on at the end, I suppose," said Festal. "The earlier work is in the libraries."

Merculan turned from the panel he was examining.

"Libraries?"

"Through that door," Festal pointed.

The door was etched with a map of sorts. He couldn't find a way to open it.

"Look for Zintilla," Festal called.

"What do you mean?"

"It's a map of other worlds, Zintilla is in the centre."

A circle in the centre had the mathematical formula etched in it. It was the formula for crystal.

"Put your hand over it," Festal said.

Merculan touched the centre of the map and the door opened. Beyond it were interlinked rooms lined with ancient recorders. Merculan entered. He stopped at random and pressed some buttons. Two screens flickered and lit with a series of diagrams. He could make nothing of them for the moment, but he was excited.

"It's all here," he called to the others. "It really is, look!"

The others hurried after him. Most of the recorders were functioning. They went from room to room touching buttons and peering at screens. Festal and Maya followed awkwardly.

"This is where I want to live," said Chareem decisively.

"You understand all this?" asked Festal.

"Not too much at the moment," Pipanda said.

"But you have the knowledge," Festal persisted. "You will understand."

"Some day, I suppose."

"We'll help you in any way we can."

Tingaal looked at the bipeds long and hard.

"What do you want from us, Festal?" Tingaal asked.

"I — I don't know," he answered.

"There must be something. Why would bipeds help us?"

"It is our custom to help Crystal Beings."

"There must be more to it than that."

Festal opened his arms.

"Make sense of this," he gestured to the laboratories and the unexplored rooms beyond. "Teach us what is useful ...."

"We do the work, you get the benefits?" Tingaal laughed.

"There are things we can teach you in exchange."

She turned her back to Festal. The arrogance of him! She pressed a button and watched the screen.

"Let me tell more of our history, maybe then you'll understand ...."

Festal's voice caught the younglings' attention with its storytelling tone. Even Tingaal listened.

*

Imo had been the Namer for the Children of the Heart, but naming confers both power and danger. Just as he forgot his origins, he forgot the purpose of the naming. He named things to separate them from origins and to separate them from each other. He divided them into categories and groups and forgot the underlying unity.

"Every suceeding generation juggled names in more complex and more abstract ways. The taller the spires of crystal cities grew, the more the dwellers revered abstractions of abstractions. They despised us for caring for the land, for soothing sorrow, cleansing rancour, making joy. They even belittled how we nurtured children! They named us Outlanders and slow-brains, and called themselves the Crystal Beings.

"We told ourselves that they were mad, that names don't count. We called them infidels, nullifidians, traitors to the Heart. But we feared we were too stupid to understand their learning.

"The cities made discoveries, developed theories, invented ingenius machines, but they needed us to bring them food.

"As they expanded into Tsa and Xemplox they wanted workers to build their palaces and halls. They lured Outlanders with promises of earthshine, rock pearl and flame diamonds. But they shackled them and made them into slaves. We rebelled, but they had powerful weapons; we had hoes and rakes.

"The populations of the cities grew and grew and we could no longer provide enough. They invented high-power fertilizers, plant-boosts, additives for animals, cunning tools in their laboratories. For a time these increased our yield. But the soil became exhausted, crops failed, animals succumbed to strange diseases.

"They said that we were ignorant, and travelled farther with their tools and fertilizers. Thousands and thousands of kenka of good land were laid waste that way. The cities felt the pinch of hunger. They burnt our homes and stole what meagre crops we had.

"At last they made a truce. They would take no more slaves from the Outlands and we could farm our land as we saw fit. In return for peace we would give a proportion of our harvests and our beasts. It was a poor bargain but we were crack-spirited and afraid. And hunger chews at any bone. But when a raining came too soon or weezfly killed our herds we felt the whip. We ate only grezzel soup and stirabout while they took away our crops.

"Yet the land stirred slowly and recovered. Purple ahli daubed the forest floor again, and harvests yielded fruit and leaf and grain. Outlanders complained that Crystal Beings had got the best of the bargain. But beings who've been slaves are not the stuff of revolution, especially with their bellies filled. Each generation spawned a hero to shout at villagers from a verandah and call for glory, blood and death. Walgur the Waddler was one, and Hapur Hagusset. But nothing changed until the time of Bewal, the one whom you call Mother."

*

Festal stretched his long arms to the darkening dome.

"There are many stories from those days," he said. "The Battle of Dappled Fivenri, Old Mistrain's boots ... renegades and

127

heroes ...."

"It sounds," Pipanda said, "like your night-fire yarnings. But it's not history. History relies on facts."

"Whose facts?" asked Festal with a smile.

Pipanda didn't answer. She remembered facts that the Kristeran had taught.

"Your history may be night-fire yarnings, too," he said gently, exactly reflecting her thought.

Abruptly, Tingaal turned her floater and left the room.

"Tingaal!" Merculan called.

He followed her down a corridor to a small empty room.

"What's wrong?"

"What's wrong?" she turned to face him. "I'll tell you what's wrong. You. That's what's wrong!"

"Me?"

"You released us. Freed us from from the Kristeran and the Cowel. But what kind of freedom is this? We're dependent on bipeds."

"They're helping us."

She turned away in exasperation.

"You don't like his version of the histories, do you?"

Tingaal glared at him.

"You act," she said, "as though every word is true. You show him a Krister's respect, and Maya too. They're only bipeds! They're full of chaos!"

Merculan was angry. He could feel the chaos rising. He hit the door with his hand. It hurt.

"Is this what Festal has been teaching you?" she said.

Merculan laughed. "That was my own stupidity," he rubbed his sore hand. "I've known Festal for three years. He is roundabout, obtuse, silent, and what Outlanders call 'mischievious'. But he is no slow-brain."

"And he wants us for his own ends."

"As far as I can tell, he speaks truth."

"He's only a biped, Merculan! You and I are Crystal Beings. We don't need them."

"I think we do."

"We have companions who are intelligent and daring. We have the Attics of the Star Vaulters and access to their information. We can start anew. We need neither Kristeran nor biped.

128

We could make our own Pool of Life."

"We cannot do it on our own."

"You and I, Merculan, we could be co-creators."

"We've left the Cowel, Tingaal."

"Co-creators, Merculan. Think what we could do."

"We can't go back, and we need the help of Outlanders."

"Have it your way then," she said and left the room.

Merculan returned to find Maya and Festal arranging sleeping couches for the younglings.

"You could do with one of those elevators," Maya said. "We won't always be here to lift things for you."

"I'll find a way to get one," promised Stipo.

Afterwards Festal brought the younglings to a nearby house. It was larger than most Outland homes, with many extra rooms.

"Tusala is a healer of animals and a teacher," Maya explained. "Her students live with her."

Afon was standing outside the door, waiting for her parents.

"What are you doing here?" asked Merculan.

"I've come to study with Tusala. She's the best. I'm very lucky that she took me."

Tusala came out wiping her hands on a cloth.

"Festal! Maya!" she called.

She was not as tall as Maya, but wider, rounder. The younglings had never seen anyone quite like her. She threw her arms round the other bipeds and asked after friends and neighbours. Then she turned to the younglings.

"So you're the rebel Glitterflies!" she said, taking each of their faces in her pudgy hands. "You're very welcome."

The Outlanders ate at a long table in the kitchen while the younglings watched. The students stared over the rims of their bowls. They had only ever heard stories of Glitterflies. Merculan tried to talk to them but they stuttered and giggled and looked away.

"What more would you expect?" Tingaal whispered.

Afterwards they sat around the fire, students, visitors and younglings.

"Have you a tale for us, Festal?" asked Tusala.

"Tell us about Bewal," urged Merculan.

"I'm teaching them some of our history," Festal explained.

"Bewal, please, Bewal," the younglings begged.

Only Tingaal remained silent.

In the Outlands we knew little of the goings on of Crystal. The cities were not worth our thinking time. No matter that they were clever-headed, they needed us to live. City people travelled through our lands from time to time but we paid them little heed. There were rumours of unrest, but it was not our business.

"The travellers became more numerous. Rumours multiplied. Instead of passing on, city folk came seeking shelter. They said that the Law forbade their having children and gave them infants from a tub instead. We laughed behind our hands. Even a frill-frill fungus knows its offspring are its future. Who would be so daft? Lop off their future's future and make babies in a bath!

"But still they came, a great flood of refugees. They said that Bewal had poisoned the water in the cities and made everybody sterile; that she raided the bodies of the dead for the makings of new lives; that her supporters, spies and toadies ruled the streets.

"Around our fires at night we argued. Could beings be so foolish? Some said it was a plot to cheat us of our land again. Others said it was to make us give more food.

"'This time,' the village councils said, 'this time, they will not trick us.'

"But the rumours were proved true. No-one who came from the crystal cities birthed a child. Many killed themselves, some, resigned to their fate, returned to the cities to take infants from the Pool. But one man wanted war.

"His name was Quingal Takh'bisa and he had a child. He was Bewal's husband and the child her son. He said Bewal found motherhood restricting. She wished to free herself and all women with her from the tyranny of the womb. The Pool of Life was her obsession.

"She gathered round her pick-thanks and toad-licks, scientists without a vision of their own. They saw a wagon to be jumped on. They scented power and recognition. They convinced the rulers in the cities to support her.

"Quingal founded a secret opposition. He encouraged protest, led rebellion. So Bewal had her spies arrange his murder. Intrigue begets intrigue, and Quingal learned of the plot. He escaped from the crystal cities with their son.

"During his first years in the Outlands, Quingal tried to raise a rebel army. But he could never muster more than a handful. The exiles were apathetic, debilitated by their loss of children and of hope. And Bewal and her spies now ruled the Cities.

"Then he met and fell in love with Zhera. She was an Outlander and a woman of great wisdom.

"'Why must you overthrow?' she asked. 'What will you gain?'

· "'Bewal's downfall,' he said.

"'And then?'

"There will be new Laws.'

"'And then?'

"'Beings must obey, they'll have to change.'

"'Laws don't change hearts and minds.'

"'We'll have information programmes, education.'

"'And if folk won't pay heed?'

"'We'll make them.'

"Zhera laughed out loud.

"'You're just the same as Bewal,' she said.

"Quingal realized that she was right.

"'Is there another way?' he asked her in their bed that night.

"'Yes,' Zhera whispered. 'If we change our own hearts and minds and our old ways first. Then maybe we can blend the best of both our worlds.'

"So Quingal taught Outlanders the ways to harness the energy of the suns and Zhera taught exiles how to till the land. There were many who disapproved.

"'A child of Crystal can't be trusted,' they muttered. 'And that Zhera is a fool.'

"But the work of Zhera and Quingal flourished. Every ten years or so another group of dissidents, clutching their belongings, sought homes among the Outlanders and settled in to learn our ways and teach us skills. The last of them were the Star Vaulters who came about the time the Cowel was built. They were willing enough to teach but not to learn.

"After the Cowel, travellers from the cities became less

frequent and Outlanders were discouraged from going in. We were left, at last, to live our lives in peace.

"Outlanders agree that unity with Crystal Beings is the ideal to be aimed for. Many think its unattainable, a pious hope. Most are too busy with their families, their crops, their terraces of fish to give it any thought. But for the Takh'bisas, descendants of Zhera and Quingal, it is a vocation. We have waited for generation after generation, tending your food beasts, your allish and your neff, and watched for signs. We watched you shrink and lose your legs and float and make your light shows, and we waited. Then Merculan began to learn from me and you rebels have escaped. I know the time has come."

*

Fendan dreamt the corridors were crowded, spangled with the light of jewelled robes, colours glinting, swirling, getting in his way. He had this dream so often now. Beings greeted him, talked, delayed him. He had to hurry but the shifting crowds slowed him down. He glimpsed Merculan resplendent in his Bajinj robe. Fendan called and tried to follow, but beings gathered in his path. He pushed rudely through but Merculan was gone. He searched side corridors and alleyways. Merculan had disappeared.

He woke with his heart thumping. All day in the corridors and labs he watched, expecting to see Merculan. He had to remind himself that it was just a dream. It was so vivid. And he could not shake off the sense of expectancy. We can ill afford to lose our Merculans, Fendan told himself. Nothing great had been discovered under the Cowel for a long, long time, nothing truly great. Fendan wouldn't say it publicly but he knew that it was true. Nothing he and Joquah' could create would last. But Merculan and Emmerlade ...

"I should have saved him," he said. "I should have saved him."

"What's that you said?" an assistant Krister asked.

But Fendan did not reply.

*

Rebels. The younglings were proud of the title. Everyone used it now and no-one called them 'Glitterflies', at least not to their faces. But living together in the Star Vaulters' quarters was more difficult than they had expected.

"You're not used to our ways," Maya warned them. "Sometimes you'll feel out of control."

"We have ways of dealing with it," Tingaal answered.

"Perhaps," said Maya, "but call on Afon if you need help."

"Afon, Afon, Afon," muttered Tingaal, "these bipeds!"

Every morning they did the exercises that Maya promised would make them stronger. They tended their plants and made food-capsules in their primitive laboratory. They explored the Star Vaulters' records and visited Afon and Tusala in the Outlands.

But Outlanders thought nothing of bouts of wild laughter, weeping and shouting. Their stride was long, their gestures big and fluid and their faces were in constant motion, expressions changing from moment to moment. It did affect the Rebels. At times they laughed a lot, everything was exciting, enlightening, wonderful. Other times they felt black despair. Sometimes they erupted into anger, blaming one another while Tingaal stayed aloof.

"It's normal!" Afon assured them.

"Not for us," Tingaal replied.

"It gets easier as you get stronger."

*

Fendan couldn't sleep. He was thinking about bipeds. Was it possible that they were capable of complex thought? They had common ancestors, after all. If they had helped Merculan then he'd live in some place with access for the bipeds. Fendan rolled to the edge of his sleeping couch and slipped into his floater.

"Are you all right?" asked Joquah'.

"Yes, I just can't sleep."

"Where are you going?"

"To my work room for a while."

Joquah' frowned and watched the walls.

In his work room Fendan keyed a recorder for the most detailed maps.

*

Afon helped the Rebels to look after their food-plants. They knew so little! She told them all the 'Gifting of Flickflies' stories. The ones Maya had taught her when she was a little girl. Chareem thought they were amusing, Kwas and Pipanda thought they were poetic. Tingaal usually drifted away to press buttons on recorders. Only Stipo and Merculan listened carefully.

"This is Outland learning," Merculan scolded. "You should pay attention."

"They'll learn anyway," Afon assured him.

Sometimes Afon brought them to the corrals. They liked to watch her working with the animals. She moved confidently among the ogra, talking to them and patting their huge heavy heads, watching carefully for signs of illness or injury. She tended an infected eye with leaves and crooned gently to a dam in calf.

"Why do you talk to them?" asked Chareem.

"They understand," Afon replied.

She checked the splint on the broken leg of a young beast.

"When you see her with them," Pipanda remarked, "it's almost possible to believe it."

"You believe that nonsense!" said Tingaal.

"Why not?"

"You're so gullible, the lot of you," she snapped. "You believe anything a biped says".

"They know more about the Outlands than we do," Pipanda said mildly.

"But it's not very logical, is it?" Tingaal moved away towards the long, low cleaning sheds.

"Don't go in without me," Afon called after her.

Tingaal did not look back.

Afon finished with the ogra and went over to the cloplinger. They twitched and stamped their feet and flicked their tails.

"I don't feel safe when they're like this," Chareem said.

"I don't feel safe with them ever," Kwas laughed.

Afon ruffled through the shaggy coats and picked something out.

"Weezefly," she said, showing the insect. "It makes them restive. Help me herd them to the sheds."

Pipanda and Chareem opened the gates and Stipo rattled a stick on the fence.

"Whoo-oop," he called in imitation of the Outlanders.

"We'll make a herder of you yet!" laughed Afon.

"Whoo-oop," cried Merculan and Kwas.

Tingaal entered the shed. It was dark inside and stank so badly that she almost left. As her eyes adjusted to the dark she looked carefully around. All she could see were the long pens for the animals and the solid wooden pillars that supported the roof. She heard the snorting as the cloplinger approached and she moved away from the pens and sheltered by a pillar.

She heard scratching noises somewhere near the roof. She fixed her headrest to look up and saw eyes, hundreds of them. It must be the bilsa. The cloplinger clomped their hooves and the ogra made that unpleasant rasping noise with their teeth as they moved into the pens.

There was a high-pitched scream. Tingaal could feel a chaos in her chest. She held her breath and tried to suture. There was another scream and another and another. Hundreds of small grey furry things jumped from the rafters and scrambled down the pillars. Tingaal remembered Afon walking among the ogra and determined she would stay. She held her breath again, closed her eyes and regained control.

The bilsa were no more than the size of a hand. They leaped onto the ogra and the cloplinger and began to snuffle in their coats. They scrabbled with their fast little claws and snatched and ate what they found. The ogra stared and chewed the cud and cloplinger snorted quietly with pleasure.

So Outlanders did use the bilsa to get rid of bump-tics, weezefly and other irritating fleeties. But it didn't mean everything they said was true. That was the problem with them, you never could be sure.

Tingaal went over to the pens to take a closer look. She wondered why Afon hadn't brought the others in. The bilsa were quite amusing the way they jumped around and squabbled. One leapt on the railing right beside her. She started back. It screamed and leapt away again. Tingaal moved down the rail a bit. Another bilsa jumped at her and tore her tunic with its claws. She moved towards the door as fast as she could. But a bilsa jumped on her head and clung there, digging its sharp little nails into her and snuffling.

"Get it off, get it off," she screamed.

A huge hand seemed to grasp her by the chest and squeeze. The ogra tossed their heads and the cloplinger shifted uneasily. Tingaal screamed and screamed. The animals began to snort and push. Bilsa jumped nervously about on the shifting and plunging herd, their black eyes wide and watchful. Tingaal crashed into a pillar and toppled over. She saw flared nostrils and rolling eyes, splayed, kicking hoofs and little scrabbling paws. The noise, the foetid air, the stench of excrement ...

Afon heard the commotion in the sheds and ran to investigate. If the animals broke loose they would stampede. She stood quite still and closed her eyes a moment. Then she sang the chanting song. Her voice was strong and low and sweet and gradually the cloplinger quietened down and the ogra chewed the cud again. She opened the doors and let them out and the bilsa scrambled back into the rafters.

It was only then that she saw Tingaal lying bloodied on the floor. She wiped the blood away.

"Oh, Tingaal, you poor thing."

"Leave me alone," squeaked Tingaal.

"They're only surface scratches," Afon reassured her. "You'll be all right."

She searched her apron pockets for banda berries and rubbed them on the cuts.

"Don't touch me, stay away." Tingaal beat at her with her hands but Afon easily held her.

The cuts were the least of Tingaal's troubles. Afon's parents had warned her that the Glitterflies might panic at any moment.

"Chareem?" she called. "Stipo. Merculan!"

"What's wrong?" Pipanda looked into the sheds.

"It's Tingaal," she said. "She needs help, get Tusala quickly."

She closed her eyes a moment and began another chanting song. Tusala came and they moved Tingaal back to the Attics, but it took many days of chanting songs and cold compresses before Tingaal stopped whimpering and twitching and screaming in fear.

*

Joquah' woke suddenly. Something was wrong. She looked around and nothing seemed amiss. She lay awake watchfully a long time. Nothing. This had happened so many times since Bajinj. As her eyes began to close again she thought there was a faint glow. Was it her imagination? She blinked hard and looked. Nothing. Then the walls flushed bright green, just briefly, and she was sure. She looked at Fendan. He was in deep sleep but his head rolled from side to side and he made a tiny mewling sound. She watched a while longer. It might be some fault in the circuits. I'll have them checked, she thought.

*

"Look," Kwas called from the door of the livingroom.

He'd been working all day on the Star Vaulters' recorders. They all took turns at it. The formulae, diagrams and graphs had been more difficult than anyone had expected.

"Look at what?" Stipo asked.

Kwas turned slowly.

"No headrest!" he grinned delightedly. "I've had it off all day."

"You're coming on!" said Stipo.

The others had dispensed with them already. It had taken a whole year of Maya's exercises.

"And it happened to me again."

"What happened, Kwas?"

"The flash, the sudden leap of understanding. Suddenly those graphs made sense." Stipo laughed.

"But it's not logical," Kwas insisted.

"I know."

*

In the Hall of Justice Haupus still wondered about Merculan. He wondered about Emmerlade too. All his contacts said they'd end up in the Chambers but they hadn't. Emmerlade had reformed, very suddenly and Merculan ... Merculan had disappeared. It was very curious.

"Watch the Supremes," he instructed his contacts, "watch for anything unusual, rumours, gossip, speculation. Tell me everything you learn."

He had many reports of Fendan's visits to the cities. The Supreme Krister was travelling more than normal. And taking a special interest in Guilds of Education.

*

Stipo moved the elevator into the centre of the livingroom and went to get the map he was making. He was drawing with great concentration when Merculan came in with Chareem. She saw the elevator and stopped.

"Where did this come from?" she asked.

"I found it," Stipo said nonchalantly and went on drawing another section.

He liked exploring and had discovered rooms leading from rooms, rooms of broken furniture, work rooms, livingrooms, viewing points, balconies and corridors. He drew them all here on his map. He marked the features of the bits he'd discovered today.

"Where did you find it?" Merculan asked.

"In Cah'ai."

"Cah'ai!" Merculan slapped his forehead the way Outlanders

do.

"Yes. I found a door. It leads straight through!" Stipo opened the door of a storage cupboard underneath the windows.

"Look!" He pointed to laboratory utensils, a visitape, a recorder, a light show, things they had missed from their old life.

"Be careful, Stipo," Merculan warned.

"I'm not called Smuggler for nothing," Stipo grinned.

*

Tingaal complained of the heat and the length of time they had been waiting for Festal to load the APT. It was dark and humid and the rain clouds obscured the moons. The Rebels were sticky and uncomfortable, unused to moisture seeping through their skin. It meant they had to take more liquids than they were used to. It made them irritable. Stipo moved around restlessly.

"Do you think the Glitterflies ..." began Maya.

"Rebels!" Stipo snapped at her.

She winked at Afon who chewed a smile off her face.

"Do you think the Rebels are really able for Rainsong?" Maya continued, as though they weren't there.

"I'm not too sure," said Afon, and continued plaiting halu threads.

"Of course we are," Merculan protested.

He was afraid the Outlanders would go without them. Maya erupted into laughter. Then he realized that they were mischieving again. It always surprised him when, in the middle of a serious talkout, Outlanders burst into laughter, finger-clicking and calling for faizle-wine.

"You're such solemn little people," Maya told him, and tapped him with a finger on the chest.

Festal's house was filled with friends and relatives for the festival. They wore only waist cloths and did not seem to mind the heat as they bustled back and forth, calling out and mischieving each other, putting rugs and baskets in the APTs.

"Hurry on, we'll see you at the lake," someone shouted and an APT drove away. Suddenly it was time to be off.

Many Outlanders had arrived at Blue Lake before them. Maya

found a place on the platform and arranged rugs and cushions for the Rebels to lie on.

"You'll see everything here," she said, and went to unpack the water-pipes. The younglings looked around curiously.

They were on a ridge above the lake. The Watersource Mountains rose sheer and black from the water. The Shergun Shroga family had been responsible for the festival arrangements this year. For a month beforehand they had worked to build the platform. It was raised on stilts and thatched with leaves to form a crescent facing the lake. The high stepped roof was crowned with carved animal heads. Inside the crescent the stands for the water-pipes stood in a circle.

The platform was filling up. Outlanders walked about, chatting and laughing. As each group chose a favourite spot they set down light globes. Children played catch-catch on the steps. Women set the pipes in their stands, running their fingers round the mouth to check the tuning. People, gathered to watch this work, held the lamps, offered advice and bandied mischiefs. There were pipes of every shape — slim, belled, fluted, bellied, plain, made from many types of crystal — each a family treasure, for crystal was rare outside the Cowel.

"The rain should come soon," Afon said, sitting down beside the Rebels. She held her hand out to the dark sky. A fat drop fell on her palm.

"The rain! The rain!" the cry went up.

Women made last minute adjustments to their pipes. Friends found one another and settled on the platform. One by one the lamps went out. Everyone fell silent. Single drops fell rustling in the thatch. Pipanda stretched her hand to catch one. It was cold, pleasant in the heat. The lake was smooth and dark. The air got hotter, steamier.

With a sudden 'shshshsh' the rain came down, surprising the younglings. A sigh went round and already the air seemed cooler. One clear, pure note sang out.

"The waterpipes," Afon whispered. "Rainsong."

The rain became heavier. A second note joined the first in a simple chord. Outlanders began to rise and move to the edge of the platform. They stretched their hands to the rain and began a soft low humming. The rain fell faster, another note joined the Rainsong and another and another. The humming swelled. A long, wild note blared out, high above the rest. The Outlanders burst into shouts of exultation and jumped from the platform into the rain. They stood with heads lolled back, drinking it. It trickled on their skin and soaked their waistcloths through.

The note resounded. Harmonies shifted in the ear. Rivulets of sound streamed through. Outlanders began to chant and sway. The swaying rippled into dance. The chant wove through the chord. The Rebels knew that this was something which they could not name.

The dance got faster and wilder. There were hoots and cheers and whoops of helpless laughter. Lightening branched across the sky. The lake and mountains flashed electric blue. Thunder grumbled and a cheer went up. They scrambled for the shelter, wrapped themselves in blankets and sat to watch the storm. The rain sang on.

The last of the lightning forked over the horizon and the thunder tumbled after it. The rain settled to a steady drizzle. Outlanders lit the lamps again and brought out fruits and soft damp cake and faizle wine. The talk and stories started, and the songs. The younglings, well wrapped in veldan blankets, fell asleep to the gentle hum of Rainsong.

At first light Sefon woke them.

"Time to go," he said. "Time to go home."

*

There was a direct link between outstanding intelligence and high chaos levels. Fendan observed it on his travels. The Kristeran reported it from the schools and Joquah' said her data showed a growing trend. Until the research gave them the genetic key, Fendan believed he should take action. As an experiment he exchanged energy with young Terevor from Tsa. He wanted to see if it would affect his own suturing in any way. He had noticed a little slippage since he had exchanged with Emmerlade. Nothing serious, nothing he couldn't deal with. And he wanted to find out if it would work with a youngling whom he didn't know. He had been careful in choosing Tsa. The Tsazian reputation for innovation had been failing and the Kristeran searched for ways to restore it. They were flattered when Fendan lingered over their ability indices and sycophantic when he asked to interview a number of their younglings.

Terevor was the obvious choice. He was too young, for his words to be given much heed by adults and his ability rivalled that of Merculan's. His chaos level readings showed a similar tendency, wild fluctuations which averaged out just within the upmost limits. Terevor enjoyed aspects of the chaos but he was ambitious.

His parents were honoured and grateful to get Fendan's help, for they feared for his future and their own. Afterwards, he told them that Fendan had a machine that sucked the chaos out.

Two months later no loosening had occurred. The reports from Tsa showed that the latest chaos tests on Terevor were satisfactory. There need be no more Merculans!

*

Joquah' watched Fendan toss and mutter. It was happening more often now. The walls glowed dimly on and off. It had to be Fendan. She had checked the circuits and there was nothing wrong. Of course many beings had bouts of chaos while they slept. It was normal. No-one paid attention to sleeping scans. But this sleeping chaos wakened her. She had watched him carefully by day and checked his day-scans. Everything seemed normal. She decided there was no point in alerting anyone at this stage.

*

Fendan's tours of the cities proved very popular. A visit from a Supreme gave beings an excuse for dressing up and entertainments. At first the High and senior Kristeran were not so pleased. They'd have to entertain the Supreme on his visits, but Fendan accepted invitations to lodge with Kristeran of every rank. Lower-rank and younger Kristeran were delighted — it was an honour, and opportunity. The High and senior Kristeran were relieved.

Before setting out, Fendan studied maps and visitapes of each city he was to visit. He noted the abandoned outrooms, store rooms, spaces in the Attics, places where Merculan could hide and each time chose an area to investigate. Then he stayed with Kristeran who lived close-by.

The slow-brains were never satisfied with the official parade and pageant. They always wanted to see more of the Supreme Krister. They crowded the corridors near where he was staying, hoping to recognize him and make urh. Fendan used this to his own purpose. Except for official function, he wore a plain veldan tunic. No-one recognised him, it made him look like a technician.

"It gives me privacy," he told his hosts.

"Of course, your Supremacy, we understand," they said.

A technician in a veldan robe went unnoticed in the Attics, back corridors and outrooms.

*

Was there a connection between Fendan's chaos and Emmerlade's recovery? Joquah' wondered. Fendan said it was a larger dose of jiwa that had cured her. Emmerlade was vague. And now there was the young Tsazian.

"What's this machine the Tsazian talks of?" she asked Fendan.

"There's no machine," he said.

"They say Terevor's reformed by the Supreme's machine!"

"You can't believe the prattle of a youngling! It was just jiwa. We'll need to re-calculate the dosage for these high-chaos younglings. I thought I might experiment and Terevor was willing. Any developments in your genetic programme?"

But Joquah' was not so easily diverted.

"I've been wakened regularly by the greening of our walls," she said. "It happens when you're sleeping."

"That's hardly unusual," he said weakly.

She decided then to keep a daily report, officially voice and hand printed, where she would record and date her observations of her husband. She would talk to him about it later but she wanted to be clear on her own position first. Even a hint of poor control, of loosening sutures, and Fendan should resign. It had happened before, he wouldn't be the first. That would leave her in a difficult position. But if she reported him in time and chose another co-creator ...

*

Fendan knew he must be careful. He couldn't tell Joquah' anything until Merculan was back and cured of all his chaos. He didn't think that she'd approve. But if his night-chaos was disturbing her it must be dealt with. A 2r drop of jiwa should be enough. But he missed his dreams.

*

Stipo slipped quietly into the empty lab. The Pool of Life hummed softly and the monitoring instruments recorded the progress of the foetuses within. He ignored it. Tingaal had told him what to look for. To his surprise the storage unit was unlocked; these Birthing Kristeran were careless! He slid out the shelves and took a package of incubation material from each shelf. Then he rearranged the remainder to cover the theft. With luck it would never be discovered and, even if it were, the enquiry would take forever and probably get nowhere. Tingaal was pleased with Stipo's work.

"Now we can start our own Pool of Life," she announced.

"Can we reverse our genetic limitations?" Chareem asked.

"That's simple," said Tingaal. "Some shift has already happened. All the continents have the same problem. The proportion of recessive foetuses is rising steadily. It's a secret that the Guild of Birthing Kristeran have kept to themselves. We'll just let them come to term in our pod."

"In the meantime," Merculan said, "we need more help out

here."

*

Reports from Tsa told Haupus that Terevor had suddenly reformed, just like Emmerlade, after a visit from Fendan. And rumour said Fendan roamed the corridors disguised in work-clothes at hours when most beings were asleep. And there was the curious tale of 'Brawnarm'. Some younglings said they saw a huge being roam the back alleys. He was waiting to kidnap them, they said. Everyone dismissed it as youngling chaos, but it puzzled Haupus. Every rumour had some basis.

Chapter 9

The gurgles, blips and rumbles were quite familiar now, close and comforting. He turned and stretched and kicked and turned again. He was cradled and stroked. Sometimes it was light and sometimes it was dark. A tingling discomfort stippled his body making him cringe and curl and beat about. *Ba-dum, ba-dum, ba-dum, ba-dum* .... He was safe again, soothed and comforted. Sometimes a surge of pleasure rippled through him. His eyes opened, he curled his toes and waved his hands.

Sometimes the far sounds were soothing and he closed his eyes in pleasure. Sometimes they disturbed him, sending jagged rhythms to shift his world. He jerked unwillingly to their beat and kicked and kicked. Sometimes sounds throbbed, vibrating through his Universe, and sometimes they spoke to him. *Ba-dum, ba-dum, ba-dum* .... Rhythms, sounds, sensations .... They merged into a trace of knowing. He was welcome. A deep calm stroked and curled him into rest.

*

Fendan paid little attention to the rhythms now, or the sounds, or light and dark. He'd lost interest in their meaning and their cause. Images, voices, thoughts, sensations tumbled through him. They came from everywhere, from Joquah', Merculan, Haupus, even from the bipeds. He was a memory transmitter now, nothing more.

*

When Chech, the assistant Krister, opened the door, the Chambers were in turmoil.

"They've gone, they've gone," the prisoners clamoured.

She paid no attention. What could you expect? Officially they weren't yet unworthies yet but they might as well be. They were difficult when the chaos levels were especially high.

She got the elevator moving and lifted the younglings from the shelves. She counted them onto Floaters to bring them to the Test Labs for their last examination.

Neth and Theelah', High Justice Kristeran of Cah'ai, made their final adjustments. Their carefully calibrated instruments hummed softly, ready for use. They had the names and details of the prisoners on screen before them and were ready to begin the final testings. Anyone whose chaos levels were reduced could be reprieved, otherwise they'd go to Haupus.

The door opened unexpectedly and Chech rushed in. She was babbling, waving her hands about, in such a state of chaos that the walls glowed green.

"They're missing," she gasped." The younglings are missing. They've escaped."

"Control yourself," snapped Neth.

The high chaos in the Chambers must have affected her. A certain tolerance was necessary. Chech held her breath and sutured quickly. The glow faded and the walls returned to their normal pale gold colour.

"Ten prisoners are missing," she reported in a neutral voice. "They are all younglings. It appears they have escaped."

"That's better," said Theelah'.

She looked at Neth and made a tiny signal.

"Wait outside," he said, "until we call you. And do not speak of this to anyone."

Theelah' switched off the instruments.

"This must be kept quiet," she said. "If it gets out, we're ruined."

"How did it happen?" Neth asked.

"It doesn't matter. There are Kristeran in Cah'ai who'd be delighted to tell Haupus about it."

Theelah' switched her screens on and off again. Neth closed his eyes and held his breath.

"We must involve them all," he said eventually. "We cannot

keep it a secret."

"Why not?"

"Chech knows. She'll tell somebody."

"Can't we get rid of her?"

"How?"

"Burn tubes."

"How would we explain the disappearance of a junior Krister?"

Theelah' realized that would be difficult. She switched her screens on and off again.

"What's your suggestion?" she asked.

"Call an emergency meeting of the Guild and let Chech break the news. Then they're all implicated so they must all hold their tongues."

Ten prisoners missing! The Guild was dumbfounded. Then they began to talk at once. Neth pressed the silence chimes five times before he got their attention.

"I suggest," he said, "that everyone with duties in the Chambers report. Tell us everything: what you saw and heard, everything you can remember about prisoners."

But when the reports were finished they'd learned nothing extra except that ten floaters were missing and the prisoners' clothes were gone.

Questioning the prisoners was slow. Their chaos levels were high and their stories garbled. All of them agreed that a being had come in and offered to help them escape and that he was male. Some said he was a Crystal Being, others that he was a biped. Many said he was 'Brawnarm'. He had manoeuvered the scoop and ten younglings had rolled onto it and left the Chambers. They knew nothing more.

The Cah'ai Guild of Justice Kristeran argued the possibilities for days.

"It must be bipeds," someone suggested. "Hoping to enhance their brutish lives."

"But bipeds show no interest in Crystal's learning," another argued. "Not even those working under the Cowel who've experienced its benefits."

"Besides," Neth added, "how could a biped find its way to the Chambers? And how could it get there without being noticed?"

"There have been many sightings of this 'Brawnarm'," Chech

said.

"Youngling evidence only."

"But we should consider it."

"We will keep it in mind," said Theelah'.

There were lots more arguments but no further suggestions. Neth called the Kristeran to order.

"There are things we have to do," he said. "We must guard the entrances to Cah'ai, epecially those connecting with the Outlands. Theelah' and I have made out a duty roster." He pressed a key on the panel in front of him.

"It is available in your own work rooms now," he said. "Ensure that only authorized bipeds enter the plant sheds. Next, contact your agents. Tell them there's another outbreak of laboratory espionage and ask them to keep a strict watch on all non-residents."

There was a murmur of agreement.

"Shouldn't we use burn tubes?" asked Chech.

Theelah' pressed a key to call an elevator. It carried a large box. From it she took a tube of plain stemple-steel and held it up for the Kristeran to see.

"Remember these from your training?" she asked.

She pointed it at the wall and pressed a smooth depression. A spot on the wall changed colour. She switched the burn tube off.

"This high-energy light concentration can burn anything within a range of fourteen dinka," she reminded them. "It's not as good as Haupus's Levigators, but effective enough."

She made a sign and Chech distributed the burn tubes.

"We must keep this business of the missing prisoners quiet," Neth warned. "Our reputation is at stake."

The Cah'ai Kristeran put their weapons in their sleeves and swore the oath of secrecy.

*

Haupus needed more unworthies to work on the manufacture of hand-levigators. Younglings were the most intelligent. He examined the lists of the new prisoners just in from the continents. The numbers from Cah'ai were down. Considering the general increase in chaos levels that was strange.

He checked the lists again. Cah'ai had at least eight or nine fewer younglings than the last time. Normal fluctuation couldn't account for it. He contacted Theelah' and Neth.

"Fendan has been here several times," they explained. "He's met with younglings every time, always the most chaotic. His visits are having their effect. Chaos levels have dropped considerably."

Haupus's smile sickened suddenly. If Fendan's visits were so effective why were the numbers of prisoners from the other Justice Guilds unchanged? His sources in Cah'ai said nothing about reduced chaos levels. Theelah' and Neth had something to hide. He would enjoy finding out what it was. He went to the new workshop behind the Chambers. His prisoners were finishing another batch of hand-levigators. He picked one up to examine it.

"Well done," he said. He put the steel tube to his eye and pointed at one of the prisoners. "Now it's time for Levigation."

The prisoner began to breathe very fast and wave his hands before his face.

"No, please, no," he begged.

Haupus put the tube down again and smiled. He liked watching their chaos levels rise. He called an assistant.

"Take them to the Chamber. Get them off their floaters and on to the shelves."

"When do you want them levigated?" she asked.

"Immediately, but I'll do it myself."

The assistant was relieved. She hated all the moaning and the hand-waving. It affected even the most experienced and best trained Kristeran.

But Haupus was unmoved. He guided the elevator to scoop them up. Any remnants of control, of suturing, were gone. They cried and beat their faces with their hands. Their chaos levels rose but did not affect the Justice Krister. Could Joquah' and Fendan do the same? Could they withstand the chaos? He thought not. A smile slit his face as he imagined the Supremes swaying and moaning and waving their hands. He could withstand any level, any level at all. For this alone he should be Supreme Krister.

Fendan heard about the stranger 'Brawnarm' on his visits. Merculan, he told himself, it had to be Merculan. The rumours had started in Cah'ai so he concentrated his search there. There were places in the Attics, likely places, places which might have access to unused space beneath the Cowel. Places where Merculan could live. Night after night he searched stores, cupboards, abandoned cellars, but he could not find the exit he was seeking.

*

Stipo tossed a cloak around himself to hide his bulk.

"We called you 'Brawnarm'," one of the new escapees from Cah'ai told him. "They said you came to capture us."

Stipo grinned. He could imagine frightened children frightening other children.

"Brawnarm, we whispered to the younger ones, Brawnarm is out tonight. He's come to take you off!' Us older ones said you were an optical illusion, a trick of atmosphere and light. But no-one wanted to go home alone."

Stipo liked the name, but it confirmed the suspicion that his muscle made him conspicious. Those reckless times when he'd roamed the crystal cities openly were over. He had to be careful now.

When he came to the door he waited, listening. It led into an abandoned laboratory in Cah'ai and was invisible from the other side, hidden in the cracked surface of an undressed wall. He could hear nothing, so he pressed the key and the door slid open. A technician in a veldan workrobe was there right in front of him. Stipo was the first to recover from the surprise.

"Who are you?" he demanded. "What are you doing here?"

Fendan looked at the creature and backed away. As he recovered from the surprise, he realized that the being was not a biped, for he moved by floater. But he had no headrest, his head was covered with downy hair, his skin was ruddy and he bulged with muscle.

"Who are you?" The creature's voice was resonant and loud.

"Merculan?" asked Fendan, faltering. It might be him. It was possible. Living with bipeds, there was no knowing.

"Who are you?" Stipo asked again.

The door was no longer a secret, Stipo's mind raced as he tried to hold his advantage. He must do something. He whirled the little technician round and pinned his arms down from behind.

Fendan wriggled but he could not free himself nor regain control of his floater. The creature propelled him through the door and steered him through a maze of corridors. The grip was like a clamp of stemple-steel. He couldn't think. His suturings pulled apart. He could feel them loosening like a faulty seam. He tried to hold his breath, draw the seam together, summon his authority.

"I am Fendan," he said. "Supreme Krister of the Radiant Orb, I am Fendan, I am Fendan, I am Fendan."

But the words would not come out and the seam in his mind kept slipping. Suddenly the stemple grip was gone. He was in a small, shelved room. It was circular and dusty and lit from the ceiling. The creature locked the door and tilted his floater to lean against it.

"Now," he said, "who are you?"

"I am Fendan," the little technician said. "I am the Supreme Krister of the Radiant Orb."

"You! Fendan!" Stipo laughed. "The Supreme Krister!"

Fendan felt his seaming slip again. Stipo grinned mischievously.

"Chaos, chaos!" he admonished, wagging his thumb at Fendan as parents do to younglings.

"I am Fendan, Supreme Krister of the Radiant Orb, I am Fendan, I am Fendan, I am Fendan ...." He repeated it over and over.

Stipo waited till he'd calmed.

"Can you prove it?" he asked.

Fendan slipped his hand inside his tunic and brought out the knuckle-wide, blue jade ring, set with the crescent cut diamond.

Stipo bowed his head and made urh.

"Why does the Supreme Krister dress like this?" he asked.

Fendan fingered his veldan robe for a moment as though he had just realized what he was wearing.

"It gives me privacy," he said eventually. "I'm watched, surrounded, followed everywhere. Are you Merculan?"

"The Kristeran say that he is dead," replied Stipo, coolly.

"He disappeared but that's no proof ...."

"And if he were alive ...?"

"I — I would like to talk with him again."

Stipo looked at the Supreme Krister for a moment, then he left the room.

Alone, Fendan could gather his mind once more in disciplined control. The door was locked. He would just have to wait until the creature came back. The shelves held nothing except dust. Light poured from the centre of the ceiling. He watched the dust motes dance and hover. He moved into the golden beam, adjusted his headrest and let his head loll back.

An irregular circle of translucent blue. Was it crystal? Finglass? Sheenstone? He recalled the refraction properties of each — no something else. Imperceptibly, a thin white smoke leaked in and undulated behind the circle. It curled and thickened, like gases in a phial, and then dispersed. It was some time before he realized that he was looking at the sky! He had never seen it this pale beryl blue before. Only black and threatening, during Bajinj Ceremonies. He noticed the golden beam was warm on his skin, comforting.

*

Stipo went quickly to find Merculan. As usual he was watching visis.

"You won't believe who I have locked in a store room!" Stipo said.

"Who?" asked Merculan, scrutinizing the images before him.

"Guess, Merculan, guess,"

"Stipo! You're as bad as an Outlander for games. Tell me."

"Think of the most unlikely person in all Zintilla."

"Haupus."

"No."

"Tell me."

"The Supreme Krister."

"Fendan!" Merculan turned from the visis. "Stipo, this isn't one of your jokes, is it?"

"I'm serious."At least I've somebody down there who says he's Fendan. And has the blue jade ring to prove it."

Merculan switched off the visis. "Show me where you have him."

*

Voices! How those resonant voices carried in the corridor! Fendan adjusted his headrest to hold his head as straight and high as possible. He had enough time to gather his wits, do a careful suturing process and think about his captor. When he'd learned who Fendan was he had shown respect. He knew the correct form of greeting, his speech and accent were refined despite the loudness of the voice and he seemed intelligent. The door opened. Stipo came in first, followed by Merculan. Fendan looked from one to the other. How strange they were, broad-shouldered, thick-necked, with their facial muscles in constant motion. They had something of the coarse physicality of bipeds, but they were Crystal Beings all right.

"You're right, Stipo," Merculan said closing the door. "It is Fendan."

Merculan was surprised at how bleached and delicate the Supreme Krister looked, waiting in the beam of sunlight. Like the insects Afon once showed him that live in the darkness underneath a stone. He observed the outsize head, blue-veined, hairless, gleaming with allish-oil, supported by the padded head-rest, the face shrunken, immobile, transparently pale.

"Yes, I am Fendan, Supreme Krister of the Radiant Orb."

The voice was a thin squeak. No wonder Outlanders laughed. Merculan and Stipo bowed their heads and made urh.

"I recognize you, Fendan," Merculan said. "But I think you do not recognize me. Have I changed so much?"

154

"Merculan!" His search was over. "My son, you must return to Breg," said Fendan. "We have need of you in our laboratories. Emmerlade needs you. I — "

"I'm not your son."

"No, of course. But I often think of you as such."

Merculan and Stipo exchanged looks and laughed.

"Careful, Fendan," Merculan said. "Crystal Beings should not be so illogical. You'll turn the walls green."

Fendan felt the seam loose in his mind. Did Merculan know about his night-chaos? I am Fendan, he reminded himself, I am Supreme Krister. He held his breath and pulled it tight again.

"Come with me," he urged. " I can save you, return you to the cities."

He moved to the door as though his words decided everything.

"In time you can tell me all that happened to you."

Stipo looked at Merculan.

"You seem to forget, Fendan," he said," that you're the prisoner. Your word is not law here."

*

"You let him go!" Pipanda was astonished. "Why did you let him go?"

"There's too much else to do," said Merculan.

"We could have taken him to the Outlands, shown him the restrictions, the hypocrisies of life within the Cowel."

"The new Rebels need our time and help," insisted Merculan. "We know too little about the Star Vaulters and we've more to learn about the Outlands and Outlanders. To convince Fendan we need all the information, all the facts, all the documentation we can get. You know how Kristeran are."

"But, Merculan," interrupted Stipo, "Fendan knows who we are and where we are. We should not have let him go."

"Just a moment," said Chareem. "A little logic, please. According to the new Rebels the Kristeran know only about Merculan, and everyone thinks he's dead."

"Except Fendan," Tingaal interrupted.

"Even if the Justice Kristeran know, they will say nothing.

You know their obsessive secrecy. We counted on it to plan both escapes! My guess is that Fendan knows nothing of the rest of us or of the newcomers."

"But the entrance, Chareem," said Pipanda. "He knows about the entrance."

"True, but Stipo tells us it's not visible from the Cowel side. And Fendan has neither the knowledge nor the key to open it."

"He's not a slow-brain, he could work it out and be back here with Haupus."

"We're stronger than them now."

"And Justice Kristeran may carry weapons," Stipo added.

"Calm down, everybody," interrupted Merculan. "Fendan has changed since I knew him. He seems obsessed with saving and his control is slipping. He wants to 'save' me, bring me back to the cities. He'll keep quiet."

The Rebels realized that Merculan was right. Who'd believe him if Fendan said he'd met the long dead Merculan?

"But we should be prepared," said Stipo. "Things are stirring underneath the smooth surface of the Cowel. Security has been stepped up and there are rumours of burn tubes."

They decided to monitor all broadcasts from the Cowel.

"I think Fendan will be back," said Merculan.

*

Fendan could see no sign of the door, and the seam in his head was loose again. A disconcerting wave of chaos broke over him. For a moment he was paralyzed and dizzy. He did not want to be found like this. The lab was abandoned but anyone might come and find him. He needed rest, a little time. He saw a door and opened it. A cupboard full of junk. He went in and pulled the door shut behind him. It was safer in the dark. He stayed there until his chaos had subsided.

Back in his bed he dreamt of gases in a bottle. They swirled and whorled and burst the bottle, the Cowel ripped wide open, crowds spilled from the buildings and ran screaming from the gases that smoked and undulated in the beryl-blue sky ....

When he awoke, the walls glowed green. Dream images

invaded him. One suturing was not enough, nor even two: he needed jiwa before he regained composure.

Merculan was alive! He'd said nothing of his present life. But he was alive, that was enough.

This chaos, he must do something about it. Some time spent back in Breg with Joquah' would help. Her calm logic would stabilize him. He'd been away too long. Adventures in the secret places of the Attics were not conducive to an ordered life.

In Breg he put memories of Merculan aside and concentrated on the work that had accumulated in his absence. But he kept an eye on the levigation lists. Too often he recognized names of younglings he had met. But these thoughts, too, he put away and continued with his work.

He'd been right about time with Joquah'. He sensed a return to the old certainties, the old stability, a renewed intellectual vigour. He and Joquah' co-created a new series of sound puzzles which became immensely popular.

But the levigation lists kept coming in and he thought again about saving younglings, about refining his method. Energy-exchange was simple. With their eyes, two beings tuned their brain energy to the same wavelength. Thoughts vibrating at the same frequencies connected and amplified. During amplification ideas and information developed and exchanged with extraordinary rapidity. To prevent abuse, they restricted it to co-creation partners, to use for the benefit of the crystal cities. Saving younglings was surely to the cities' benefit.

Fendan began travelling again and meeting younglings. He got them to focus on control, gave them exercises and jiwa. Then he calibrated crystals to help them tune their eyes to his. And when the two waves met he transmitted a stream of suturing thoughts. He had to adjust the jiwa dosage and fine-tune the crystals separately for each individual, and he could never be sure what chaos levels they transmitted to him. But it worked.

Requests for help came from younglings, parents and Kristeran. They questioned Fendan about his method and, when he said his research was not complete, they were satisfied to wait. They were pleased with the results. But Joquah' was not so easily satisfied.

"Is it wise, Fendan?" she asked.

"I believe so."

"You've been having chaos problems," she warned. "It started after Emmerlade and got worse after Terevor of Tsa. There must be some connection."

"I am using unorthodox methods. Some Kristeran would object if they knew, so I must be very sure of my results before I say anything. That's why I must keep travelling to the cities."

"Stay, Fendan," Joquah' asked. "Take care of your own youngling and let other parents do the same."

"Emmerlade is an adult, my duty is to all our children."

"Even though you get night-chaos and dose jiwa like a trancer? I know, I've been recording it. And if I must, I'll pass the information to the Assembly. It's not what I want but it is the Law."

Fendan seemed unconcerned.

"Do what you must, Joquah'."

"Haupus will be pleased," she said.

"I've discovered something about Haupus that should keep him quiet."

"I hope you're right, Fendan, I hope you're right."

*

Everywhere he went parents and younglings lined the streets. Many wore their ceremonial robes to show respect. They bowed, made urh and called him the Supreme Father. There was great speculation and discussion about Fendan's methods. Local Kristeran monitored the progress of their own 'saved' younglings. Fendan welcomed the follow-up and examined their reports on subsequent visits. They were very satisfactory. But every continent had a core of younglings refusing to be helped. Like Merculan. Maybe it was time to contact him again.

"Talk to the biped Festal," Merculan had said before they'd parted. "You'll find him in the plant sheds of Breg."

The plant sheds were cold and Fendan shivered. A biped moved slowly down the rows of allish, peering at the plants and poking the soil around them with his stubby finger.

"Festal?" Fendan asked, looking at the creature with distaste.

With smiles and nods the biped indicated he was Festal.

"Tell Merculan," he said, speaking slowly and carefully, reducing his message to a simple command, "Fendan."

The biped stood fingering a leaf and frowning. Fendan wasn't sure if he had understood. He was searching for another simple formula when the biped spoke.

"Go to the place in Cah'ai. Stipo awaits you."

·The biped had looked him straight in the eyes. Fendan was taken aback. Bipeds do not look at Crystal Beings. He could feel his eyes drawn into the biped's as a nail might be attracted by a magnet. He closed his eyes tightly and the biped turned and left the plant sheds, chuckling. Fendan stayed there staring at the allish. He had never before noticed the pattern of leaf veins nor the faint blue haze of down.

*

Fendan lay on the couch after his visit to Merculan, his mind racing. His suspicions about Haupus had been right! Stipo was an escaped prisoner. And there were more who had escaped from Haupus's Levigation Chamber! Merculan had arranged it. Fendan wasn't interested in the details. All he could think of was Haupus. Prisoners condemned to Levigation had escaped and he had not reported it to the Assembly!

There had been a biped with Merculan. He was large and dark like all bipeds. Fendan hardly noticed him until he spoke.

"Supreme Krister," the creature said, bowing and making urh. "I bid you welcome to the border of the Outlands."

Fendan smiled politely. Bipeds usually spoke in simple words and gestures, but this one expressed his thoughts in a queer, oblique way that had a certain lumbering rhythm. And his articulated limbs moved with an admirable economy for such awkward things.

"What do you think of us, Fendan?" the biped asked.

Fendan was shocked that the biped addressed him as an equal.

"This is Festal," said Merculan. "He is a leader in the Outlands."

"Festal?" Fendan said.

The biped smiled and looked him in the eye.

"We met earlier in the plant sheds," he said.

Obviously this was a brighter specimen than most.

Merculan had talked of Birthing, chaos and saving young-lings. Most of it was nonsense. Fendan only half-listened. The biped watched him steadily and he could feel a loosening in the seaming in his head. He focused all his power to pull it closed again. He would insist on seeing Merculan alone the next time.

Then there were the visis. Merculan semed to think that they proved some point. But they were old Star Vaulter material. Fantasies no doubt, nightmares of their addled trancer brains.

The important thing was to pinpoint the thought he and Merculan had in common, thoughts he might use for an energy-exchange. Merculan was concerned about chaotic younglings, that was certain. It was a place to start.

*

The youngling stayed awake until the adults had gone. She waited to be sure they were asleep before she ventured from her couch. She got on her floater and slipped quietly to Fendan's door. Her parents had warned her to be on her best behaviour for the Supreme's stay. Mostly she stayed out of the way, but she was curious to see what he looked like sleeping. She opened the door a crack. Fendan was asleep. She opened it a little more and stared.

The Supreme's head lurched from side to side, he mumbled and groaned and his hands waved in spasm. The walls pulsed faintly. The youngling's eyes widened. The walls were glowing a pale green!

In school next day, nobody believed her.

"It can't be true," they said. "He's the Father, the one who saves us."

"He was tossing and talking in his sleep!"

"Don't believe you, don't believe you," her classmates jeered.

"All right. Somebody come and stay with me tonight. See for yourself."

That night four younglings stayed awake and waited. It was a long wait. Fendan did not return for hours, then they had to wait for him to sleep. When at last they peered into his room they saw him toss and mumble and the walls glow green. They watched and listened fascinated, hoping to catch something, anything, of what he mumbled. But the only word they could make out was 'Merculan'.

*

Haupus rubbed the fingers of one hand on his other palm. He always did that when he was displeased.

"How many this time?" he asked.

"Three in Xemplox, four in Breg," his assistant answered.

"I don't like it."

"The citizens do. They're calling Fendan 'Father'."

"I know what they call him," Haupus snapped.

The assistant kept quiet and listened to the dry sound of Haupus's fingers on his palm.

"One other thing," he began.

Haupus turned to look at him.

"There is a rumour going about, I can't verify it. It only comes from younglings ...."

"Get to the point."

"They say Fendan has night-chaos."

Haupus fingers stopped rubbing. He pressed a key to summon Dilh'.

"See if you can have it checked," he said.

"It may only be youngling fantasy."

"Now!" The assistant left hurriedly as Dilh' arrived.

"News?" she asked.

Haupus smiled.

"This might be our chance," he said.

*

The Star Vaulters' quarters seemed at first to be a random maze. But, as the Rebels explored further, Stipo added to his map and a pattern developed. It began to look like the great odar tree that cloplinger sheltered under in the rain. The lab where Festal first brought them formed a core. Corridors and rooms branched from it and the branches branched again. Whole sections of the Attics could be closed off by locking one door. Stipo had developed a talent for locksmithing and had opened many doors, but there were many more to be unlocked. Merculan found a great collection of visis. Some were recordings of events around the time of Bewal and the making of the Cowel. They were different from the versions that he'd been taught. It confirmed their mistrust of Kristeran. Other visis related only to Star Vaulters and their lives.

Throughout the maze there were notes of experiments, diagrams, descriptions, summaries, extracts and so on, neatly arranged but in no apparent order, everything left as though their owners had just gone out for a moment and would return.

As they read and collated information, patterns, some faint, some broken, began to emerge. What looked like the confused disorganization of jiwa-trancers turned out to be a sophisticated system of information storage, designed to prevent outsiders gaining access. A jigsaw picture of Star Vaulters' history, lives and work began to form.

It seemed they had their origins in the scientists of the Space Travel Programme. They had opposed Bewal and formed a secret sect when she banned their work. That was in about 230 B.Co. The sect continued through every generation, sometimes openly, sometimes in secret, and members were involved in every coup, every protest movement, every rebellion. They travelled far beyond the crystal cities and kept accounts of their journeys.

*

JOURNAL OF NARDO NARDERER
(THE VOYAGER)

I wandered the Outlands observing the countryside, the villages and the people. Outlanders are unfriendly and uncivil, but not unwilling to converse. They are obsequious in their offers of food and shelter to Crystal Beings and treat us with a fearful reticence. By contrast, when among friends, they greet each other with great whoops and claps and laughter.

After some months I decided to move on. A young man asked if he could travel with me. His name was Shatim. He had been an orphan and, as is the custom here, he had been reared by the village. He offered me his services and begged to travel with me, for he was restless to see the dapple of the world.

He had a cart and a team of sturdy cloplinger. Each of his animals had been a sickly suckling which the villagers had left to die. Shatim had cared for them and nursed them to health, so the villagers let him keep them. He had a gift for helping helpless things.

The elders objected to Shatim leaving. They said they'd reared him and he should show gratitude and stay. They wanted him for their village healer and they showed their knives and threatened to hunt him through the whole world if he came with me. Shatim just laughed.

"They'll hunt as far as the next village," he said, "then they'll be back to their ogra and their allish."

We packed in haste and fled the place by stealth, at night.

On the road to pass the time, he told me tales he'd heard from travellers. He knew of sailing folk and broad flat boats, of singing stones and swalley holes, of dangerous beasts and the Inland Isles where beings flew beyond our planet to the stars. Because of our interest in such matters, I questioned him closely about these last but all he knew was that the Inland Isles were far beyond the ocean. I determined there and then to find them.

The journey to the coast took several months for Shatim

could not bear to see any living thing in pain without stopping to help. It made our journey slow but a welcome in the villages certain. Everywhere we went they wanted Shatim to stay and be their healer.

As we travelled the weather became warmer and the suns rose higher in the sky. We passed through towering mountains and desert plains until we came at last to the sea-roads. These roads wind for many kenka through dunes of mauve-pink gravel. It was growing time and the dunes were hazed with the white flowers of sea-nimbus. An old man whom we met advised Shatim to make for Parsal, a town renowned for sturdy ships and skilful sailors.

We left the cloplinger and cart in the care of a tailor whose pet bird Shatim had cured, and sailed in a cramped trading ship with a cargo of foul-smelling hides. Shatim stayed on deck, chatting and joking, but I did not like the ocean. On landing we set off through the villages with Shatim healing as he went. We parted company when a laughing Yal woman wooed him with her eyes.

There are many travellers and traders in Yal and I questioned them closely about the Inland Isles. They were three months' journey to the west, I was told. Some said the islanders could truly fly up to the moons. Others laughed and said it made a good tale for nighttime yarning.

After many difficulties I reached the shores of Lake Pakitata and saw the islands grey and hazy in the evening mist. I found a boat to take me to the Middle Island where their chieftan lives. She welcomed me with flowers and food and asked if I had come to witness flying ceremonies. I told her of my interest in space travel. She said they tolerated no gawpers at the ceremonies but if I wished to I could stay and study.

For three years I lived there learning many curious facts about plants and mosses, practising healing arts and committing to memory the many songs and chants which the islanders consider essential for proper function in the world. When the chieftan held that I was ready I was initiated.

First, she brought me in her painted canoe to an island where little grew except the dull brown spines of jiwa among the cracks of healing-quartz. She stood chanting to herself while I harvested the grey-green encrustations that grow on mature spines. Then she took me to my sleeping hut and showed me how to make the trancing drug.

The Initiation Festival begins before the dawn, the time the islanders call the seda-time, when the stars are fading. The sky is not yet light and the air brushes your face like the finest seda cloth. Three elders came to my hut. They were robed in black with nothing showing but the glitter of their eyes. They stripped me bare and chained me to a pallet and carried me to the place outside the chieftan's home where all important meetings of the islanders take place. They put my pallet down on the hard trodden earth, beside the other two initiates, inside the circle of white stones.

As the first beam of the first sun struck the ground the islanders gathered round. They pounded the earth with their sticks and danced and chanted. The chieftan came and placed three drops of pure jiwa on our tongues. Our chains were loosed and we hovered over the village. I could see our bodies lying inert on the ground, each one attended by a black-robed guardian. I wanted to go back to it but my guardian told me sternly to fly. I left my body in the guardian's care and soared with the others, swooping and diving over the islands. Then I flew beyond Zintilla to the Red, the Ringed and the Broken Moons. I bathed in a fountain of stars and saw Zintilla floating in the zaffer sky, blue and beautiful.

For three more years I stayed in the Inland Isles, learning about the jiwa plant. When I had learned all they had to teach, I said farewell and, taking many choice spines with me, returned to the crystal cities.

*

The story seemed to confirm that Star Vaulters were jiwa trancers. They got their name from their boasts of flying beyond the stars. And yet, Merculan was not convinced that that was all they were. Jiwa was certainly introduced to the crystal cities about the time of the Voyager's story and there was controversy about its use until it was controlled by law.

But the details of experiments they found suggested that the

Star Vaulters were involved in all forms of energy research. The evidence was there in hard scientific research. They did pioneering work on solar, lunar and crystal energies, and all their work seemed to be aimed at finding the best energy to travel far in space. There were references to a major breakthrough, but no hard evidence.

"You'll find it's just more jiwa trancing," suggested Tingaal.

"No, no," Merculan said excitedly. "Listen to this."

He read from a screen:

"After the building of the Cowel we moved into the Attics of Cah'ai and devised the system for storage of information. All applicants must now complete a rigorous apprenticeship of study and examination. As each test is passed, the successful applicant will be given a key to the next level of information."

"Don't you see," Merculan said. "This place was designed to protect information. To keep the secrets from the Kristeran. We must search farther."

"They were jiwa trancers," Tingaal insisted.

Pipanda keyed a screen.

"Now we can truly call ourselves Star Vaulters", she read, "for we have journeyed in the stars. Now the heavens are indeed ours, we can travel where we will. We have been there and have returned. The journey went according to plan. There are some details that need attention. We lost consciousness during the exchange. Orbit round the Red Man was wider than we had planned. Objectives 8 and 9 of mission had to be abandoned."

"There are hundreds of reports," she said to Tingaal. "Visits to other planets, other galaxies."

"But are they real or jiwa journeys?" Tingaal asked.

Nobody could answer.

*

Fendan scanned notes dutifully and watched the visis. He was not particularly interested but Merculan had insisted, and he wanted to know Merculan. He must discover everything possible about the youngling's thoughts so that he could tune in easily, synchronize when the time for mind-fusion came.

"What do you think?" asked Merculan.

"It's about time you thought of returning."

"I'm not going back, I told you."

"The cities need you," Fendan said gravely.

"How can you say that?" Merculan was exasperated. "After all I've shown you here?"

"Any being with ingenuity could concoct those visis. The fact that they exist doesn't prove that they are true. I would have thought you would understand that, Merculan. The truth of history is in the crystal cities, safely preserved from one generation to the next."

Every meeting with Merculan was the same, a duel of minds, a trial of strength. Fendan was enjoying it. It was a challenge. It was more interesting than any of his work in Breg, more interesting even than saving younglings.

"Come to the Outlands," Merculan pleaded. "It is nothing like you think. I promise, it will change your mind."

"No." Fendan had seen the Outlands from the windows of the Attics. It was wide and inhospitable to Crystal Beings. It was bad enough to have to converse with Merculan's bipeds. Granted, they were more intelligent that he'd expected, but obtuse and childish, constantly playing silly word games and tricks. How could Merculan tolerate it? But he said that he enjoyed it. He even treated bipeds with a kind of deference.

Yet Fendan was quite taken with the accounts of Star Vaulter voyages. There was a strange attraction in their tales of being lost in other worlds, of mirage galaxies shimmering at the edges of their vision, of marbled planets, strange landscapes and stranger life-forms.

"Have you discovered any more travellers' tales?" Fendan asked.

"Nothing new," said Merculan. "There's nothing dated after 215 A.Co. What happened then, I wonder?"

"They just died out. You must know that. They could find no more recruits. Beings were no longer interested in jiwa-trancing."

"But the Attics look like they were abandoned suddenly. And there is only one space rider! The records suggest many more."

"It's all fantasy, the stuff of jiwa-dreams."

"Is it?"

"They had no Pool of Life."

"Perhaps they were in danger, left in haste, migrated to another world."

"We have no record of anything like that."

"No, Fendan, of course you don't. Your histories record nothing that you don't want to know about. That's the point. That's why we left the Cowel. Everything is ... is ... reduced. We've cocooned our cities from the world. Reduced our bodies: we've even shut off parts of our brain. You Kristeran talk of objectivity, the scientific method, truth, but only your truth. No questioning allowed. No challenge permitted."

There was a long silence.

"What's your solution?" Fendan asked.

"I have no solution. Generations of tradition won't suddenly be changed. And there's no one solution to cure all ills. We are all infected. We must heal ourselves."

"For one of your intelligence, " said Fendan sternly, " you talk a lot of nonsense."

"For one of your intelligence, Fendan, you dismiss a lot of facts."

Fendan turned and left the visis viewing room. Merculan followed him to the central lab. The space rider stood in the centre, the steps up to it had been replaced by an elevator. Fendan mounted it and entered. He took his time examining everything and then descended again.

"It's beautifully made," he said. "There's no doubt about that."

"Yes," said Merculan."

"But I could find nothing to power it. If they were not jiwa trancers, Merculan, what did they use for fuel?"

*

"The walls of Fendan's room glow every night!" Haupus told Dilh'. "I have reports, it's well substantiated."

"Night-chaos is tolerated," she replied. She was not as excited as Haupus by the news.

"In the Supreme Krister? I don't think the Assembly would

like it. Besides, I have heard another secret."

"What?"

"Joquah' lodged documents with the Assembly's secretariat."

"What documents?"

"Even I could not find that out, but I could guess."

"Fendan?"

She began to understand.

"I believe our time is coming," Haupus said.

They smiled deep into one another's eyes.

Chapter 10

Sometimes, borne by the rhythm, he left his familiar, gurgling darkness. *Ba-dum, ba-dum, ba-dum* .... It carried him to places bright with movement and vague beckonings. And he floated there and stretched and waved his hands. *Ba-dum, ba-dum, ba-dum, ba-dum* .... It bore him back to the warmth and the safety of the dark.

Turning was an effort. He kicked and wriggled until he was comfortable again. *Ba-dum, ba-dum, ba-dum* .... Things prodded him so he kicked and shifted.

Ba-dum, ba-dum, ba-dum .... Something caught him, squeezed: he kicked but the squeezing persisted. Then it let go.

Ba-dum, ba-dum, ba-dum .... He was in a different darkness, loud and heaving. There was brightness somewhere, drawing him towards it, dazzling him with sparkle and promise. No, no, not yet, he wriggled back into his familiar dark. *Ba-dum, ba-dum, ba-dum, ba-dum* .... His head was cradled. He was safe. He must rest now. Gather up his strength.

*

A small child stood on the path, swathed in layers of cloth. His eyes, huge and grey, stared at Fendan in that steady, all-absorbing way of biped children. The sun was warm and healing and a soft breeze lifted the child's bright hair.

"You must be hot, wrapped up like that," Fendan said. "Here, let me help you. The sunlight will be pleasant on your skin."

He reached to unwrap the layers but the child said, "No!" and ran away.

Abruptly the image disappeared. Fendan was in the pulsing darkness. What memory was that? *Ba-dum, ba-dum, ba-dum* .... The rhythm throbbed around him and the things he thought of as the works rumbled, squeaked and clanked. An Outland memory? The eyes, the hair, the layers, they were different from the biped children he had seen. Perhaps something from beyond the heaving Ocean ... then he remembered what was different. There was only one sun!

A dream. It must have been a dream. Well, enough of that. The time was getting shorter and there was more to tell.

*

Joquah' lay in the pleasuroom alone, considering what to do. The elegant lightsounds showering round her went unnoticed. Fendan was in trouble, serious trouble, she was sure of it. All he talked of was saving younglings: he was obsessed. He neglected everything to travel the cities. And his night-chaos ... Others knew about it now, she'd heard the rumours. Night after night, no matter what precautions he took, she watched him groan and toss and mutter to the greening walls. His hands made jerking silhouettes against the glow and the name he muttered constantly was 'Merculan'.

Merculan! Why had they ever brought him here to Breg? Jergul had been right. They should have left him in Aluu. By now he'd have been levigated and everything would be fine. Since he'd disappeared that Bajinj Day she'd thought of him as dead. But what if he were still alive? Supposing Fendan somehow had had news of him. Rumour had it that Fendan roamed the edges of the Cowel by night. That was dangerous in his present state. It could make his fragile sutures snap.

She was right to take her records to the secretariat. It was for her own protection. Fendan might believe that his saving younglings would be approved by the Assembly, but she was not so sure. And if he failed, she'd end up in some laboratory in Tsa, checking nutrient levels. She stared into space for the longest time. The lightsounds had finished. Then the shadow of an idea flitted faintly in the silence.

*

Scientific espionage! There was no research in the cities worth spying on. What slow-brains they were. Did they really think he could be fooled so easily? Oh, the Kristeran did their best to keep it subtle. Most beings wouldn't notice. But Haupus's business was to notice everything in these unsettled times. He'd seen Justice Kristeran at every boundary conversing casually while they watched the passersby. He'd observed the secret signs, the finger flick, the shift of an eye that sent a follower after someone. And it wasn't only in Cah'ai. He summoned all the High Kristeran of Justice to Breg.

Faced with Haupus's information what could they do? Prisoners had escaped from all the continents. As each Krister related the details the others relaxed in the knowledge that they were not the only ones.

"How many are there missing?" Haupus asked.

"Cah'ai ten, Aluu twelve, Tsa thirteen, Xemplox fifteen."

"And Breg?" he turned to Dilh'.

"None, I believe," she replied with a smile.

Haupus smiled too. He looked at each of his High Kristeran in silence. The silence stretched into discomfort.

"That's fifty prisoners missing in all," he said at last. "Now, about this Brawnarm."

They told him all they knew – sightings, descriptions, areas where he was most likely to appear, the rumours of the younglings and the theories of the Kristeran.

"So, it seems this Brawnarm is the danger."

Hands jerked up and fingers spread in unanimous agreement.

"Yes, yes," they answered hastily.

"He's somehow stolen prisoners from all the Chambers except ..." he did not finish the sentence.

The Kristeran's hands closed limply in the silence, waiting.

"He could be a type of biped, but I doubt it. Besides, they say Brawnarm moves by Floater."

"It was a biped who captured Merculan," said Theelah' of Cah'ai."

"Yes, I remember clearly. It was said that he was killed but the evidence, unfortunately, was circumstantial. It is possible he survived. If so, well, he's lived among the bipeds now so long anything could have happened." Haupus paused to let these words sink in.

"The Education Kristeran were never happy with his chaos levels," he continued. "I wonder ..."

Their hands rested on the circular table as they considered the implications. Each had thought of Merculan before.

"Could a being survive outside the Cowel?" asked Selucid

"Let's not speculate," Haupus replied. "Let's deal in what we know. We've learnt that Fendan has been wandering the corridors by night and in disguise. But I expect you all know that."

He paused and glanced around.

"There have been rumours."

"And talk of night-chaos too!"

Everyone had heard some version. Haupus watched the agitation of their hands as they talked and caught Dilh's eye and smiled.

"It was Fendan who kept Merculan from Levigation."

"Of course! He was a protégé."

"Maybe he's met Brawnarm!"

"Maybe Brawnarm and Fendan are in league."

"Fendan has scant respect for Justice Kristeran. That's no secret."

"Now, now," said Haupus smoothly. "Let's not hasten to conclusions. We have no evidence. The Supreme Krister acts in the best interest of the cities as he sees it. We must gather facts, wait, observe, question discreetly. Listen, and report to one another regularly. Knowledge is the key. And we must secure our borders."

He touched a button and the surface of the table lit up from below. It showed a detailed plan of the Cowel with certain areas marked in green.

"We will carry weapons", Haupus said, simply, "for we must protect ourselves against this Brawnarm and perhaps against the bipeds too. We will patrol every crevice that could conceal an exit — I've marked them on the map. Guild members will carry burn tubes and I have levigators for the border guard."

He could not believe it had worked out so easily.

*

Emmerlade lay huddled in her cupboard waiting for the chaos fit to pass. She had had tremors since her Bajinj but she could control them easily. Over the past year, though, they'd been more frequent. She had told no-one of it. Treat it logically, she told herself, assemble facts, then talk to Fendan. But chaos tremors started when he returned home and continued until he left again for the crystal cities. She did not know what to do. This one was the worst.

Joquah' had told Emmerlade everything, the progress of Fendan's chaos, the dossier she'd given to the secretariat, the rumours, her questions about Merculan.

At the mention of Merculan, something stirred in Emmerlade, a memory she could not catch but which made her chaos surge. Joquah', absorbed in her own concerns, did not notice. Emmerlade controlled herself as best she could until Joquah' had finished. Then she came straight to the cupboard.

She'd forgotten how dark it was in here with the door closed. She'd not been here for years, not since ... Merculan. What had they talked about there in that cupboard? There was confusion in her head. Thoughts, words and images whirled in a blur. Some formed tantalizingly for a moment only to disappear again, leaving her with a sense of loss.

*

Two Kristeran insisted on accompanying Fendan back. They exchanged courtesies and made urh several times. When he travelled in the continents he had to visit important Kristeran in their homes and attend official functions. It was expected. And the Kristeran had lists of younglings for him to save. It took time, there were examinations, training and his own recovery period. This evening had been boring, with no decent entertainment. But then all the entertainment he'd seen lately seemed stale and flat.

174

At last the formalities were over and he could go to his room. He took off his robe of tiny yellow sheenstones and changed into a veldan tunic. It was some time since he'd seen Merculan. They'd made no arrangement but Stipo kept a watch for him at certain times.

He liked the corridors shining and empty like this. It was how they were designed to be, shimmering with reflections. As he neared the Attics, he wondered if Merculan had learnt more about the Star Vaulters. Perhaps he'd found new tales of journeyings. They were entertaining, more entertaining anyway than the pretentious drivel he'd had to listen to tonight.

He hardly noticed it at first, the sound behind him. Then he heard it and stopped. The sound stopped too. He moved slowly and heard it again. Then it registered, the 'shshsh' of another floater. Who was it at this hour? He looked back and saw no-one. Was he being followed? Cautiously he changed direction and moved sedately down a corridor. The sound was fainter now, he went some distance and listened closely. It had ceased. Slowly, carefully, he made his way back but, as he neared the entrance to the Attics, he heard the sound again. Best to give up, he would not make it tonight. He returned to his lodgings.

He could not make it any night. Cah'ai was guarding its borders. Fendan smiled to himself, the Justice Kristeran had not told the Assembly about the border guards! And they had not reported the escaped prisoners either. But Fendan knew about the prisoners, he'd seen them with Merculan. The Cah'ai Guild must be worried. Later, when he was in Tsa, he could try again.

But there were border guards in Tsa also. And in Xemplox and Aluu. None of this was reported to the Assembly. But then Justice Kristeran was obsessive about secrecy. Maybe they were right. It was easy to upset the slow-brains. He wondered if Breg too, guarded its borders. He decided to return to Joquah'. He needed to rest and think carefully.

*

Derow and his friends had been among the first to glimpse the big dark figure. They used to wait in alleys hoping to catch sight of him and, when they did, they would dash off screaming. But as they grew bolder they waited and watched him as he passed, daring one another to speak. Rumours were rife among the younglings.

"Brawnarm is our saviour," some whispered. "He can save you from the Kristeran."

"Brawnarm comes to kidnap and destroy!" others said. Derow wanted to know what was true.

Each time they saw him, Brawnarm greeted them formally, in the way you greeted strangers, but said nothing else. Then he was gone before anyone could formulate a question. Once, though, he'd stopped and looked at them. It was almost as if he could see into their minds.

"If you should ever need to leave the Cowel," he said, "seek a biped."

Then he left. They swore by the Great Crystal to keep this message secret.

Derow's parents were not pleased when he'd refused Fendan's offer.

"You need his help," they scolded. "Your chaos levels are far too high, you'll end up in the chambers."

Derow did not reply. They wouldn't understand. He did not want to change. He had seen what happened to the ones who went to Fendan. Overnight they became like Kristeran, narrow-minded, rigid, boring. He questioned the value of so much control. And he wasn't the only one. Most younglings did if they were in any way intelligent.

When he refused a second time it brought a visit from the Justice Kristeran.

"Do you understand your positon?" they asked, but Derow refused to answer. "If the next tests don't show a marked improvement ...."

"Do you understand?" his father interrupted. "You'll be sent for Levigation if you don't take Fendan's help!"

But Derow had decided to take Brawnarm's advice instead. It took ingenuity to dodge the guard and find a biped.

*

"I've reached a crucial stage in my research," Fendan said, "I cannot be disturbed."

"You're going to the Outlands, aren't you?"

"No."

"You're going to look for Merculan."

Joquah' guessed too much, but he had expected that.

"I will remain under the protection of the Cowel," he said. "There's no need for concern."

He left without further explanation.

As Supreme Krister his business could bring him anywhere but the exits in Breg were guarded. His visit to the plant sheds would be reported to Haupus. It was a risk he had to take. A few moments with Festal would be enough.

That night Fendan entered the service basement quietly, watching carefully and listening for any sound of guards. Festal had suggested an air-vent which led from the service area to the Outlands. He heard the hum and gurgle of the rows of pipes and the steady 'chukeda-chukeda' of a pump. He moved cautiously to the air-vent. The service door was open and he peered inside.

It was wide and high as a corridor, stretching away into gloom. At regular intervals light domes cast a yellow-brown glow on the rough, grey walls. A service track ran down each side, some height above the floor. The bottom of the vent was littered with brown debris. He moved inside and stopped once more to listen. He heard strange sounds, whispers, moans, shrieks and whistles. The sound of air, thought Fendan, rushing through the filters.

He took the track on the right and moved into the gloom. Out of sight of the entrance door, he went from light-glow to light-glow. Everywhere looked the same and he lost all sense of distance. Disorientated, he heard a kind of rattle. It started low. What was it? Should he hide? Before he could decide, the sound got louder and a gust of air whooshed past, blowing him against the wall. It flung the debris, dry and sharp as knives, against his face. He raised his hands for protection while the pieces whirled, slashing at his skin. When the air calmed again, his hands and face were bloodied with stinging cuts. He looked at the brown thing still clinging to his robe and recognized it as a leaf.

The track wound smoothly, sometimes to the right sometimes to the left. Each time he rounded a curve, Fendan hoped to see the light of Outlands in the distance. Each time he saw more light-globes. His cuts were painful now, as though a bright, sharp flame leaped from every wound. He stopped to search for his jiwa, a drop or two might help. The sounds in the vent were strange. He thought he heard the mumble of a distant crowd, the whispering of Kristeran, an infant's cry ...

But there was another sound. He listened a moment and dismissed it, but it came again. It was regular and coming towards him. He stopped and paid attention, 'shshsh, shshsh, shshsh'... the sound of floaters. And there were voices too, real voices. Guards! He should have known that Haupus would be thorough. He had to hide. He looked around. Beneath the service track? It meant a leap to the floor of the vent. He had seen the Rebels make leaps like that but they were practised.

The voices came closer. He had to do something. 'Shshsh, shshsh, shshsh.' The wind sighed and moaned, a leaf blew against his face. He brushed at it but couldn't move it, then another leaf and more and more. He began to flap his hands in panic. The seams in his head tore open. He was blinded, paralyzed. The 'shshsh, shshsh, shshsh' was nearer now. Without thinking he leaped from the track. His floater hit the bottom at an angle and toppled over. He lay stunned and winded in the thick leaf bed.

The guards patrolling the tunnel heard the thud.

"What was that?"

They hurried forward with their levigation tubes at the ready.

"I don't like this place," said one.

"Nor I."

A gust of air came whining through and the leaves whirled and crackled.

"I can see nothing with those leaves."

"There's nothing much to see."

"This place is full of Outlandish sounds."

"I'll be glad when this duty's finished."

"Me too." The 'shshsh' of their floaters faded slowly.

Fendan pushed some leaves away. The guards hadn't noticed him. He tried to roll over but he couldn't. His body hurt all over from the fall. For a while he lay there dazed with pain. But he mustn't rest long, there was no knowing when the guards might return. Another dose of jiwa would help him. The pain began to ease.

First he must get upright. He removed his floater, adjusted the body-cup to its lowest point but could not drop into it as he normally would. He needed the height of his bed or couch. Anyway he could see no way to climb back on the service track. The wind still whined and moaned. He struggled for a time but the pain was too great and he collapsed into unconsciousness.

*

Ba-dum, ba-dum, ba-dum, ba-dum .... Five years old. He just knew the child was five years old with his solemn little face, standing under the sun, one sun, against a gate of ornate metal. A woman came, she leant her elbows on the gate and called the child. Then she lifted him up to sit on top of it and, laughing, pointed away at something Fendan couldn't see. The child laughed too. *Ba-dum, ba-dum, ba-dum* .... Another dream, but not his dream, not from his old life. Was it from the new?

*

Voices! The guards were coming back. They wouldn't be able to lift him themselves, so they'd have to go away to get an elevator, and tell Haupus. Fendan scrabbled wildly at the leaves trying to cover himself again. Silence now. No 'shshsh, shshsh, shshsh' of floaters. But another, unfamiliar sound, soft and regular. It was coming from the direction of the Outlands. He listened, trying to identify it. It teased the fringes of his mind, not familiar, but he'd heard it somewhere.

"There he is," someone whispered.

"Where?"

"Look ... in the leaves."

The beings jumped lightly on to the floor of the vent. One bent to brush away the leaves.

"Fendan?"

Bipeds. Of course! Their feet on the service track, that was what the sound was!

"Are you all right?" one whispered.

She picked him up, frowning slightly at the cuts. The other lifted his floater and rested it on his shoulder.

"No talk until we're outside," he whispered, and led the way through the air-vent to the Outlands.

"I am Afon, Festal's daughter," said the one who'd carried him out, "and this is my brother, Sefon."

She lowered Fendan to the cushions in the back of their APT.

"You drive," she told her brother. "These cuts need attention."

For many days he lay in the huge, soft, biped bed, tossing and mumbling in fever, speaking to the images in his head. For a time Maya was afraid that he might die. She bathed him with agenon and inger-water and cleaned the cuts with dap-bark. His bruises faded, the cuts healed, but the fever still tormented him.

The fair-haired biped child ran away. Fendan tried to follow, but the terrain was rough and he fell and tore his skin. He looked at the cut. His skin began to peel away exposing raw flesh. The flesh was moist and bleeding. He tried to hold the skin in place but it slithered off again. The child was there, stopped at a distance, staring at him. Fendan looked from peeling flesh to those wide eyes and was afraid.

He woke with a start. Apprehension gripped his chest. Walls glowed green and faded. Then it was dark. A noisy dark, surrounded by pipes burbling and grumbling and beyond, a regular hypnotic thump. *Ba-dum, ba-dum, ba-dum ...*

He tossed in the big biped bed, unsure if he were awake or dreaming. His body felt peeled. Even the soft covers burned him. Bipeds came and whispered in the shadows. Someone bathed him and soothed his head with something fragrant.

The child was in the corner, staring. Fendan knew this child could see right through him, read his every thought.

"I am the Supreme Krister of the Radiant Orb," he said aloud. "I am Fendan. You must not stare like that."

But the child did not move or shift his gaze.

"Yes," the child said, strong and clear, and Fendan felt that everything he stood for was denied in that one 'yes'.

He wanted to grab him, shake him, kill him, anything.

"Merculan, Merculan," he cried. "I must get to Merculan."

His head, hot and turbulent, rolled from side to side.

"Maya," a rich voice nearby sounded. "Maya, come here, I think he's coming round. He's called for Merculan."

Merculan came into the room and waited by the bed.

"So, Fendan," he said smiling. "The Supreme Krister of the Radiant Orb has survived!"

"Merculan," said Fendan weakly. "Where am I?"

"You're in Festal's house. He sent for me immediately. We were not sure that you'd survive."

"I've had such strange disturbing dreams."

"I know. I saw you toss and rage and scream."

"Enough," said Maya quietly from the door."He'll need a lot of rest. Don't tire him out."

They left the room and Fendan slept again. Merculan was relieved that he was better. He'd watched him anxiously these past few weeks, pestering Maya about his condition.

Since Fendan's last visit, Stipo had opened another sector of the maze and found further information. They were still studying it. The bulk was lists, the EI factors for all kinds of substances and related research. They hadn't understood it because no-one knew anything of Energy Interchange. Fendan, however, was the authority. But this was not the time to talk to him. Maya insisted that he still needed rest.

"He's had a wearisome time," she said. "You'll have to help him to get better."

"Of course, what can I do?"

"His sutures snapped, all at the same time. His mind broke open suddenly and the shock almost killed him. A being cannot drop defences suddenly like that. And, as well you know, being close to us does not help, either. Remember when you Glitter-flies first came?" She laughed at the memory. "He must build more defences quickly, but our Outland ways will make them all fall down! Take him to the Attics, it'll be easier amongst his own. But you must help, he can't do it alone."

*

The tests were very satisfactory. All 'Fendan's younglings', as they were known, showed improvement. The Education Kristeran, relieved to find a solution, did not question Fendan's methods — especially as he'd saved many of the best. But the Justice Kristeran were not pleased. At the meetings of their Guild they talked only of the other younglings, the ones who had disappeared.

"Has Fendan no suggestions?" asked one member.

"Our Supreme Krister is not available," Dilh' replied. "He's doing crucial research and will not be disturbed."

"We haven't seen him for weeks."

"I know," said Dilh'. "It's most unusual, but that's what Joquah' told me."

"Now," said Haupus, "I understand that fifteen more have disappeared. Two were levigated while trying to escape and seven were arrested.

"I've questioned these seven at length. They talked the usual youngling nonsense about questioning the Law and the pursuit of truth. But when I asked them how they intended to survive outside the Cowel they didn't know. They said a biped would take them to where Brawnarm lived."

"There have been no reports of Brawnarm recently," said Teelah'. "At least not in Cah'ai. Not since we placed the border guard."

"Nor in Xemplox."

"Nor in Aluu, nor Breg, nor Tsa."

"What more can we do?"

"We must continue to be vigilant," said Haupus, "and levigate all younglings who refuse help more than once."

The injunction caused a clamour.

"We'd never get away with it."

"Other Kristeran would protest."

"Parents too!"

"The Assembly would consult the Laws."

Haupus waited for the protest to die down .

"We have the future of Zintilla to consider. These younglings are a threat. Too many have already disappeared. If they're allied with bipeds who knows what they'll do. We can't afford to allow any more to escape and add to their numbers."

The silence seemed to signify agreement.

In the Attics, away from bipeds, Fendan felt better.

"I must go," he said. "I've been away too long."

"Not yet, Fendan," Merculan replied. "You still have bouts of chaos. Haupus would have you levigated within a week."

"Nothing that a little jiwa can't put right."

"Be careful with the jiwa, it can work both ways, especially in your weakened state. Take more time and continue the exercises. You can do them by yourself now."

"You're probably right."

Merculan moved Fendan's couch over beside a recorder.

"While you're here," he said, " I want to show you something. Tell me what you think."

It was fascinating. Fendan read it through and then went back to examine it more carefully. EI factors for every substance, systematically tabulated. Experiments to find which ones were sympathetic. Details of all mutually energizing combinations.

"They were searching for a self-renewing fuel!" he told Merculan.

"For space riders, perhaps?"

"It's possible." Fendan considered.

"Is there any relationship between this," Merculan indicated the information on the screen, "and energy exchange?"

"The principles would be the same."

"Teach me, Fendan."

"About energy-exchange?"

"Yes, and about mind-fusion."

"What has that to do with space riders?"

"I don't know. But we should know how to use it. If we could exchange our knowledge like co-creators do, it could help us in our work. Will you teach me?"

Fendan could hardly believe what he was hearing. It was his opportunity.

"Better still," he said, "I'll do it with you, if you're willing."

"But I thought it only worked between male and female," said Merculan.

"Well, I've discovered different."

Merculan would return to the cities yet! And the other Rebels too. Where he went they'd follow. Haupus wouldn't like it, nor the Guild of Justice Kristeran but they'd be disgraced when it was discovered that their prisoners had escaped.

Star Vaulter records, the Rebels' knowledge of the Outlands and the brightest younglings saved! There would be new research in the cities, another age of learning could begin. All because of Fendan, Supreme Father of Zintilla. Joquah' would be proud to take her place beside him once again. But first he must be careful, prepare Merculan well.

Merculan had been surprised at Fendan's offer. If it was true that mind-fusion really could be done with same sex beings then the possibilities were endless. But he knew he must be careful. Fendan's loyalty was to the crystal cities; there was no knowing how he would try to use it.

The more Merculan learned, the more convinced he was that mind-fusion was how Fendan had 'saved' Emmerlade, and Terevor of Tsa and all the other younglings. Much of the preparation was designed to allow Fendan to penetrate his mind. He must not let that happen.

"We'll need time and privacy," Fendan said when he thought Merculan was ready.

"I'll arrange it."

Merculan thought he understood enough to plunder Fendan's knowledge and resist intrusion.

"How about tomorrow then?"

"Tomorrow," he agreed.

Each time they tried they failed. The rainbow beams were out of phase, bouncing round the room. Merculan's eyes engaged again and again but Fendan could not draw them in. They sucked his energy and sent back chaos. Merculan would not, could not, merge.

Merculan stared hard at Fendan trying to fish his eyes from their protective glaze. He was impatient to dive in, to penetrate the Supreme's brain, to give him knowledge of the splendour of the Outlands, the wisdom of its people. Then, maybe, the Supreme Krister would understand. He would know why Merculan could not return to crystal corridors, sterile research, abstractions of abstractions, the rigid laws of birth and death and

Kristeran. Who could tolerate that after the freedom of the Outlands?

If he could only get past those eyes. But Fendan's eyes remained untouchable behind their glaze.

"This isn't going to work," said Fendan and he turned away, "you're trying to dominate me, it doesn't work that way." They were equally disappointed.

"Maybe another time." Fendan made to leave the little room.

"No, let's try again."

Again the rainbow beams were out of phase. "Do not resist!" said Merculan suddenly.

"I'm not resisting ...."

"No, it's something Maya says. We do it all the time, resist."

"Merculan, will you concentrate! We must agree a common thought. Transmit on the same wavelength."

"It's like Muayli!"

"What are you talking about?"

"Muayli, it's a discipline. Outlanders learn it as children."

"Outlanders are irrelevant. You're here to learn energy-exchange. Now concentrate. The EI factor of speckled quartz, let's use that to start."

They found a contact. It was difficult to maintain and neither had enough attention left to slip past into the other's mind. Then it happened. The contact suddenly relaxed and then expanded.

"Now," thought Fendan, "now's my chance." He pushed hard past the rainbows of Merculan's eyes, into his mind.

Merculan felt the push and wanted to resist. He remembered Sefon lying winded on the oval floor. He saw Festal standing, laughing.

"Too rigid," Festal said. "Do not resist the blows, flow with them."

And Merculan relaxed, stopped resisting and gave Fendan the freedom of his mind.

There were no sutures, no resistances. Fendan had never met a mind like that. He felt helpless in its presence. The push he'd given seemed too much. He had gone too far. He began seeing things with Merculan's mind. It was a strange experience, strange and frightening. The thoughts were loose, chaotic, free, a heaving ocean. Tossed on their waves he saw rainstorm, lightning and heard distant thunder. He saw three pale moons, scuttling from cloud to cloud. He saw sea surf pounding stones. The surf broke over him and he drowned in a surge of unspoken freedoms. Haunting music called, dancers whirled their wild, brightly-coloured skirts, shook ribboned tambourines. Cloplinger plunged and rutted. A sweating woman squatted and a baby, all wet and bloody, cried.

"I am Fendan, I am Fendan," he repeated, panicked by Merculan's thoughts. "I am Fendan."

He looked and saw himself, pale, worn out, pathetic, and for one clear instant he understood. He knew why Merculan had chosen as he did.

Fendan collapsed and the connection short-circuited. Merculan brought him to a couch and laid him down. He bathed his head with inger-water and lightly stroked his hand.

Merculan had remained within himself while he looked into Fendan's mind. It was closed. He had images of windows, barred, meshed and curtained, behind which something ghostly flitted in the dark. He felt repelled, wanted to break the connection.

"Flow with it, flow," Maya's voice said in his ear.

He took a breath and looked again. Behind the window was a criss-cross patchwork in the colours of dried blood. Black seams were roughly sewn, some loose, some torn and some pulled too tight.

So that was mind-fusion. He used to think how it would be with Emmerlade. We were of a kind, we two, he thought, we had a common destiny. But ... Fendan's eyes were fluttering.

"Are you all right?" asked Merculan.

The Krister's eyes opened but they were glazed once more with fever. He had failed. He closed his eyes again. He had had the opportunity and failed. That mind was strange and full of awful things. The plunging, rutting cloplinger, the teek, teek, teek of Glitterflies mating on the wing, sinuous dark creepers twining trees, the fruit of odar opening to expose their flesh, a woman cradling a baby to her naked breast, stroking it and crooning. It would take time to get used to such a mind but he would. He must bring Merculan back.

It was very dark and hot. Hot and cramped. A door opened making an oblong of light. He was on a flight of stairs. The child peered round the door post, laughing up to him and calling something. He couldn't make out what it was. He wanted to follow but he couldn't move. Outside, the sky was blue, the sun was shining yellow. The door closed with a bang and the sun and sky were gone. Fendan in the heat and dark yearned for the blue, the yellow and the light.

It was days before the fever abated and many more before he had control.

"You must return to the Cowel soon."

"No, I wish to stay."

"You're not used to the Outlands, Fendan," Merculan said gently. "It is a place of much chaos for us, we need a long and careful training to adapt. Without that, your sutures will burst open unexpectedly, giving you more fever and a lot of pain. If you want to stay you'll have to choose to be like us, for you'll no longer be welcome in the Cowel."

"Come with me, Merculan. Come back to the cities, back to Emmerlade."

"No, Fendan, you know my life is here."

The mention of her name made Merculan wish to see Emmerlade once more. He dismissed the thought. If she came, it must be of her own accord.

Late that night, when the Rebels were asleep, Fendan took a double dose of jiwa and did a long and complex suturing process. He went to where Stipo kept the keys, took one and, with his headrest set to hold his head up high, he let himself out of the Attics. As he passed into the corridors of Cah'ai, the guards arrested him.

*

"He is the Supreme Krister," Theelah' said. "We cannot hold him prisoner."

"But what was he doing there?" asked Neth.

"How can I know? He will not say. He will only say he was doing research. We need say nothing about it, just let him go."

"And what about the Kristeran who found him? There's bound to be talk. A Supreme Krister in our chambers is too dangerous for my liking. Let's pass him on to Haupus, Fendan is a citizen of Breg after all."

"You're right. Pass him on to Haupus. I'll contact him immediately. Let him deal with it."

*

"He was caught in those junk rooms near the Attics by the Cah'ai guards."

"Was he was coming from the Attics? Did he say?"

"He says nothing, but where else could he have been?"

"Is it enough?" asked Dilh'.

"I think so."

"What will you do?"

"Nothing."

"Nothing! Haupus, this is our chance, how can you do nothing?"

Haupus smiled his knife-like smile.

"The Assembly of Kristeran is meeting shortly. We may have some questions to put to Fendan then."

"Ah, yes," Dilh' smiled also, "the Assembly."

*

"You were in the Outlands?" said Joquah.

"Yes."

"Meeting Merculan?"

"Yes."

"Oh, Fendan, what's to become of you? Of us?"

"I need more time but I can save him."

"I don't think there's much time left," Joquah' said quietly.

She said no more. He'd refused to talk much since he had returned. Just said that he'd been ill these weeks and needed rest. She'd have to make a decision soon. She must submit her notes on Fendan to the Assembly a week before it met. Once she did that everything was lost. That gave her four days to find a way to bring him back to normal. The shadow of an idea she had had before returned.

Fendan heard music as he passed the pleasuroom. Joquah' must be playing lightsounds. Pleasant but insipid, he thought. She called him and he opened the door. She was lying on the couch.

"Come here."

He went to her.

"Lie down," she said.

As he removed his floater she uncapped the jiwa phial. And when he lay beside her she took four drops herself and put four more on his tongue. Steadily she held his eyes, then slowly, half against his will, his eyes enlarged and rainbow colours flowed.

"Let us unite our minds once more," she said, "It's been so long."

"Are you sure you want this, Joquah'?" he asked. "There have been things — research — changes in the workings of my mind."

"All minds work the same," she answered. "You know that."

Eyes held eyes and lurid rainbows on the walls glowed acid. She drew his eyes deeper into hers.

She wants to change me, Fendan thought suddenly. He pushed her rainbows out, hauled back his eyes.

"Do not resist," a voice said. "Let it flow, do not resist."

One moment she was fighting his resistance with all her mind, the next she was in his head. Everything was alien. Ogra tossed their heads and flailed their lethal hooves. Foodbeasts jostled in a pen. They stretched their necks with rolling eyes and yawled hoarse and loud. Bilsa squealed hysterically scrabbling in the rafters. Suddenly she saw herself frail and brittle and as she watched she fell apart and the pleasuroom glowed green.

Her collapse did not last long, but afterwards tiny chaos flashes assailed her. Now she was sure. Something hideous had happened to Fendan, he was beyond help. Her submission must go forward to the Assembly. From now on she must fend for herself.

*

Before the first Kristeran had arrived, beings gathered outside the Assembly Hall. The meeting would probably last all day but there could be news earlier. It was not official yet, and only Kristeran were supposed to know, but the rumour was that Fendan was accused of chaos.

Kristeran of every rank were present, from every Guild and every continent. No-one was going to miss this extraordinary Assembly. Each had a copy of Joquah's submission. Every time someone entered, the robes of the Kristeran sparkled, swished and tinkled as they all strained to see.

Fendan and Joquah' were last to take their places. Their arrival caused a hush. Instead of going to the speakers' table, they waited with the rest of the Kristeran. Orgolon of Aluu directed the business of the Assembly instead. He lowered the Crystal from the ceiling. The Kristran bowed five times in greeting and made urh. The Assembly had begun.

Joquah' spoke first, her voice quiet and measured.

"I know that Fendan has always had the interests of Zintilla in mind," she said. "It was his duty as a Krister. Whether you agree with his interpretation is not for me to judge. My duty is to bring some facts to your attention. It started first with Emmerlade .... "

When she had finished, there was a buzz of comment and a tinkling of robes. Orgolon called for questions. Silence. Everyone looked straight at Fendan.

"Is there anything you wish to say, Supreme Krister?" Orgolon asked.

"Before Fendan speaks", Haupus interrupted, "there is more that you should know."

Robes tinkled as the Kristeran turned expectantly to Haupus.

"You have all heard rumours of Fendan's night-chaos," he said, "that's no news. Neither is his wandering by night. But there is more. Do you know of Brawnarm?"

"The being that the younglings talk of?"

"You've heard their stories?"

"Of course, but what has that to do with Fendan?"

"Hear me out. The Justice Kristeran have investigated Brawnarm. He does indeed exist. He comes here from the Outlands but he's not a biped.

"You also know of Merculan's disappearance. There was never any evidence that he died, that was an assumption that we made. We are now sure that Merculan, Fendan's former protégé, is Brawnarm."

There was a buzz of comment.

"What has this to do with Fendan?" intervened Orgolon. "Neither he nor Joquah' were Merculan's parent-educators. This is another issue altogether."

"I have not finished yet," answered Haupus. "It is dangerous to have Merculan stalk the alleys — "

"Refer to him as Brawnarm," snapped Orgolon. "You have given us no proof as yet of your claims."

Haupus lowered his eyelids at the reprimand.

"Because of the danger to our cities from a possible agent of the bipeds," he continued, "the Guild of Justice Kristeran decided to guard the exits to the Outlands and watch for those who came and went. That is how we discovered that Fendan travelled to the Outlands regularly!

"For many weeks he has not been seen in the cities. Crucial research, we were told. But the Kristeran in Cah'ai discovered him coming from the Attics and arrested him. He was not doing research. I believe he was in the Outlands, that's why we have not seen him. And I demand to know what he was doing there."

There was uproar in the hall. Orgolon rang the chimes several times before order was restored. Haupus, in the ensuing silence, turned to Fendan, made mocking urh and sliced him with a smile.

"What do you have to say, Supreme Krister?"

The 'shshsh' of Fendan's floater seemed very loud as he went to take the speaker's place.

"I have much to say, High Justice Krister," he said. "I had hoped to wait until my work was finished to tell you of it, but now it seems it is time to speak."

He faced Haupus.

"You are wrong about Brawnarm," he said. "He is not Merculan. He is Stipo of Tsa, also known as Smuggler."

"But he was levigated years ago," a voice interrupted. "I brought him to the chambers myself."

"No, he wasn't levigated," continued Fendan. "He was imprisoned in Breg but he escaped."

Orgolon had to ring the chimes again to restore order.

"Haupus is right," Fendan continued. "Merculan did not die.

On his Bajinj Day he chose to leave the Cowel. But before he left he went to the chambers and helped Stipo to escape along with Chareem of Cah'ai, Kwas and Pipanda of Xemplox and Tingaal of Aluu. They are living in the Outlands and call themselves the Rebels."

"Haupus lost prisoners from Breg!" exclaimed Teelah' of Cah'ai.

"Not true," Haupus looked to his assistants for confirmation.

"It can be proved," said Fendan. Everyone began to shout. Orgolon rang the chimes again and again.

"No interruptions, please," he ordered. "What Fendan says has serious implications, please hear him out in silence."

"Since then," Fendan continued, "the Rebels have rescued fifty or more younglings from the chambers."

"Why would they want to leave?" asked Orgolon.

"They are critical of our ways and want access to a wider range of knowledge. To this end they co-operate with bipeds."

"But their chaos levels — "

"Certainly, their chaos levels were high, but they are our most intelligent. Is Levigation the solution?"

There was silence. Fendan looked around the Assembly.

"I think the Rebels can be saved," he continued. "They've acquired much knowledge that we do not have. They have access to Star Vaulter libraries and a new understanding of the Outlands. We have much to learn from them."

"How can they be saved Fendan?" Orgolon asked quietly.

"That's what I've been researching. You already know how well it works."

"Describe it to us."

"Certainly."

When Fendan had finished, Orgolon opened the discussion. Some cautiously approved, some demanded his instant Levigation. Many spoke approvingly of his work with younglings, more advised caution. Haupus insisted that he should be brought to trial.

"Haupus is right," Fendan said. "I am willing to stand trial for my actions. With the energy-exchange I broke the Law."

"What about the Justice Kristeran?" asked Joquah'. "Shouldn't they be brought to trial?"

Haupus glared at her while Orgolon thought a moment.

"The Assembly must investigate," he said, "but the Justice Kristeran haven't broken any law."

Fendan left the hall surrounded by guards, Joquah' followed, alone. Orgolon brought up the rear. The crowds were silent as they passed, then broke into a gabble of speculation. As the other Kristeran emerged they were besieged with questions. And as beings learned the details — prisoners escaped from Justice Kristeran, Brawnarm, Merculan, Fendan's chaos and his way of saving younglings — the disagreements started.

Late into the evening, the corridors were still crowded. Beings quoted Law to neighbours, swapped theories about bipeds and argued with strangers. And when they finally went to their couches, they tossed and moaned and dreamed strange dreams. And a great many walls glowed green.

Chapter 11

There was a change. A shift. His body was held snug, too snug, and something pressed, uncomfortable in the dark. He pushed, nothing happened. He pushed again. Still it pressed. He gathered all his strength and wriggled vigorously. An arm released, a leg .... *Ba-dum, ba-dum, ba-dum* .... Reassured, he settled, comfortable again.

*

Joquah' was busy. There was Fendan's work as well as her own to do. In his absence she was responsible. If they were no longer to be Supreme Kristeran, there were the records to be checked and put in order.

All day she noted data from the cities, monitored research, met delegations. And in the evenings when she returned home she went straight to her work room to scan recorders. She checked for files not up to date. She marked errors, noted omissions and sent meticulous instructions. But, when her head was lolling in its headrest and the screens were just an out-of-focus blur, she had to stop. All she could hear were voices, thoughts and arguments: Fendan talking to the Assembly, an argument overheard in the corridors, the grey-blue gleam of a High Krister's earthshine robe, a hectoring voice addressing the Assembly .... Fendan might go free, but her position was intolerable. Dilh' and Haupus wanted Fendan in the Chambers and the Justice Guild was hostile. What could she do? She went to her couch and hoped for sleep but tossed and turned instead.

Her walls glowed green, flashing danger in the dark. Even

with her eyes closed, the light disturbed her. Jiwa helped, of course, but she didn't want to become like Fendan. Eventually she took it and fell into a tumbling, dream-infected sleep.

But Emmerlade was awake. She woke often now in the night. Dream-shreds hung in her head and a chaos lingered in her chest. She rose and wandered from sleeproom to work room to pleasuroom. She called up information on recorders, played snatches of lightsound tapes, peered in at Joquah' — anything for distraction. That was when she saw her mother's walls glow green. Joquah' too! Her mother had always seemed so stable. So serious. If she was affected, how many other beings tossed and dreamed? How many other sleeprooms glowed bright green?

Each morning Joquah' checked the chaos ratings. The screens flashed scores for Xemplox, Tsa, the continental averages, day figures, night figures. All of them were rising sharply. She checked her own score — rising, and Haupus's — rising too.

*

Ba-dum, ba-dum, ba-dum, ba-dum .... It clutched again, shattering his safety. Tight, tighter than the other times, it squeezed. Fear streaked all through him, and the grip released. He listened. Yes.... *Ba-dum, ba-dum, ba-dum, ba-dum* ... and wriggled into comfort once again.

*

Fendan, dressed only in a prison shift, lay staring at the wall. At least he was alone. They had put him on the highest shelf with a guard outside the door. In case he should escape, he supposed. Should he have told about the Rebels? All they wanted was their freedom, mountains, black and purple jagged against a green-gold sky, the scent of odar blossom after rain, the night-sky's gaudy glitter, the adventures of Star Vaulters ... Haupus would destroy them if he could.

He stared at the granite vaulting of the ceiling. A fevered

chaos stirred, voices whispered to him from the corner, a child laughed and beckoned, the earth began to tremble. No help from jiwa now, they'd taken it away. The flecks of granite glinted. To distract himself he identified components — quartz, feldspar, orthoclase and mica. And, as he stared, the coarse grain swelled and ebbed, like something live and breathing.

Ba-dum, ba-dum, ba-dum .... Each breath brought the granite nearer, lower, closer, until it pinned him to his shelf, pressing him tight. Fear streaked in every artery, every vein.

"Fendan!" called a voice.

He blinked and rubbed his eyes and looked around. He must have been asleep.

"Wake up, wake up." A young Justice Krister looked up at him. "Your trial is today."

His trial.

"Have you brought my robes?"

"Yes, Supreme Krister, they are here."

"A mirror?"

"Yes, that too."

"Leave me alone for a while," he said when he'd been lowered from the shelf onto his floater. "I wish to prepare."

He raised his floater to its highest — only his most sumptuous robe would do for this occasion and it needed height. The rubies, garnets and flame-diamonds cascaded to the floor, red torrent over cliffs, foam boiling around rocks, flinging hazy rainbows to the spume. No, no, he must control himself. Meticulously, he adjusted his headrest, his headcovering, its jewelled fringe, his earpieces and armlets, and surveyed them in the mirror. He was satisfied.

"Enough of chaos," he said aloud. "I must be in control today."

He repeated a long suturing process several times, then looked his image in the eye.

"I am Fendan, Supreme Krister of the Radiant Orb," he said. "I am — " A guard came in.

"Supreme Krister," he said. "It's time to go."

Fendan went to the door. The guards moved back respectfully and made urh. They were unsure as to how to proceed. The Supreme Krister looked imposing in his robes. They could hardly treat him like a common prisoner and bind his arms.

"I won't escape," Fendan said, resolving their dilemma.

Along the corridors from the chambers, through the Amethyst Arcade, past the gleaming polyhedron of the Music School, the tiered light sculptures, the square outside the Hall, everywhere, crowds had gathered. This was no ordinary court. Fendan must be tried amongst his peers, not in the Hall of Justice but in the Hall of the Assembly of the Kristeran of Zintilla. There had been other such trials. The histories recounted them in the sparse language of facts. This was a chance to see what it was really like.

Haupus swept past, greeting no-one, and Dilh' hurried to keep up with him. Beings jostled one another for a view, small younglings darted around their elders' skirts, and Kristeran appealed for order. Then, flanked by guards, Fendan arrived.

The crowd fell silent and made urh.

"Supreme Krister," a voice called out. "You have saved my son."

There was an agitation in the crowds and a being struggled through, pushing a youngling before her.

"Move back, move back," the guards called, keeping them at a distance.

"Just let him speak to Fendan," said the mother.

"All right then, speak."

"I am grateful for your help," the youngling said. "You saved me from the Chambers."

"May you be Supreme Krister until the Child of your Life is placed in your arms," the mother added.

"Zhenta, zhenta, zhenta," murmured voices.

"All right, all right. Move back," the guards said, pushing mother and son into the crowds.

*

It came again. Gripping longer, harder, tighter. Fear scorched again. No .... He struggled to escape but he was caught, imprisoned. No, no, no .... The grip relaxed, softened into a stroking and with it the fear subsided.

Ba-dum, ba-dum, ba-dum. He curled to rest.

*

The Rebels gathered to watch the trial. They watched on Star
Vaulter equipment adapted by Chareem. Things were changing
in the cities, especially since Fendan's last visit.

Dilh' and Haupus entered the Hall together wearing matching
robes of flame and white-fire diamonds.

"Some display!" said Chareem.

Joquah' had chosen the subtly shifting colours of grey opals
that sometimes flared into a brilliant hue. The Hall was crowded
with Kristeran. Communicards talked urgently, speculating on
the outcome of the trial.

"Look at them," said Tingaal. "Idiotic!"

"All show and flash and scoring points," agreed Stipo.

"Hush, watch and listen, this is interesting," commanded
Merculan, and his eyes grew larger.

Fendan requested a committee of High Kristeran to judge
him. Haupus argued fiercely against his request but was over-
ruled.

"Look," cried Merculan. "Look at Haupus! Can't you see the
chaos? He's angry."

"You're right!" Pipanda said. "And Dilh' too, look!"

They were all watching closely now.

"I wouldn't trust that Haupus," muttered Stipo.

"Yes, Fendan may need our help," Merculan said.

"Do you think so? The Kristeran are already arguing, he's
sure to win."

"Yes, and that makes Haupus more dangerous."

At the end of the day, Fendan's return to the chambers was
slow. The corridors were crowded once again and younglings
pressed forward to thank him and make urh. There was little that
the guards could do to stop it and they seemed unsure as to how
to act.

"We must discover what Haupus is planning," Merculan, said
to Tingaal.

"That's impossible, how can we?"

"We can find out from the Justice Kristeran."

"They won't talk to us. Besides, they all have weapons."

"Then we must plan carefully," said Merculan.

*

He lay there staring at the ceiling. It had been a long and tiring day. So much chaos amongst the Kristeran, even Haupus. His eyelids fluttered. The granite ceiling swelled and ebbed again .... *Ba-dum, ba-dum, ba-dum,ba-dum.* The walls expanded, breathing too, *ba-dum, ba-dum.* He tried to push them back but they would not be held. Some contrivance of Haupus to engender chaos, or to kill .... It caught and crushed him once again.

"Let me go, " he screamed. "Let me out."

It crushed him tighter. His neck was twisted, his hand jammed tightly to his face. He could not breathe. Fear tourniqueted his chest, streaked electric to his head, his hands, his head. He couldn't breathe .... The gripping softened a little and he gasped for air, and then a little more until it stroked him calm. *Ba-dum, ba-dum, ba-dum, ba-dum* ....

The sound woke him and he looked around. The sound? *Ba-dum, ba-dum, ba-dum, ba-dum* .... He listened carefully and realized it was his heart, loud in the silence of the prison.

*

"It was the action of a slow-brain," Jenta said. "We should never have agreed."

"Well, it seemed a good idea at the time," Jergul snapped back.

"To you it did, not to me. You can never trust a Krister."

"Fendan and Joquah' are not just any Krister."

"Supreme Kristeran, least of all. Fendan always was too tolerant. If it were up to me I'd have accused him in a flash. Merculan was wild, just like that Emmerlade, but what happens in the end? He saves her and sends our son to the Outlands! Don't talk to me of Kristeran!"

"And what about the walls? Since we've heard the news we've had night-chaos too. Every night I wake and the walls are flashing — not glowing — flashing, and don't you know that Joquah' checks all that. We'll be blamed, just mark my words, we'll be blamed for this."

"But the visis, Jenta? You have seen the visis. Fendan is mobbed by younglings showing gratitude and parents asking for his help. They call him Father of Beings, Saviour."

"Well, he didn't save Merculan, did he?"

*

Haupus went to the Levigation Chamber. He often went there to think. It was a place he liked to be. The moaning prisoners pleased him and the controls of the levigation equipment gave him a sense of power. But not this time. The trial was going on too long. Too many beings believed Fendan had a case. And there was this unprecedented rise in chaos. He had tried asking Joquah' for the figures, but she avoided answering. There must be something he could do. The noise of the prisoners made him restless so he left to roam the Hall of Justice instead.

"He should be here, right here, before me," he said aloud to the empty Hall. "I would apply the Law verbatim."

And there wouldn't be these younglings making urh. He'd come straight here from the chambers. No journey through corridors, no crowds of slow-brains and gawking younglings. It was a problem for the guards, too. He'd increased the numbers but he must be very careful. All Zintilla watched to see how he and his Kristeran would behave. And if Fendan persuaded the Assembly, what then? A chaos fluttered deep inside and the Hall of Justice echoed with a howl. He turned around to see where it came from then realized it came from himself. He left abruptly.

"Have you noticed Joquah'?" Dilh' asked when he returned. "She accused him to the Assembly, but now she acts as though he will be freed!"

"She's keeping all her options open."

"She intends to remain Supreme Krister, Haupus, and we cannot let that happen."

"I know."

Haupus looked around him.

"But what do you suggest?"

*

The granite glinted in a cave, dark, deep underground. He heard the rumble, felt the tremble at the centre of the earth. Rocks crashed and tumbled, crushing his frail body, contorting him. The cave walls, no longer stable, groaned and shifted, inching closer, closer until they caught and ground him, slowly, slowly, in their boulder teeth. The pain, he couldn't bear the pain, but the boulder teeth ground on. He couldn't breathe ....

"This is the end. Oh please, just kill me quickly."

But no death came, just pain and fear and suffocation and somewhere, far away, the muffled cry of some other living thing, trapped. He couldn't breathe .... The earth sagged a little and relaxed, the boulders eased their bite, the rumbling died and he could breathe again. *Ba-dum, ba-dum, ba-dum* .... He could breathe but he was still imprisoned in a tiny crevice, no way to move, no exit, no escape. Fear tore him like a wild thing caged inside his chest as he waited, dreading the earth's next convulsion.

Ba-dum, ba-dum, ba-dum .... The sound woke him. He looked at the vaulted ceiling not knowing who or where he was. Then he remembered.

"I am Fendan .... I am Fendan the ... the ... transmitter."

*

For the fourth night in a row the relief watch was late. The guards on duty, already fretful, were getting nervous. The dim glow of the entrance globes leaked into the dark, casting uncertain shadows. They were the only lights permitted in the sheds, for the plant schedules must not be interrupted. It was very quiet. Minute sounds made the guards go tense and feel for weapons,

201

but they were reluctant to investigate, to move beyond the light. Behind the raised beds of food plants, Merculan and Stipo watched and listened. The new guards arrived making excuses and asking how things had been. The old complained, said all was well and left. Everything was hushed. The guards stationed themselves at either side of the entrance and chatted quietly for a while, then silence.

Merculan signalled 'ready' and picked a pebble from the plant beds. He threw it, hard, against a wall.

"What's that?" The guards spun round, fumbling for their weapons. Levigators drawn and pointing in the direction of the sound, they peered anxiously into the shadows. Silence. They patrolled the borders of the light uneasily. Still silence.

"Just one of those night noises," one said loudly.

They returned to their places, watchful.

Merculan threw another pebble.

"There it is again!"

"Turn on the light."

"We can't, slow-brain, it's programmed. We'd have to go into the labs."

This time they ventured cautiously into the dark. The silence stretched, elastic, fit to snap. They drifted back to the light again, all eyes and tension. Deftly, Stipo tied a fibre string around a plant stem and tugged it. The plant, tall, strong-leaved, filled the dark shed with sibilance. The guards listened, seeming paralyzed.

"Who's there?" they called.

No answer came, just a rustling. Cautious, they moved forward, slowly, wary, weapons pointing. And in the shadows Merculan and Stipo waited.

The Kristeran moved along the rows of plant beds towards the sound. Merculan and Stipo silently manoeuvered, using the string to keep the plant leaves whispering. When a guard came close enough, Merculan grabbed a wrist, snatched the weapon and propelled his captive outside. He removed the guard's floater and left him lying in the back of the waiting APT. It was easier than he'd expected. Stipo pinnioned the other guard's arms from behind and his levigator fell to the floor.

"Where's the weapon?" asked Merculan as Stipo removed his captive's floater.

"I'm going back to get it now."

"And don't forget the string," Merculan called after him.

*

"The education of younglings is our concern and Fendan should have consulted with us first."

"Yes, yes, but as Supreme Krister he must do research. He was within the Law."

"Of course, but that's not the point," a senior Krister interrupted. "The real point is, what will happen if he goes?"

The Guild of Education Kristeran was silenced. The arguments, flung back and forth all day, ceased abruptly. They might not agree on Fendan, but the prospect of his successor united them.

"It can't be Dilh' and Haupus."

"But who else could make a claim?"

"One of us, perhaps?"

"Not very likely!"

"But can Fendan still hold office after the trial? Apart from the younglings, there is the charge of chaos."

"Night-chaos, true," the senior Krister interjected, "but which of us is without it now? No, think of it this way, Fendan's research was pioneering work. He did not want to involve others in the dangers and thus exposed himself to chaos, 'in the interests of Zintilla'. As a result we live in a new era of effective chaos control which saves gifted younglings, releasing their talent for all our benefit. Could that, perhaps, summarize our position?"

The Kristeran considered this a moment.

"We may need to rephrase it," the High Krister said.

"Of course."

"And Fendan must consult us in the future."

"We will remind him of his debt to us."

*

It began again, the gripping, squeezing, crushing, crushing. Oh pain, and fear and life cut off .... Oh pain again and pain and fear, locked, caught and held, a need to push and push. Oh let me out, cut off, cut off .... And then he pushed again, head first and pushed ... there was no 'out' and he was crushed and caught, compressed, constricted. Anger flashed. He pushed. No good. His anger was doused with danger. He was in danger now, all life cut off, cut off .... *Ba-dum, ba-dum, ba-dum, ba-dum* .... The rhythm was still there, life seeping through again, danger deferred. He was exhausted now and still caught. No way out, nowhere to go. *Ba-dum, ba-dum ba-dum* .... He had to rest.

*

She woke. Where was she? Not on her own couch, it was too soft for that, too big. She lay propped on pillows under soft coverings. Curious, she turned her head. A rectangle of light on the rough floor, it was cast by the bright rectangular light source on the wall. Too bright, inefficient, it made the rest of the room seem dark. She watched the bright patch creep across the floor, making idle calculations about the nature of its source. The room was warm. A movement caught her eye. There was a being in the shadows, large and lumpy. It rubbed its eyes inelegantly with its fists. A biped. Chaos surged and she remembered she was in the Outlands.

She had no control over the chaos. Attempts to curb it failed. Sometimes, when she was alone in this room, it faded enough for her to do a suturing process, but when one of Them came near it fell apart again. And They were there all the time, shuffling and whispering in the shadows, releasing strange and soporific odours, giving her nutrition capsules, bathing her with liquids. So far they hadn't hurt or injured her, despite their bulk. But they tortured her with chaos. Like Haupus did with unworthies in the Levigation Chamber. She wondered how they did it, how they loosened her controls. It was terrible and filled her with unfamiliar sensations and confusion.

She must remember exactly how it had happened. Haupus would expect a clear report. We were on guard, she reminded herself, we heard a noise, we went to investigate and in the dark both of us were captured. That was all she could be sure of, that and a hazy recollection of sharing this huge bed with another.

"You!" she called out sharply to the biped in the shadows. "Where is he? What have you done with him?"

"The other Glitterfly, you mean?"

"Glitterfly? The other guard! I demand to know."

"He's dead, the fever took him," said the biped.

"Fever?"

"What you've been suffering from. The reason that you're here. But you're getting better now."

She was confused. She did not understand the creature's words. No, she understood the words, but the meaning made no sense, or was it the other way around? She was tired, her head hurt from the effort and she closed her eyes. The door opened.

"Merculan," the creature who was with her rose in greeting. "She's better now, much better. But mind you take it easy, she's still weak."

So this was Merculan! Chaos surged briefly and memories of that awful journey quivered in her brain. It was him, the leader of the Rebels, he had done it! What could he want with her?

Merculan came close to the bed.

"You won't be hurt," he said and smiled. "We're not barbarians."

She said nothing, but noticed his lack of a headrest, the muscle development in his arms and shoulders, the colour of his skin. Even his head grew hair like bipeds. Not one to trust ....

"I need some help," he said. "Fendan is in danger."

"If he is, he put himself there," she replied.

"Oh, you mean the trial! He is in no danger from the trial. From what I hear, he'll be released. The danger is from Haupus."

"Haupus is my High Krister. He is just."

"Haupus plots to be Supreme, everyone knows that. He has plans for Fendan's downfall."

"That's jiwa talk. Haupus has no plans. His sole aim is justice."

"What orders has he given to his Kristeran?"

"The orders of a High Krister to his Guild are secret. I cannot say."

"Well, then we'll have to make you."

The biped in the shadows moved forward.

"That's quite enough, Merculan," he said sharply and led him from the room.

"What do you think you're playing at?" asked Festal when they were outside. "You don't have to push her so hard. The other one is dead. Do you want her to die as well?"

"She's a Justice Krister. She must have information. How else can I get it?"

"The question really is why do you need it?"

"To save Fendan, you know that."

Festal laughed.

"He's desperate to save you, you're desperate to save him!"

"But he's changing. I think he wants to join us. He could help us with our work. And think of the effect it would have! Don't you see, Fendan is the key. Everyone would follow him. Outlanders and Crystal Beings would be one again. You do want that, don't you, Festal? All Children of the Heart."

"I don't think it can happen quite that easily or that quickly. It's like the harvest, Merculan. It needs its time. Time to clear the soil and sow it, time to sprout the seed, time for the flower to blossom and grow seer. Only then the fruit begins to swell and sweeten. And when it's ripe, it needs no force, but falls into your waiting hands."

But Merculan was in no humour for Outland imagery.

"You're far too cautious, Festal," he said.

"Perhaps," said the biped.

*

A change! *Ba-dum, ba-dum, ba-dum* .... He wriggled, testing the restrictions. Something had changed! He gathered all his strength and pushed. Nothing. He pushed again. The gripping came, a volt of fear, pain, pain and purchase! It gave him purchase with the pain! He pushed and pushed until it caught and crushed him like before and held him impotent and angry. *Ba-dum, ba-dum, ba-dum, ba-dum* .... He had to rest. *Ba-dum, ba-dum* ....

He had to gather strength. The next one came too soon. He

wasn't ready. He pushed and pushed but now could find no leverage. Oh help me, help me.

*

The guard didn't want to see him so she closed her eyes. Merculan came every day to torture her with chaos, ask her questions. Questions about Breg and Emmerlade, about Haupus and the Guild, things she couldn't know and things she shouldn't speak of. She tried to keep control and keep her silence, but sometimes when the chaos overtook her she talked and talked and did not know what she was saying.

"That's enough," Festal said, and led Merculan by the elbow from the room.

"I was right!" Merculan said. "You heard her, Haupus has some plan. All the Justice Kristeran are armed. He told them he has word of a Rebel plan to capture Fendan and that they must be ready. He even gave a date! It's an excuse to murder Fendan, I'm sure. What would be easier than to fake a kidnap and have him killed in the chase? Now you've got to help us, Festal. We will be saving Fendan's life."

"And what about her?" Festal asked, nodding in the direction of the bedroom door.

"Can't she stay here?" said Merculan.

"You know she can't! You'll have to take her, help rebuild her control. The chaos here would kill her."

"Just for a little while, until this is over?"

"Even that might be too much," said Festal.

"Very well, we'll take her to the Attics."

*

Fendan lay once more staring at the ceiling. He was pleased at how things were going at his trial. The Education Kristeran were definitely in his favour, and the Birthing Guild too. He had taken on the youngling chaos for the future of the crystal cities. That's what they had said. Joquah' too had met his eyes today. He stared at the granite, remembering Joquah's eyes. The granite swelled and sighed.

And the earth convulsed again. Boulders growled and shifted, grinding him in his crevice. Oh the pain, the pain, and he couldn't breathe, he couldn't breathe, he couldn't breathe ....

Then there was air, a shift, a change. A crack opened near his head. He could feel the thin draught. He pushed against it hoping it would open more, but nothing happened. Then he heard faint voices calling and he awoke. He was lying on his shelf. No crack, no voices, no escape. But curiously, a strange new sense of hope.

*

"You know exactly what to do," said Merculan. "Follow the plan precisely. Stipo and I will be at the Amythyst Arcade."

When he'd asked for volunteers everyone had offered. He chose younglings whose size would let them pass unnoticed in the crowds of Crystal Beings but who also had the strength, the discipline and the nerve to rescue Fendan.

"We'd best be going soon," said Festal. "I don't much care for travelling once darkness falls. These no-moon nights are dangerous with spinwinds."

"We could enter through Cah'ai if you'd prefer," said Merculan.

"No, security is sloppiest in Breg because of all those extra visitors. You'll stay in Takh'bisa's tonight and get a good sleep."

"Zhenta, zhenta, zhenta," Merculan agreed.

"Make sure you wrap up well. The season of Landrest can be very cold, especially this late in the day."

It was indeed cold. The younglings, packed into the back of Festal's APT, were glad of the extra blankets he'd provided. The sky was fluorescent green and streaked with violet. Bare trees, like gnarled hands, clawed the sky, the distant mountains black and glowering. Sometimes in the fields they saw thin black spirals, tall as trees, speeding across the grey-brown earth.

"Spinwinds," murmured Festal. "Hold on to your boots, I may

have to swerve suddenly."

"If we had boots to hold on to!" laughed Stipo. They held on to a bar instead, but even Stipo and Merculan, the strongest of them all, had difficulty when Fendan swerved and bumped off the roads.

"It may not look like much," said Festal, pointing, "but that slender spinwind could overturn us all."

They got to Festal's house without mishap and Maya welcomed them to the fire-bright hearth. Sefon, Irthon and Rithon were arranging pillows for the younglings to lie on. Afon was there, too.

"I have your Justice Krister outfits for you," Maya said. "You'll have to try them on."

She had taken the clothing of the captive guards and subtly adjusted it to suit the bulk of Merculan and Stipo.

"They'll do," said Festal, critically, when they tried them on. "I think you'll pass, but I'll have to shave your heads if you're to look like proper Glitterflies."

Stipo still had half a head of hair when three Outland neighbours came through the door with a crock of faizle-wine.

"We've planned for songs and night-fire tales," said Afon, "and games of mischieving."

"It will keep the Glitterflies from brooding," laughed Maya.

It was true, the Rebel younglings were nervous, unable to relax. More Outlanders came with bells and pippin pipes. Rithon got his tabour out and Sefon his viol and they played lively dance tunes. Festal and Irthon cleared the floor space. Outlanders jumped up to dance, the formations weaving patterns while their feet tapped intricate rhythms on the floor. More neighbours came and eventually even the younglings were up, learning the patterns of the dances while Outlanders laughed and clapped and encouraged them.

The dancing gave way to mischief games and laughter and then to stories by the fire. And, when the flames sank to bright embers and white ash, the neighbours left in ones and twos, bidding a quiet goodnight and slipping into the dark. Many of the Rebels were already asleep on their cushions, but Merculan and Stipo talked quietly together, rehearsing, one last time, their plans for Fendan's rescue.

"Go to sleep, you two," Festal said. "Being tired won't serve your cause. You have done all you can. Sleep is your best rehearsal now. Rest easy, I'll make sure you get to Breg in time. Their sunless day starts later than ours this time of year. You'll have all the sleep you need."

*

The rumble started in the earth again. His crevice creaked, heaved and crushed him, rammed his head against the rock. Oh the pain, the pain. He couldn't breathe .... Panic, and his skull must split! He couldn't breathe, he couldn't breathe .... Boulders pressed down on his chest and shoulders. Then the thin draught once again. The earth rumbled and convulsed once more, the crack widened just a little. More air, enough to stay alive. The heaving eased, the earth grumbled to a rest and left him battered and exhausted, waiting. *Ba-dum, ba-dum, ba-dum, ba-dum* ....

"Wake up, Fendan. Wake up, wake up."

He was impatient at the interruption and his head hurt.

"Wake up."

He opened his eyes. For some moments he could not fathom where he was. Then his eye caught a movement of his guards, waiting silently for him. He pulled himself together to do a suturing process.

Each day of the trial brought more visitors to Breg. Those who could travelled to the capital every day; those who lived too far away looked for lodgings in the city. Every room in Breg was taken, every home was full. Crystal Beings were curious to see for themselves what was going on. Before the Assembly opened they were there, lining the corridors, and there again when it finished for the day. They came to see the Kristeran in their ceremonial robes and speculate about their attitudes. They came to see Fendan, surrounded by younglings, making his way from the Chambers. And they came to hear the gossip about the Assembly. The latest was that the old Kristeran alliances were breaking up and each day new ones were beginning. Big changes must be coming if the Kristeran were in so much disagreement.

Haupus asked all the juniors in the Justice Guild to assist with crowd control in Breg. They were to clear a passage for the

Kristeran to pass, but allow beings to greet Fendan, as long as order was maintained. He gave no directions about limiting the numbers coming into the city. Crowds and confusion suited his plan.

*

The crushing came again. No, no, no! He was angry now and kicked and pushed and found it gave him leverage. He kicked and pushed and yes, there was a little give, a little movement, some way out! He gathered strength and pushed.

*

All day the sense of hope he had on waking filled him, fueling the answers that he gave the Kristeran. The Education and Birthing Kristeran were definitely behind him. The rest were unable to agree amongst themselves. That much was obvious. And Joquah' — Joquah's eyes had met his time and again. She was with him now. What of Emmerlade, he wondered?

By evening, so many beings had come to greet him that it was difficult to keep moving through the grateful younglings, parents and petitioners. The guards did little to help. Gradually he began to feel uneasy. He could not get enough air. Beings crowded ever closer, hands opened, eyes searching his. He wanted them to go away but they milled around him closer. He tried to move on but he was trapped, suffocated, he couldn't breathe, he couldn't breathe ....

Suddenly he could breathe again. Had he lost consciousness for a moment? A group of younglings had formed a tight circle around him, giving him a little space and moving him through the crowds.

"Thank you," he told them gratefully.

"Supreme Krister," a familiar face said quietly. "Be prepared, your rescue is at hand."

"Rescue?" He was surprised. "I don't need rescuing."

"We have word that Haupus plans to kill you."

He recognized her now, one of Merculan's Rebels! He looked closely at the others and thought he recognized them too, but he wasn't sure. He was confused and felt a chaos rising. Not now, not here, he begged, and held his breath and sutured quickly. Another Rebel moved close.

"You are in danger, Fendan," he murmured in his ear, "but do exactly as we say and you'll be safe."

While Fendan puzzled over this, they arrived at the Amythyst Arcade. The crowds were densest here with beings pushing and swaying. There seemed to be some kind of disturbance. The Justice Kristeran shouldn't allow this kind of incident to develop. Haupus should have forseen the crowds. Then it came to him: crowds and confusion would make perfect allies if Haupus planned to kill him. He was glad when his escort closed in protectively and moved him to the shelter of a wide Arcade pillar.

*

Ba-dum, ba-dum, ba-dum .... The rhythm throbbed inside his head as he lay resting on the heart of all the world.

*

The young Kristeran were concerned. This was the worst day yet. It was difficult to keep Fendan in sight, what with the younglings and the crowds. The jostling and the pushing made it impossible to keep any sort of control. They shouted, "Order, Order," at the tops of their voices, but it had no effect. They'd have to speak to Haupus. The numbers in the corridors made their task impossible. Besides, beings would get hurt.

*

212

He knew it now. There was an out, he felt it. The crushing was his ally now, it helped him. He rested, expectant, hopeful, waiting for the next.

*

Beings hurried down the alley towards the Amythyst Arcade. They saw figures in the doorway, but took no notice.

"They think we're Kristeran on guard!" grinned Stipo.

"Let's hope they're all in the same rush," answered Merculan.

The other Rebels had gone on to mingle with the crowds, but they had remained in the alley. Their headrests felt impossibly restrictive and chaffed their chins and necks. Their shaven heads were prickly and cold, uncomfortably exposed. They waited until the crowds in the Arcade were at their densest.

"Time to go," said Merculan.

There were Justice Kristeran everywhere. Haupus was taking no chances. Merculan and Stipo moved purposefully through the crowds. As they passed along, they pushed floaters, causing a wave of movement and confusion in the crowds, beings bumping into one another.

"Stay back, stop shoving!" those in front called back.

"Order, order," cried the Justice Kristeran, "Order or we'll clear corridors."

But no-one paid any heed. Merculan and Stipo moved in behind two guards and waited. Fendan approached and, as he passed, they stretched their strong arms. Each grabbed a Krister's floater and toppled it. In the following consternation they moved off through the crowd.

"Order, order," they shouted as they went, pushing more floaters and causing more disruption. They reached Fendan at the pillar.

"Quick," said Merculan.

He ducked into the circle and lowered Fendan's floater. Stipo followed him, his arms locked around a protesting onlooker. Without a word, they removed Fendan's jewelled head and earpieces and put them on the captive, raising his floater to its maximum height.

"Now you can be the Supreme Krister," Stipo said, removing the being's robe and slipping on Fendan's. "Not many get that chance!"

While Merculan and Stipo bustled Fendan through the crowds, the Rebels held Fendan's substitute in a tight circle. After an agreed length of time, one by one they made urh and slipped away.

As they raced through the alleys, Fendan felt his chaos level rising. He had to stop. His suturing was slipping .... Boulders shifted once again, rumbled and pushed, jammed his head against the crack. He couldn't breathe, he couldn't breathe, he couldn't ....

"Breathe, relax, remember what I taught you," Merculan said urgently in his ear, keeping an anxious watch on the corner. "Fendan, pull yourself together."

But it did no good. He took a phial of jiwa from his pocket and put a drop on Fendan's tongue.

"Let's hope this works till we get him out of here," he said.

Two of Cah'ai's junior Kristeran watching from the edges of the disturbance were uneasy.

"There's something going on," one said. "I know there is."

His companion agreed. They could see Fendan's jewelled headcovering glittering among the younglings and yet ....

"Perhaps it's just the numbers in the corridors."

"No, it's more than that .... Two guards have disappeared and ... that's not Fendan! The Rebels! They've taken him, that's what Haupus said."

"But Haupus said tomorrow!"

"He was wrong. Get over there. Arrest the imposter. Tell the others. I'll make for the alley and get as many as I can to chase Fendan."

"But – "

"Just hurry."

It was impossible to get through the crowds quickly. Four junior Kristeran managed to struggle into the alley beside the Amythyst Arcade but there was no sign of Fendan.

"Come on," the one from Breg cried. "They'll make for the Food Laboratories and Outlands. Follow me, I know the quickest way."

They rushed in pursuit, pulling out their burn tubes.

Fendan, gasping for air, trailed after Merculan and Stipo through the alleys. The jiwa worked a little but soon he felt his chaos rise again. His head was hurting, throbbing. He was stuck again and there was no escape. An anger rose. He would batter his way through if he must. Fear grasped his heart and throat. He couldn't breathe ....

He stopped, collapsed against a wall and, unconscious, tumbled to the floor. Stipo and Merculan lifted him between them. They struggled on as best they could but Fendan's dead weight slowed them down. As they got to the entrance of the Food Laboratories he regained consciousness.

"Leave me," he gasped. "Go on yourselves, it's me they want."

"We want you too, Fendan," said Stipo. "Come on, we're nearly there."

"No, no, I must stand trial, it's the only way."

"The trial's not your problem, it's Haupus."

The first shots singed their clothes and sprayed scorch marks on the walls. The guards came rushing round the corner.

Merculan and Stipo grabbed Fendan and dragged him through the labs to the plant sheds where Festal and Sefon were waiting. The Kristeran burst through the entrance after them. Flame streaked and hissed around the sheds and plants began to burn. Festal grabbed a water-hose and turned it on the Kristeran while Sefon shepherded Fendan, Merculan and Stipo to the APT. Blinded by the water, the Kristeran dropped their weapons and retreated, leaving the burning sheds behind them.

Fendan lay fevered and chaotic in the back of the APT.

"We must get him to the Attics immediately. He needs quiet and to be amongst his own."

"And Stipo?" asked Merculan anxiously. "What about him?"

"He's stronger, and Sefon's taking care of him."

"But will he be all right?"

"He'll need a lot of care," was all Festal would say.

*

He had moved! He pushed again and moved another bit. Then

it grasped his head and held it tight, tight and he was stuck.

*

The weather had been calm when they had started but now spinwinds were rising. Festal was worried. Another no-moon night and spinwinds growing taller .... He watched a spiral tear through a field and rip out a tree before it disappeared. Clouds, like thick black smoke, coiled and spiralled in the dirty sky. Rain should bring an end to spinwinds but the clouds were still high. There was no telling how long it might hold off.

Merculan was worried, too. The eerie sounds all round made him nervous.

"The lament of the spinwinds," Festal had explained lightly.

He did not remember a noise like this last night. He was sure they were in danger. And what was happening to the other Rebels? They were to go to Tsa and Xemplox and exit through their plant sheds. Had they made it? They were supposed to wait with Outlanders until Festal picked them up, but would they get caught in spinwinds? Stipo's arms, shoulders and head were badly burned. Every jolt of the APT was agony for him. Sefon had bathed and bandaged him and put jiwa on his tongue but still it hurt horribly. Sometimes he dozed and woke uneasily with that discordant, high-pitched wheening in his ears.

Fendan, too, was in pain. In pain and pinnioned. Boulders heaved again, crushing his head into the crack. It opened just a little more and took his temples in its grip. Oh the pain, the pain ... but he was moving. He waited for the next contraction and when it came he used the leverage to push ... and push again ... and once again. The spasmed earth became his ally. Now he welcomed the heaving, the rumbling and the crushing pain. His head inched into the rock, tight, so tight, like a vice, clasping so tight he could not move. The pain, the pain, he couldn't breathe, he couldn't ....

"Let me out," he gasped. "Oh, let me out."

"Fendan's very feverish," Merculan said anxiously. "Will I give him more jiwa?"

"Ask Sefon," Festal replied, wrestling with the steering. "I'm busy trying to keep you safe."

The spinwinds grew taller. The clouds were still too high for rain and darkness was creeping from the far horizon.

"No, no more jiwa," Sefon said.

*

"What now?" asked Dilh'.

"I don't know, I'll have to think," Haupus snapped.

"Chaos, chaos!" she admonished, waving her thumbs at him as though he were a child.

"Stop that nonsense, Dilh'," he said and left for the Chambers. The moaning in the Chambers soothed him a little. He had to get Fendan. He'd made a slow-brain of him with this escape, a laughing stock of him and all the Justice Guild. Fendan must not get away with it. But all Zintilla watched. It would be difficult. So many were on Fendan's side in this messy business.

He listened to the moaning while he wondered what to do. It got louder and louder until it filled his mind. He must find a way into the Attics, for that's where Fendan was hiding surely. He'd take a trusted lieutenant, but who could he trust? The moaning of the unworthies drowned his thoughts. Oh, stop that noise! Where was he? Yes, a lieutenant. No, better, he'd take Dilh'. They'd use the levigators to blast their way in and find Fendan. Afterwards they could deal with Joquah'.

"Stop that noise," he called. "Shut up, you miserable unworthies!"

He would be Supreme Krister of the Radiant Orb, he would, he would.

"Don't howl like that!"

Then he could deal with Merculan — and all his so-called Rebels. Yes, yes, that's what he'd do.

When he did not return home, Dilh' went looking for him. The first place she went to was the Chambers. There she found him by the levigators, in turn whimpering and howling and babbling wildly to himself like any unworthy, completely lost in chaos. She got him outside and into the Hall of Justice. There she forced some jiwa into his mouth and led him through a suturing process.

"You do not deserve the honour that you're seeking," she told him sternly. "I know that these are strange, disturbing times, but never, ever, let that happen to you again!"

*

He could push no more, he was exhausted. The gripping urged him, pushed him on but he must rest. There was an out but he must rest. His head was squashed, his body caught, held, restricted, hurting, but he had to rest.

*

Rain came at last. It slashed down, bouncing on the road, streaming on the window, making it hard for Festal to see ahead even with the powerful lights of the APT. In parts the road was flooded and verges churned into mud. But at least the spinwinds had died down. Or so he thought. Suddenly the APT swerved off the road and whirled round in the mud until it stuck there, leaning at an angle.

"Is everyone all right?" Festal called.

"I think so," Merculan's voice was shaky. "Stipo, what about you?"

Stipo groaned in reply.

"Stipo, tell me you're all right." Merculan began to sound hysterical and he shook the groaning Stipo.

"Stop that," snapped Sefon, struggling from the floor. "I'll look after Stipo, you tend to Fendan."

Fendan was all right. Bruised perhaps and dazed and a little more feverish. He had been asleep when the accident had occurred. Stipo was in great pain and groaning.

"I think there's something broken," Sefon said quietly.

Festal started up the APT again but it would not move. The broad wheels, designed to cope with all kinds of terrain, were too deep in the mud.

218

"There's nothing for it," he said. "I'll have to get out and find a home and see if I can borrow a team of cloplinger and a harness to pull us out."

He threw a hooded cape over himself and squelched away into the dark.

The rain shshsh'ed like a thousand Floaters. Stipo cried and groaned. Fendan's head was hot and throbbing and he was cramped and sore. Something was pushing him, pushing him further and further into the crevice in the rocks. His whole head was in there now, face flattened against the wall. And still the earth heaved and pushed and drove him on. Somewhere beyond he heard a scream of anguish, as though his passage through the earth had caused it pain. Fear gripped and spurred him. He must get out, he must get out or die. Progress was so slow, each tiny movement forward fought for with his life. And yet he knew for sure there was an out, a place to go, a place to learn.

It was three hours before Festal reappeared. His hair streeled down his face in wet black rivulets and he looked tired. Behind him were two hardy Outlanders and a team of cloplinger. The animals were already harnessed, black and snorting gently in the dark. Quietly, efficiently, the Outlanders hitched them to the APT. The mud squelched and sucked but the cloplinger's big splayed hooves prevented them from sinking.

"Hey-bla-ha!" the strangers cried to the animals urging them to pull.

The powerful haunches strained and strained, until with great splutters, splash and squelch the APT was back on the road. Festal, Sefon and the two Outlanders examined it with torches to make sure it was roadworthy.

"We'll need to hurry, father," Sefon said to Festal when they were sure the vehicle was all right, "Fendan is really bad with fever and Stipo must have attention soon."

The rain had stopped by the time they reached the entrance to the Attics and a gentle wind arose. Stars glittered through the cloud breaks. Merculan rushed on ahead, leaving Festal and Sefon to follow with Fendan and Stipo. Kwas met him in the main lab.

"Are they back yet?" Merculan inquired.

"Yes, most of them," Kwas replied. "But there's something else ...."

"What do you mean, most of them? Who's missing? What has happened?"

"Merculan, listen, there's something more important. Haupus is here!"

"Haupus!"

"Yes, he's here with Dilh'. They blasted their way in with some weapon that they have. Not those burn tubes, something else that totally detroys. The exit to Cah'ai is just a hole and a pile of dust. They've destroyed Tingaal's Pool of Life. Pipanda found them blasting any doors that wouldn't open, demanding to see Fendan. When we told him he wasn't here, he killed Pipanda, blasted her to nothing. He would have killed us all only Dilh' restrained him."

"Where are they now?"

"We thought it safest to let him look through the Attics himself. Tingaal and Chareem are with him now."

Just then Festal and Sefon arrived carrying Fendan and Stipo.

"Where will we put them?" Festal asked.

"Bring Stipo to his room, but we must hide Fendan immediately, Haupus is here and wants to kill him."

Merculan looked around distractedly.

"Then I'll put him in the space rider," said Festal.

He climbed the steps to the entrance, opened the door and placed Fendan gently on the couch inside.

"I'll take the steps away," he said. "You hide that elevator. Tell Dilh' and Haupus that the bipeds have him. And while we're at it, open the roof and let the stars shine through. The view of the Abyss of Chaos should distract them for a bit."

Fendan was very hot and feverish and his head ached horribly as he lay in the space rider looking through its dome at the starry sky. The Abyss of Chaos was what he used to call it. He smiled as he remembered, such a long, long time ago. The stars, how he really loved the stars. They were small and manageable, not like the fat cracked moons. They shone inviting, glistening and blinking in the blue-black sky, invitingly, calling him to join them. Oh, that he could! He must show Joquah' this, she'd love the wide magnificence of skies. And as he lay there he began to see her eyes among the stars, Joquah's eyes looking deep into his and growing larger. His own eyes widened in response to hers and then the skies were filled with rainbow hues. Her eyes drew him in and then their chant began.

"Let us exchange our energy. May our energy be exchanged.... "

When Merculan returned with Dilh' and Haupus the Space Vaulter had disappeared and Fendan with it. There was nothing but stars, shining down kindly.

*

Emmerlade stayed in her room until she had control again. She needed to be clear about her decision. Fendan had disappeared and the cities were in chaos. No-one knew where Haupus and Dilh' were and as for Joquah', she worked obsessively at her recorders while her work room walls glowed green all round her. She decided.

"I must find Merculan," Emmerlade said aloud, and made her way cautiously towards the plant sheds.

*

The out was tight, even tighter than the gripping had been before. It held and squeezed and moulded him, forcing him to struggle, to strive and persevere for every small advance, to push and wrestle for the slightest progress. But the millimeter gained was victory, bringing the out of space and light and cool a little closer. He could sense it already on his head.

Push and wriggle, rest, then push again. Somewhere from behind, the gripping helped. It urged him on and upwards towards the light. The pressure on his head was torture but he only had one objective — out — and this fierce, single-mindedness accepted all conditions.

Another push and then his head was free! But oh, the cold, the light. It seared his eyes and made him close them fast. But still it seared his eyelids. And the cold, his head was cold. He'd seen enough. Brightness, harsh, hideous and sterile, and the cold! Ungainly somethings, massive, swathed and wrinkled, stared at him from a height. And oh, the noise, the noise, the awesome noise. A something gripped and pulled him, rough and painful. He was out, completely out. It was cold, so cold, so bright and cold. Oh let me back, let me return to dark and warmth and comfort and my rhythm. *Ba-dum, ba-dum, ba-dum* .... No longer there, oh let me back, oh take me back!

They grasped him once again, his skin all tender from the journey. Then life cut off, his rhythm gone .... He gasped for air in desperation. Life returned but with such pain inside. He didn't want to gasp again, he just wanted to go back, go back ....

They wouldn't leave him be. Oh let me curl up and go back .... But they took him by the heels, his soft spine jolting. They held him high and terrified. No, no .... An unexpected smack made him cry out in shock. There's no respect, they do not want me here. Air rasped inside, harsh, smarting, horrible with stench, and then he cried. He cried and cried for protest and his lost, dark paradise. They took him up and put him down and took him up again. He closed his eyes tight all the time, his body curled, stench lingering in his nostrils. Then they wrapped him up in something tight and scratchy and laid him down to rest, at last. *Ba-dum, ba-dum, ba-dum, ba-dum* .... His rhythm, it was there! Fainter than before, but there. He opened his eyes cautiously and looked. And as he looked, another old familiar rhythm started.

"Welcome, little one, my darling, welcome ...."